BOOK 3 OF THE

WHITE HOLE

KITTY KING

Copyright © 2023 by Kitty King

All rights reserved. Printed in the United States of America. No part of this book may be used or reproduced in any manner whatsoever without written permission except in the case of brief quotations embodied in critical articles or reviews.

This book is a work of fiction. Names, characters, businesses, organizations, places, events, and incidents either are the product of the author's imagination or are used fictitiously. Any resemblance to actual persons, living or dead, events, or locales is entirely coincidental.

For information contact:

http://authorkittyking.com

Cover Design by Gemini Designs

Copyediting and Proofreading by Indie Proofreading

ASIN: B0C2ZS3C24 (eBook)

ISBN: 979-8-9880503-2-2 (Paperback)

First Edition: January 2023

10 9 8 7 6 5 4 3 2 1

To those who felt like they could never say anything... this is your sign to speak up.

AUTHOR'S NOTE

This is the part where I **warn you** that this is a **very dark** book. It covers topics including:

- Taboo relations
- Grooming, sexual abuse, and rape of a minor
- Sexploitation
- Serious car accident
- Body dysmorphia
- Opioid abuse, including injecting
- Domestic violence
- Depression

You have been warned.

This book does *not* glorify these topics. This book deals with the resulting trauma of those events. As always, I am not writing a relationship manual, nor a sex kink manual. This is **fiction**.

It helps to have read *Red Night,* the first book in the

AUTHOR'S NOTE

series, and *Blue Film*, the second, but this can be read as a standalone. Please understand that some events may seem rushed or out of place if not taken into context within the series.

PROLOGUE
KINSLEY

MAYBE *TUTA*? Was that a word? *Attuna*? Lining up the little tiles, I played *taunt* before sitting back with a sigh. It was a good play, but I would lose again to an 82-year-old woman wearing a red sweater with a puffy brown reindeer. In March. "Christmas is every day when you have joy in your heart," she would say.

"Excites. Triple letters on 'X' and 'E.' You sure you're feelin' okay, sweetie?" Ms. Lawson sat back with her winning look of glee, mauve lips spread flat and wide.

"You know this is a volunteer position, right? Maybe let me win some, or I won't offer my generous services again."

"So competitive, Kinsley, darling. I like that." Picking up wooden letters and sliding them into the cloth bag, she said, "All I have is time here to practice. *You* are busy with your studies, I hope. The world needs your talents in the operating room, young lady, not here."

Putting the board back in its box, a grin crept over

my face. "Yes, I got straight A's again. Mom and Dad were proud, so losing to you in Scrabble won't derail my dreams, Ms. Lawson." She snapped her eyes to mine. "I mean, Edith."

"And you're practicing your cross stitch? I heard that helps surgeons. What I wouldn't give to be able to do that again." Looking at her bent fingers, mangled from arthritis, she let out a small sigh.

"Yep! In between tennis and Cale and student government. Over the summer, I plan to shadow a few physicians, too. Before university applications."

Ms. Lawson shook her head, fluffy white curls turning with her, stiff with setting spray. "Cale... you couldn't date someone *not* named after a vegetable?" I threw her a warning look.

Glancing over to the table across the room, I watched my boyfriend's thick brown eyebrows furrow as he contemplated his move on the chessboard spread between him and Mr. Gentry. Feeling my gaze on him, his dark blue eyes met mine. I greeted his look with a smile, but he returned to his game.

"Let's talk about the game. The *real* game. When does practice start up again?"

"Next month. My instructor says I have a great chance of getting a scholarship." After sliding the box back on the shelf with the other board games, I returned to my plastic chair. It was almost time for us to leave.

"But you're not dropping your elbow anymore? Let me see the video." Ms. Lawson had played tennis in her college days. She made the all-conference team and we bonded over our mutual love of the sport. I pulled out my latest training video, filmed by my instructor. Edith watched, enraptured. "Yep. So much better than last year. Oh, to be able to play again. I miss it!"

I would, too. Tennis was the outlet I reserved for times I needed to hit something. Like before a big test, or after arguing with Cara Renfroe about how we should allocate funds to the junior dance this year. Besides, the scholarship would help with Ivy League tuition.

"Well, I'll see you next week. Can we play Chutes and Ladders or Clue next time? I may have a chance." Edith grabbed my hand as I bid her goodbye and squeezed. Her skin felt like plastic wrap.

"Doubt it. I play Sandra and Marv in Clue every other day. It's their favorite. See you next week!" A hum filled the air as she motored her wheelchair toward the hall.

Cale stood and grabbed our coats from the wall rack. The weather was warm during the days but could turn to icy rain at night. Slipping on my gloves, I asked, "Who won?"

"Who do you think, muffin?" Cale smirked towards Mr. Gentry, who didn't wave as he scooted his walker to the TV room.

I slapped Cale's arm, covered by thick wool in his coat. "You should let him win sometimes."

"Oh, is that what you do with Edith? *Let* her win?"

"Yep. She likes to win, and I like to watch her smile." It was a complete lie. I hated that I couldn't beat her in Scrabble. Or any games. I didn't want Cale to know the truth.

He led me to the front entrance of the nursing facility as we waved to the front desk staff. "You know, Kinsley, you don't have to be the best at everything. It's okay if you're not as smart as you think."

I snorted. "This, coming from you. Mr. 'I published my first research paper in seventh grade'."

He opened the door for us, and we stepped into the black night, sleet sparkles visible in the pale moonlight. We carefully high-stepped to the parking lot. "You don't have to compete with me, Kinsley. I'm your boyfriend."

Standing between our two cars, I crossed my arms over my chest. Who was he to talk about not competing? He constantly strived to one-up me. I was elected vice president of the junior year student council; he was elected as president. I won the city tennis tournament our sophomore year; he won state. My stomach tied in knots at the possibility he would get accepted to Harvard pre-med and I wouldn't.

"Come here." Given the thickness of our jackets and sweaters, he gathered me into as tight an embrace as we could muster. A spackling of freckles crossed his nose, just visible in the yellow light of the streetlamp as he leaned in to suck my pouting bottom lip. "When are your parents out next?" Blowing a crystalized breath in my mouth, he leaned his forehead against mine.

"Um, I think in three weeks. Maybe we could *watch a movie* in your basement on Saturday." The sucky part of still being in high school and living with our parents was how to finagle our trysts without being seen. We had sex for the first time two months ago after I'd researched everything about it—positions so it wouldn't hurt, how effective birth control methods were, angles for best female orgasms... I'd done the same when we started having oral sex the year before. With how Cale reacted to my blowjobs, it seemed my reading had paid off.

"Ugh. Tyler's still living down there. He's doing this whole *independent* act, pretending he's going to pay rent with his grocery store job. The Honda again?"

Cale's younger brother would tattle on us if he saw us having sex, aiming for brownie points with their parents, or possibly a higher allowance. I hated that my boyfriend and I had to resort to our cars. The fit was never quite right. Usually, I was stuffed in the passenger's seat or the back, trying to do cowgirl without hitting my head on the roof. I sighed. "I guess."

"I got that hotel room for after junior prom. We can spend all night there if you tell your parents you're at Becca's place." Lightly tapping his cold lips to mine, he walked around to his driver's side door.

"I already did. Text me you made it home safe."

He nodded, then drove off.

Getting into my little sedan, I buckled my seatbelt and cranked up the heat. The freezing rain was coming down faster, so I eased my foot on the gas pedal. So much for a beautiful spring night.

Carefully pulling onto the main road, I crawled to the next stoplight. The usually busy four-way intersection was deserted as I sat and found a new song to listen to on my phone through the car's speakers. Cara would choose a stupid music theme for our prom. I was going to stop her.

Headlights blazed into my eyes. Blinded by the white flashes, I held my hand to my brow as I looked through my window. Tires squealed on the slick pavement before a loud crunch deafened my ears. My car was thrown into a spin for what seemed like an eternity. Around and around and around. Gripping the steering wheel, I was terrified at what would happen when I stopped whirling.

My windshield fractured in such a way as to create a beautiful prism of red that turned green when the traffic lights changed. Such a silly thing to focus on, but it must have taken away the fear that hit my chest when my airbag deployed. Then the impact of metal surrounding my body.

The car had stopped, wrapped around the side of a corner store on Main Street.

Hot liquid rolled into my eyes, but I couldn't move to wipe them. It was blood. A man's face peered into my side window. Before I shut my eyes, I memorized it: soft jawline, baby smooth skin, delicate lips, green eyes lit by the streetlamp, and a wild display of brown hair atop his head. The man, probably only in his early twenties, was wearing a houndstooth blazer and an expression of terror.

"*Heyyyy*. You okay?" As his breath crashed through my smashed window, my nose tingled with the ripe smell of alcohol. My mouth wouldn't open, and something held my chest so firmly that I could hardly get any air. After getting a peek at me, he stumbled away with his hand running through his hair, back to his black car, hazy in the distance.

The darkness overtook me.

☽ ☽ ☽ ● ☾ ☾ ☾

"No. *You're* the one who thinks I'm not doing enough. She can't just force herself out of this, Jeff. Have some empathy."

"*Me* not have empathy? All I've done is have compassion for her. And you, for what it's even been worth. Not that you've ever reciprocated."

"Please. This cannot be good for her."

"You're right. Jan, I think you should wait outside. I'll stay here with her."

"Me? Wait outside? I'm her mother!"

"Well, I'm her father."

My eyes flittered open slightly, but I quickly shut them. The intensity of the light hurt. Surely, I was having a nightmare. I recognized my parents' voices but not their tone or the words they were saying. I'd never heard my parents argue before. Not with each other.

"Oh, my God. Kinsley? Baby?" my mother sobbed.

Furrowing my brow with strain, I peeled apart my dry lips to try to speak.

"Shh. Honey, rest. I'll get the doctor." Dad's comforting tenor soothed my bones.

Someone clicked a button over my head, and the room became darker behind my lids. I could open my eyes without pain, but everywhere beneath my waist was screaming at me. "It hurts."

"Here, I'll call the nurse. Oh, baby. Baby, I'm so sorry. We'll get you some more medicine. Nurse!"

A robotic voice called from a speaker near my head, "Can I help you?"

Mom's voice quavered. "My daughter says she's in pain."

"I'll be right there."

I must have drifted off to sleep because I awoke some duration of time later, and a young woman wearing pink scrubs with teddy bears on them was pushing medicine into an IV attached to my arm. When I looked down, my hands were lying on my blanket near my waist, both wrapped in thick bandages and splints. Despite my brain telling them to, I couldn't move them. My legs were also immobile.

"What happened? What's going on? Why can't I move my legs?" My throat was dry, which made it difficult to speak. Like I hadn't had a drink of water in days.

"Baby, wait until the doctor gets here." Mom stood on one side of the bed while the nurse fussed with the IV machine. Her fingers grazed gently in circles on my upper arm.

"Hey, Kinsley. I'm Maddy. I'm your nurse tonight. Can you tell me your full name?"

Clearing my throat, I swallowed the minimal spit I had left to get some lubrication for my task. "Kinsley Alice Whittemore."

"Great. When's your birthday?" Maddy was half paying attention to my face and half to the wristband wrapped above my hand bandages.

My mother held a cup of ice water to my lips, and I

sipped. It was the most refreshing thing I'd ever tasted in my life. I could answer clearly. "September third."

Maddy laid my arm on the bed and asked, "What is today's date?"

Behind her, I could see a whiteboard with her name written on it, and above that was the date. Attempting to jolt up in bed, the pain prevented me from moving as I yelled, "It's *March twenty-eighth?* I've been laying here for *three days?*" I'd missed three days of school!

Would Cara have taken over as vice president while I was out? Ugh, I bet she'd love that. I wondered if Chloe had hit on Cale. Probably asked if she could suck him off in the locker room first gym class I wasn't there. Horror struck me as I feared he would let her.

My father and a woman wearing a long lab coat rushed into the room. The woman introduced herself as Dr. Sanchek and asked me questions to test my brain function. Although sluggish, I could answer most of them, except where we were.

"It's a hospital, I'm assuming it's General, but it doesn't look like the rooms I've volunteered in."

"You're at Mercy Trinity." Dr. Sanchek answered. My parents were standing in the background; Dad looked like he might give me the answers so I'd pass the test with one hundred percent, mouthing words at me like he used to do in my school spelling bees.

"That's an hour away. Why was I moved?"

The hospitalist informed me my hands had required extensive surgery due to their crush injuries, and the closest hand surgeon was in Springfield, an hour away from my hometown. My legs were broken but would heal "just fine, but may require plastics to take a look."

"Plastics?"

"Plastic surgery. The abrasions, the glass… it was extensive. You may have scarring. But you're young, so the skin will likely mend itself over time."

"But tennis…" I pondered how soon I could return to the court. Harvard wanted a well-rounded applicant. Tennis was my outlet for everything.

Dr. Sanchek looked at my parents. My mother popped over to my bedside. "Sweetie, we'll have to think about tennis later. You're going to need rehab after this."

"She can talk about tennis now. She needs to get back to it. She needs that scholarship." My father nodded at me to emphasize his point. Dr. Sanchek and my mother snapped their heads to him.

"F-for how long?" I asked. I couldn't be out of school for much longer. Prom was coming up, and Cara would pick *Wind Beneath My Wings* as the song. Oh, my god. What if she chose the *Pirates Prom* theme?

Dr. Sanchek said, "It depends on how well you're healing. Take one day at a time. The physical therapists will work with you. Don't give up."

Don't give up? Who was giving up? I was ready to go and get back out there now. Sure, I couldn't move my legs or hands, but I knew if I worked hard enough, I could return to the shape I was. My father looked like he agreed with me.

"But, Kinsley. I need you to be prepared. Holding a racket as you did, your legs jarring in changing directions... You may not be able to move like that for a while. Give yourself a break." The concern on the doctor's face made me question my new reality. What if I *couldn't* play tennis anymore?

I gasped.

What if I couldn't walk?

The doctor told me to rest and that I would begin therapy the following day. Maddy adjusted my pillows and said she would bring in a cafeteria menu for me since I was starving. I wasn't even sure how I could eat without using my hands.

I had taken my abilities, hell, my entire existence, for granted. Did that mean I couldn't be a surgeon anymore? Who was I then? My mother stroked my hair, then walked to the small adjoining bathroom to wet a washcloth.

Dad slid to the side of my bed to take her place. "Listen to me. You get back out there and fight. Do what it takes to earn your spot back on the court. Cale brought over some of your classwork yesterday, and I'll have him bring over the rest tomorrow. You can start working on it while you're lying here." My father's brown eyes glanced down at my bandaged hands. "Well, maybe you can use one of those speech-to-text programs to type up your notes and papers."

"Jeff, seriously? Stop. Just—" Mom returned from the bathroom with another towel.

"What? What am I saying? I'm just encouraging her!"

"No, you're not. You're trying to *pressure* her—"

"She can handle pressure. She knows..." My father

let his voice trail off as Maddy came back in, who probably heard the rabble-rousing from the hallway.

Maddy opened the dining menu for me so I could see the pictures. She eyed both of my parents. "I think Kinsley needs her rest." Her small hand lightly patted my arm. "Sleep after dinner. Right, Kinsley?"

"I'm heading home, anyway. Are you staying?" My father gathered his coat and a bag from a bench near the hospital bed.

"Of course, I'm staying." My mother settled into a recliner chair covered in a floral shiny plastic.

"Don't say it like that. I'll stay tomorrow." Dad turned his attention to me. "We've been swapping nights. I stayed last night. I was here all night with you." He glared at Mom. She huffed and shook her head.

"Thanks, Dad. And Mom."

I ordered something I thought would be easy for my mom to feed me: chicken nuggets and French fries. By the time I got them, I had lost my appetite.

"What about the other guy?" I asked my mom, shaking my head as she tried to put a fry in my mouth.

"Hmm? What other guy?"

"The guy. The other guy in the accident. The drunk driver that crashed into my car. What happened to him?"

My mom looked utterly confused. "Kinsley, honey, the police said—" She paused while watching me with a wrinkled brow. "The police said you slid on the ice and crashed. They didn't say anything about another car."

"What? No. There was a black car, a BMW. A guy, a young guy—he came to my window to check on me." Lowering my voice, I whispered, "He smelled like alcohol." My mother shook her head, and her confusion made the fury within me unleash. "Did they check camera footage? Did they look at any tracks? I didn't slide! He hit my car!"

"Shh, shh. It's okay, Kinsley. Your father asked about it. The police said they watched the camera footage, and you slid off the road. We will buy you a new car. You don't need to worry about that."

She thought I was concerned about a *car*. I was worried about the asshole that left me lying in a hospital bed… possibly never able to walk again.

PROLOGUE
GEORGE

WHY THE FUCK was I hosting when I didn't even like parties? Sighing, I leaned back harder against the couch cushions in my garage-turned-recreational room, taking a drink of my dry stout. I knew why. Xavier needed this.

Ever since his mom died about a year ago, he'd been an automaton. Not like a droid, but more like a Stepford Wife, doing everything everyone expected of him with a weird smirk on his face. Levi and I could see the truth. Probably Mason, too, if he was capable of thinking of someone other than himself. Xavier was in pain.

Sipping warm beer and watching some dimwitted cheerleader grind on my crotch irritated me. She couldn't handle what was underneath my denim. Despite my annoyance with the whole scene, I would put up with it for my best friend. Besides, my father said I could have some guys over for once. It wasn't my fault the boys invited the entire football team. And Dan asked his baseball team. At least my youngest brother was with Mom. I hoped.

"Do you like this? Is this good for you?" The blonde leaned forward to whisper in my ear. She was barely doing anything for me. I grunted at her.

"Big G, my man. I heard you weren't playing for Northview University next year. Why not? Talented linebacker like you could have made division one." One of Dan's baseball friends, a junior named Bodie, passed me a fresh Guinness. I shrugged at him.

He was right. It would have been easy to try out and get a scholarship to any division one school in the country. Maybe even gone on to the national league in the future, but I couldn't. And I didn't want to; I had other aspirations.

"Where's that stepsister of yours? What's her name?" Bodie asked the real question he'd wanted to when he brought me the new bottle—trying to appeal to my narcissism first by talking football. Asshole.

"You mean, Alenna? She's just a freshman, Bodie." The girl on my legs paused her writhing long enough to look at him. "Besides, she's not even that cute." Her big eyes searched my face as if asking for permission to insult Alenna. Oh, she was desperate *and* jealous.

My latest stepsister was probably trying to get with one of these horny bastards. I'd need to keep an eye out for her. Scanning the room, I couldn't see her from the couch, so I slid what's-her-name off my lap and stood.

Alenna's mother and my father had only been together for a year and a half, but it was long enough to cause ripples in the fabric of my life. If something happened to her, I'd be the one in trouble.

The garage was packed. Some dudes had apparently called all the cheerleaders over. And the dance team. I even spotted some theater girls shooting pool. There was a crowd around the foosball table and a Mario Kart tournament on the big screen. The entire place reeked of stale beer and bongwater. But there was no little russet-haired Alenna.

"Big G! Why do they call you that?" The cheerleader stood in front of me with a coy smile, her head barely clearing my pecs. I was six foot six and had 230 pounds of muscle. But that's not what she was asking. Grabbing her tiny hand, I placed it on my thickening cock that she'd worked so hard to arouse. Her red stained lips parted into an "O" as she gasped.

Our running back, Kevin, was lounging on the couch and slapped the tight-end, Mitch, sitting next to him. "Cherry, there's a reason we call him 'horse cock' in the locker room." The guys around the sofa laughed as the little girl's cheeks flamed the color of Mars. Snatching her hand back, I smirked. Just as I thought...

Exiting the garage, I wandered towards the house. The weather was freezing for the end of March, but I didn't need a jacket; I radiated enough heat, like I was my own sun. Despite the weather, the black sky was clear enough that I could make out Virgo, then Hydra leading to Cancer.

It had been hours since I'd seen Levi, Mason, *or* Xavier. Usually, they would smoke the good weed in my room, far away from the vultures. Once I entered the house, I headed up the stairs. My legs stopped when I heard moans filtering out of the guest room before I even reached the hallway.

Mason strolled out of the upstairs bathroom down the hall. "*Dude*! G. Uh, they're all busy in that room. I walked in *purely* by accident, but they wouldn't let me watch. Told them I'd be quiet and everything—"

Brushing past him before he could stop talking, I rushed towards the door. Levi Joseph was a whore. Couldn't keep it in his pants. I'd seen him eye my stepsister when she moved in. If Alenna was in there with Levi, my father would blow up if he found out.

The door wasn't locked when I swung it open. I knew I wouldn't gag, but could have. In the center of the bed lay my friend, Levi. Buck naked. Fortunately, I couldn't see much of him because his face was covered by my stepsister's pussy, his dick obscured by my stepmother's. Alenna's nude body writhed on him, facing the head of the bed where Xavier was standing, shoving his cock in her mouth while holding her head and thrusting in harshly. Gianna, my stepmother, rode Levi reverse-cowgirl style, facing the foot of the bed. I'd seen her do the move before. The fact that she was doing this to my friends made me rage.

"Get the fuck out, Levi," my voice boomed as I went to pull my buddy off the bed. I wouldn't kill him, but I needed to scare the shit out of him so he would be safe. He had no idea what he was getting himself involved in. Xavier, I'd excuse; the man was grieving. Levi was thinking with his dick, and it had a bigger brain than his head. "Levi!" I knew my voice was scary.

Gianna slid off Levi's cock slowly. At the same time, Alenna screamed, then grabbed her clothes from the floor and ran out of the room. Xavier jumped off the bed and quickly pulled his pants back on. Levi lay there like a possum exposed to headlights in the dead of night. Grabbing him by the neck, I yanked on him as he shuffled off the bed by his knees.

"Oh, shit, G. I'm so sorry. So sorry."

"You dumb motherfucker. You fucking asshole. Can't you keep it in your pants for just one night? One night, man!" I was shoving him out the door while Xavier gathered his clothes. Gianna pulled up her negligee I'd guessed she'd worn for the show. "I'll fucking kill you. Get the fuck out of here." Levi paled to the color of paper and ran down the stairs. Xavier slid by me, slinking along the wall, and sneaked away out the door.

"Georgie. Junior…" Gianna's sugary sweet voice made me look down and clench my jaw. *Fuck*. Levi had *no* clue what he was getting into. "Georgie. Look at me, sweetie." As I turned around, Gianna reached up and tucked a piece of my long blond hair behind my ear. Like she was a mother. "You're not going to say a word, are you, Georgie?" My eyes kept staring at the hardwood floor.

Gianna's voice made my stomach knot. Sidling up to me, I had to meet her face. She said, "Because you know what happens if you do. You've been down this road before." She crawled her red fingernails up my chest. Jutting her painted bottom lip out, she gazed at me with her almond-shaped hazel eyes. "Besides…

your friend didn't get me off. You know whose job that is."

This bitch.

Licking my bottom lip, I contemplated my next move. She was right. I wouldn't say a damn word. I hadn't in years. I lived in Hell every fucking day, but I would never tell.

Images of the eight-year-old version of myself flashed in my mind. Little George wandered into his father's office downstairs to see him banging his future ex-wife number two. Dan was six, and Aaron was just a toddler at the time. I stood there for a while, watching my father pump into Mindy on his desk. She had babysat us all a few times when my parents were out. My father was panting, and she was screaming. I thought she was hurt, so I went to help her, but my dad yelled at me to leave the room.

My mom came home from the grocery store soon after with Aaron, and I ran to tell her a hurt woman was in dad's office. I'll never forget the ire that set in on my mother's face as she marched toward the door and threw it open. Mindy shrieked and gathered up her clothes before sprinting out. My father pulled up his pants and yelled at my mother. I'd never seen them fight like that, only heard it behind their thin bedroom walls.

My mother slapped my father, and then he punched her. Her body was flung by the impact into the bookcases before sliding down to the floor. Little Aaron waddled to me, his eyes filled with tears. Grabbing him, I ran upstairs to make sure Dan was safe. Shoving the three of us into the closet in my room, we huddled together, listening to the terrifying screams and pounding sounds resounding from downstairs. I put my body in front of my brothers', guarding them. It's why I made such a great linebacker. No one was getting through Big George Turner.

I couldn't call the police. My father *was* the police. So, we hid behind the clothes until the noises died down. Mom eventually found us hunched together there. Aaron had fallen asleep in my arms without dinner. Mom didn't look right, her face reddened with tears and marks. She grabbed Aaron and then Daniel. I wandered out of the closet behind her. She hugged the two of them, but wouldn't look at me.

"Mom." She didn't respond, just kissed the tops of my brothers' heads and hurried to her bedroom. I followed as she pulled out the suitcase she used when we visited Grandma. "Ma," I said again. "Mommy!"

Finally, she snapped her head at me and shook her finger. "I wished you never told me. I wished you'd just kept your mouth shut! Do you have any idea what you've done? You've just killed your mother. You've given me a death sentence, George."

Tears burst from my eyes. My young brain couldn't comprehend what was happening. I didn't want to kill my mother. "No! I don't want to kill you! Please don't die! Where are you going?"

Tossing things from around the room into her suitcase, she turned to depart, but spoke to me one last time before heading out of the door. "Keep your mouth shut and stay out of trouble. You're staying here and I'm leaving."

Sprinting over to her, I tried to grab onto her shirt and pull, but she clutched my wrist, so my fingers had to release her. "I'll get my suitcase, too! Wait, Mommy! Wait!" I darted to my room as fast as my little legs could go, pulled out my backpack we used for family trips, and threw random things into it, including my Millennium Falcon Lego set that my dad helped me put together. It wouldn't fit. As I debated which of my robots to bring, I heard the garage door close, the humming of the mechanics causing my heart to race.

I ran downstairs as my mother's car pulled away from the house. Standing at the dining room window, Dan stood beside me, and we both cried for her. Aaron couldn't make it in time to watch her leave.

My father came in behind us. "Stop that crying. Boys don't cry. Stop it. I don't want to hear any of that nonsense. She's gone, and good riddance."

He married Mindy a week after his and my mother's divorce was final. She was a good babysitter for a while. At least she fed Aaron when he was hungry. She left when Dad had sex with Candace, his friend's wife. They were married for a few months before she left, too.

My mother moved to a tiny studio apartment with roaches under the sink. Dad said she was "mentally ill," and we couldn't see her often. He'd had her committed to a hospital shortly after their fight, saying she was suicidal. His lawyers argued she couldn't get custody rights because she was "a danger" to us.

When we were allowed to visit, Mom sat in a

recliner and watched TV all day without moving. The place chronically smelled like rotten food. The sink was always filled with dirty dishes, and she had no snacks for us. Over the years, I learned to pack some for my brothers in my backpack. I'd clean the apartment so Aaron wouldn't get sick. There wasn't really a place for us to sleep. We would pile on the floor in sleeping bags, but the carpet smelled like cat pee.

Mom would hug Aaron and Dan, but ignore me. She would wait until I had tidied up her kitchen and my brothers were asleep. Then, I'd hear her mumble, "I wish you'd kept your mouth shut."

So I did.

From the day my father beat my mother, I stopped talking. Mindy and my dad went to see my school counselor because I stopped giving answers in class. Mindy talked about me like she was a pretend mother. Teachers noticed I wouldn't respond to the other children. My friends eventually gave up on asking me questions. By the time I was in high school, I was just known as the big, silent guy.

What did it matter if I did speak? I had Levi and Mason; both said enough for ten people. Xavier and I could sit in silence for hours, unspoken understanding traveling along wavelengths between each other. I communicated when it was necessary. But most words weren't. People were always waiting for the other person to finish so they could talk. I learned to listen. And in doing so, I learned a lot about human nature.

I preferred silence.

"So, what's it going to be, Georgie?" Gianna backed

up to the bed, pulling my hand to accompany her. She laid on her back and lowered her lingerie, spreading her legs wide open and exposing her core. "Eat." She commanded. Kneeling at the foot of the bed, I pulled her by the legs closer to my mouth.

In my fantasies, I had a real girlfriend. One that I wanted. One I had chosen. I figured I'd be pretty good at pussy eating by now with all my practice. Keeping that image in mind, I got her off as she demanded.

"That's a good boy. Now, go. Run along and play with your friends." Gianna dismissed me with a pat on the head. Hurrying to my bedroom, I locked the door and reached the attached bathroom before puking in the toilet. I fucking *hated* her taste. After brushing my teeth twice and washing my face, I felt somewhat normal again.

Football season was over. Drug testing was done. Rolling up a blunt, I laid on my bed, and smoked it. Then, I watched the stars through my telescope until I passed out, not caring that the party was still raging in my garage. Dan could take care of it, for once. Dad let him get away with everything.

The next morning, I awoke to screams and glass breaking—ah, the telltale signs of the end of another relationship for Chief Turner, Senior. Gianna was clever, more cunning than any of his other wives. She could cause a serious problem for all of us. Eavesdropping from my cracked bedroom door, I had to listen to ensure I wouldn't be roped into her manipulations.

"Who is she?" Gianna screamed from the kitchen. Alenna peaked her head out of her room, hair in a tangled mess. When her eyes spotted me, she shut the door with an embarrassed squeal.

"There's no one else. Things are not working between us. I want a divorce." My father was using his patronizing voice.

"Bullshit! Who is it, George? You know I'll ruin you if you get rid of me."

There was a long bout of silence. "Then you know what kind of man you're dealing with, Gianna. Maybe you should be more careful about what you say."

"Are you *threatening* me? That would not be wise." Another long pause. "Did you *fuck* my sixteen-year-old daughter, George?"

Oh. It all made sense. That *was* what he probably did. Was Alenna going to be my next stepmom?

"Gianna. We're done. Pack your shit and leave. Alenna is welcome to stay if she wants or go with you."

Gianna cackled like Harley Quinn. "Oh, I'm sure Alenna could stay... My underage daughter is coming with me, you sick fuck." Gianna's hypocrisy was a double-headed, fire-breathing dragon. Something shattered, then rapid footsteps pounded up the stairs. Gianna stood at the end of the hall and glared at me, her green eyes blazing. "Don't worry, Georgie. I'll be back."

CHAPTER ONE
KINSLEY

PAY ATTENTION, *Kinsley*.

The Russian literature professor was prattling on. My hand cramped from taking notes and I stretched out my fingers, glancing around the room, welcoming any distraction. The class was one of my non-major degree requirements before enjoying all chemistry classes for the three semesters I had left at Northview University. Chemistry was my favorite subject, so I couldn't wait to be able to take what I was interested in.

Sitting in the back row of the auditorium, I had an unfortunate view of Cale with Sydney, his girlfriend for the last two years. Sydney had a whittled waist and big breast implants. Her blonde hair was perfectly highlighted, and she wore a full face of makeup to each class. Every outfit she wore matched whatever color of nail polish she had on. Matched!

Cale was always touching her in some way: playing with her ponytail, kissing her neck, smiling like he'd never been happier. Why was she taking Russian literature when she was an interior design major? An interior design major! I was fucking pre-med with a perfect GPA!

But I didn't have breast implants. And my giggle didn't sound that cute when he used to kiss me. My nails were short because organic chemistry lab kept my hands stinky. And I usually looked like I had just rolled out of bed and put on sweatpants to come to class. Because I usually had.

Despite the distracting show, I was doing well in the class so far. I received an A on my first paper. There was only one class I struggled with, or had struggled with, my entire college career at Northview University... Astronomy. For some reason, I couldn't see the patterns in the sky. Rotating bonds? Double helices? Those made sense. My mind could envision the shapes. Venus? Ursa Major? I was lost.

After class, I hurried to gather my things before Cale could catch me. Today, I had put in effort to get myself together by wearing an argyle sweater vest over a white Polo shirt with navy blue slacks. I even took the time to put on some eyeliner and colored lip balm. But it wasn't cut-off-shorts-and-tight-V-neck-shirt sexy. She probably smelled like vanilla, or some exotic perfume Cale got her for Christmas.

Cale spotted me, and I groaned internally. "Hey, Kins. Wait up!" Sloppy tongue-kissing his girlfriend goodbye, he gripped her ass cheeks that were hanging out of her shorts. She walked down to the front of the room while Cale made his way up the risers to me. I didn't even want him. I was just hurt he didn't want me.

"What's up, Cale?" My toes tapped when I slung my bag over my shoulder and waited for him before we walked to inorganic chemistry. I hated that I had almost every class with him. Despite my enmity for the stars, at least astronomy was one hour I didn't have to look at my ex-boyfriend.

"Just hadn't spoken to you in a while. You look nice today, by the way. Big date?"

"Um, yeah." Cale broke up with me after our high school senior prom, saying I had changed and he couldn't take the "scars" from my accident (I assumed he was referring to the ones all over my legs).

After that, I had only been with one other man. Matt was a three-night stand and one of the best weekends of my life. He picked me up at the Ginger Lizard Lounge after a set he played on his guitar for open mic night. I had never been with anyone other than Cale, so I hadn't known sex could be so good. Matt had a huge schlong and knew how to give me multiple orgasms.

When we tried to go out on a date after our weekend in bed, I couldn't stand being around him. Matt and I had nothing in common besides needing each other's bodies for a short while, but he had been a nice way to get over my sadness about Cale. The last time I looked him up, Matt was in culinary school in New York City. Sometimes I wondered if I could put up with him to get more dick, but then I remembered what an insolent imbecile he was, and my impulses would be squelched.

It was disheartening after my car wreck when I wasn't accepted to the Ivy League schools I wanted. Still, I was secretly delighted when Cale showed up for orientation on the Nighthawks' campus during my freshman year. He said he didn't go to Harvard because he was trying to "save money." At least I got a full academic scholarship to NU. I had given up caring where I got into medical school, just so long as I did. Hopefully, one far away from Cale Dafoe.

Walking over to the science building together from our last class, Cale pushed the door open for us. As we entered, I accidentally dropped my bag in the hall. Cale bent over and picked it up for me, placing it back over my shoulder. "Sorry," I mumbled. It was embarrassing that my hands didn't work right—that I kept dropping things or couldn't open jars... or hold a tennis racket.

"I was going to ask you about something." Cale paused before we took our seats in the small chemistry classroom.

Was he always this annoying? "Then ask."

"Do you remember that amethyst charm I gave you for your bracelet at junior prom?" Did I remember junior prom? Let's see. I was hopped up on morphine and riding in a wheelchair and had to wear some weird dress I could sit in all night. And we didn't get to have sex because my legs were still in casts, and I couldn't open them wide enough for any action.

"The charm for the bracelet you gave me our first anniversary? Yeah, I remember it."

Cale sat down next to me like we were friends. "Do you still have it?"

"Um, maybe at my father's house. Why?" *Please don't make me go over there.*

"Well, I, um. Kins, there's no easy way to say this. My grandmother's good luck charm was on that bracelet, and I need it back." Cale's phone lit up with a text message from Sydney. The background of his phone was them kissing in a highly provocative pose near a waterfall. I could read her text to him. It said:

HONEYBEAR
Did you get the charm back?

"Sure, Cale. I'll get it back to you." I remembered the feeling of smacking a new tennis ball against a wall. Except, I imagined Cale's face instead of the wall. Turning in my seat, I focused my eyes on the whiteboard so he wouldn't be in my periphery when our teaching assistant, Sanjay, approached him.

"Cale, congratulations. You deserve it." He patted Cale on the back, and Cale thanked him.

"What was that about?" I asked when Sanjay walked to the front of the classroom.

Cale cleared his throat and dropped his gaze to his desk, pulling out a notebook. "Oh, I, uh. I got that research project. With Dr. Britt."

Perhaps a tennis ball to the face was not enough. "Research project? *My* research project? The one I have been aiming for over two years, Cale?" Cale looked straight ahead. "You're unbelievable."

"What?" Cale pulled his innocent, but totally not, look.

Gathering all my stuff, I moved to the last empty

seat in the classroom, just as Dr. Legget started his lecture. Now I remembered why I had such a great time with Matt that weekend. He wasn't Cale.

I couldn't believe they would pick Cale Dafoe over me. Sure, he played tennis for the university's team, but did Dr. Britt really care about that? Did Cale really think I'd roll over and not come back swinging? I had taught myself to walk again, for fuck's sake. Cale Dafoe had no idea whom he was messing with.

The class continued, but I was unable to concentrate. My mind raced with ways to get him out of my life and show him up at the same time. The first step was flushing that charm bracelet down the toilet, even if I did have to visit my dad to do so. Next was making sure I made perfect scores on midterms. Inorganic chemistry, physics, genetics, and Russian literature were cake; no problem. I had to find a way to memorize stupid star pictures. The third step was to ask for Elle's help.

As soon as class ended, I dashed out of the room before I committed murder. I jogged back to the campus apartment I shared with my three roommates. Sharice was there cooking our meals for the week.

"Hey, girl!" She smiled. "Making pineapple chicken with basmati for lunches."

I placed my schoolbag on the hooks near the front door and shirked off my sweater vest. "Thanks. How much do I owe you?"

"It's on the fridge." She half-pointed with her hands stuck in some sauce.

The refrigerator held the grocery receipt. I always

threw in extra money because Sharice prepared my food. Cooking was another side effect of my "accident." My hands couldn't grip a knife properly or for very long. She was kind enough to make extra servings of everything she ate so I could avoid frozen dinners and the college cafeteria food.

Heading to my room to change, I called to her, "I'm going for a run." Since I couldn't hold a racket, running was how I learned to purge my frustrations. I completed a couple of marathons the year before and was planning another before the winter set in.

Running through campus always gave me time to think. Depending on my mood, I could go hard or take it easy. Today was definitely a sprinting day. Donning my leggings and sports bra, I headed outside. After popping in my earbuds, I cranked up the music. No podcasts or audiobooks today.

Maybe I wouldn't have become so bitter if anyone had believed me about the drunk driver that hit my car that night. I'd probably be at Harvard, ready to apply for Harvard medicine or Johns Hopkins. Perhaps I'd have a boyfriend who kissed my neck in class. I'd probably even be one of those girls who dressed up for lectures. One that wasn't embarrassed to wear cute shorts or skirts.

No one ever searched for the other driver again, and no one admitted anyone else was there. The police were convinced my car had just spontaneously slipped on the ice. I knew. I saw the guy and memorized his face. It wasn't just my imagination, or some weird chemical reaction, or some trauma shock, like people told me. He was real. He was there. I just wasn't sure how to prove it.

The wreck forced me to change the course of my life. I couldn't become a surgeon, no. But there were plenty of other medical specialties I could pursue. With everyone trying to assure me I had imagined a man that hit me, the study of neurology was my main focus. Some days, I worried my mind had hallucinated a man at my window. I needed to understand what the human brain was capable of under extreme duress.

Being a patient in the hospital for so long, then rehab after, taught me a great deal about medicine. My desire to become a physician had only increased. Before the collision, my goal had been something competitive, something expected by my father. Now, it was personal.

After my seventh mile, I headed back home. It was getting dark, and I still needed to study. And talk with Elle, who would be at the apartment when I returned.

Arriving back at the kitchen, I opened one of the pre-made meals Sharice left inside the fridge and devoured it. Elle walked into the living room from her bedroom just as I cleaned up my dinner.

"Elle! I need your help!" Plopping down on our denim blue sofa, I sat next to where she lounged scanning social media on her phone.

"What's up? You're kinda ripe, by the way." Shoving her long, blond hair over one shoulder, she laid back on the couch, stretching her long legs up on our glass coffee table.

"I know. I just ran fourteen miles. I'll shower... after." Putting down her phone, she waited for me to continue. "I need you to set me up with someone. Like someone hot. You know? Someone top tier caliber."

Elle's big blue eyes sparkled. "Oh? Oh my gosh, I'm so excited! You trust me? Let's see…" She began listing off potential suitors. Matchmaking was one of Elle's talents, and she loved to do it. Plus, she looked like a Barbie doll and knew tons of attractive people like herself. Elle sat up excitedly. "Got it. How about the mayor's son? He's a bit older, but only 24."

"Mayor Grant's son?"

"Yeah, his name is Barrett Grant. He's very attractive. Just out of law school and joined Smith & Goldstein. Rich."

"And you say he's attractive?" Elle flipped her phone around and showed me a picture of a man lying on a beach, taking a selfie of his body from the neck down. The body was ripped and tan. Not as big of muscles as I preferred, but other than dumb meatheads at the gym, not many men had that kind of physique. Besides, the mayor's son? Cale couldn't compete with that. "Sold."

"Let me text him real quick."

"Wait, have you… have you been with him before?" Elle liked to party. I respected her, but couldn't compete with her experience or her likely bedroom skills. I'd hate to disappoint the mayor's son in the blowjob department or be the runner-up after receiving what I would assume to be a professional job.

"No. I prefer older men." She smiled shyly.

"Oh. Good for you." I jumped up to head to the shower. "Let me know what he says!"

After I got out of the shower, I wrapped my fuzzy towel under my arms. When I reached my bedroom, there was a tap on my door. I opened it for Elle.

"Barrett says he'd love to take you out. He wants to meet at the club on Friday night if that's cool. We're all going to be there. I'll even drag Marissa."

"Sounds fun."

☽ ☽ ☽ ● ☾ ☾ ☾

Friday night, I spent extra time getting ready for the dance club. I barrel waved my dark brown hair and chose a sexy lavender top to accentuate my pale skin. The blouse had a wide-open V that reached a banded waist, exposing my little more than modest cleavage. Tape secured it to my breasts so I wouldn't have a wardrobe malfunction. I paired it with tight white jeans and silvery jeweled high heels.

Glancing at my friends, ready to head out, I was jealous of their short skirts and dresses. Hopefully, the mayor's son wouldn't be turned off by the old cuts on my legs. It would take a while before I felt comfortable showing my body to a stranger. Or lots of alcohol, like the weekend with Matt.

As if sensing my hesitation, Marissa grabbed my hand and squeezed. "You look awesome!" Elle shuffled us all out the door, and we made the short trek to the warehouse on the edge of downtown.

Slinking back to the bar to grab a drink, I was stopped when a soft hand slid along my exposed lower back. A higher male voice said in my ear, "Let me buy you one, honey." I recognized the guy from my Russian literature class waving the bartender over. He wasn't unattractive. Thin, tall, and wearing a backward baseball cap and NU T-shirt. He just wasn't my type. But I'd take a free drink.

"Sure, thanks. Vodka soda, please."

The man ordered one for me and a beer for himself. "I'm Eric. I've seen you in class."

"Yeah, I've seen you, too. I'm Kinsley. I have to tell you that I'm meeting someone here tonight, though."

Eric nodded. "Of course you are. Boyfriend?"

Shaking my head, I told him, "No. Kind of a blind date, actually."

"Well, if it doesn't work out, I'm here. With my boys… over there." His long finger pointed to a corner table where a group of Theta Rho Zeta guys sat. My eyes were immediately drawn to a giant muscular brute taking up a side of the booth by himself. His face was the most handsome one I had ever seen, with a long, squared jaw covered in stubble. Long, shiny blond hair was wrapped in a low ponytail. A quick inhale caught in my throat.

"You're in TRZ?" Theta Rho Zeta was a notorious Greek fraternity on campus. The minimum family income for acceptance was probably a million a year. All those guys were known for throwing wild orgies and crazy parties. Almost certainly, none of them would be going into medicine. They probably bought their test scores from smart kids like me if they were.

Eric followed my eyes. "Yeah. You know G?"

"Who?"

The bartender handed us our drinks, and Eric took a swig with a smile and snorted. "That's Big G. We also call him 'horse cock.'" He looked at me knowingly.

"Oh, no. I don't know him." He was probably a dumb jock for the football team or studying geology. Likely spent all his time in the gym. Maybe even had a small 'roids penis, and they just said he had a big dick as a joke.

Elle sauntered up and placed her hand on my shoulder without noticing Eric. "Hey! Barrett's here. Over there, come on." Sliding her hand into mine, she tugged me away from the bar. I gave Eric a small smile goodbye.

"Come find me later, after your shitty date." One corner of his lips lifted into a smirk as I was pulled away.

Elle walked us over to one of the side tables in an alcove. My friends were sitting down at the table with some other guys there. "Barrett, this is my friend Kinsley."

A man with baby-smooth skin, a soft jawline, delicate lips, and green eyes peered up at me behind round tortoiseshell glasses. He was even wearing the same houndstooth blazer. The drunk driver! It was him! He was real.

I waited for him to have some recognition of me, but his eyes wandered down my chest. "*Heyyy*, Kinsley. So nice to meet you." Every syllable he spoke was slurred and his eye lids looked heavy.

"Barrett Grant? The mayor's son?" I bit my lip trying to keep from screaming.

"Yeah, sweetie. That's me. You wanna sit?" One of his palms opened, indicating his crotch.

"No. I want to know why you hit my car three years ago and drove away."

Barrett narrowed his eyes and scanned my face, but there was still no acknowledgment there. "I have no idea what you're talking about, but if you want me to hit you, I know a better place than your car." He patted his lap as the vodka smell rolled off him like ocean waves.

Glancing around the table, everyone seemed to be confused staring at our exchange. I wasn't sure how to handle the situation. He was going to deny anything ever happened. My friends looked at me with pity, and his friends seemed amused. Things were starting to get awkward as the tension between us intensified.

I decided to take him up on the offer, try to corner him, and get him to confess. Maybe he wouldn't in front of his friends, but if I got him alone... Sliding into his lap, he pushed my hair to the side and nuzzled my neck. If I lit a match, his alcohol breath would ignite in flames.

"There now. Isn't that more comfortable?"

Turning my face towards him, I whispered, "I think I'd be more comfortable if we could be alone." I grabbed his hand that was snaked around my waist and stood, putting on a flirty smile. He smirked and followed me while his friends leered and laughed at his good luck.

Pulling him into the darkened hall near the restrooms, I pushed him against the wall and glared at him. Thrusting a finger in his face, I said, "I know who you are. I know what you did. Admit it. Admit you hit my car, you fucking bastard."

Barrett sniggered, but something behind his eyes held a tiny fraction of the same terror from the night he gazed into my car window. "Lady, I don't know what you're on about. I just wanted to fuck." Skinny fingers wrung around my neck. Tightening the grip, he flipped us around, so I was pressed against the wall instead of him. He thrust his erection into my belly and licked the side of my face.

"Ew! Stop that!" Sliding my hands up his chest, I shoved, but he wouldn't budge. "Stop! Don't!" Even though I thrashed with my legs, he sucked hard on my cheek, writhed his hips more firmly against my core.

Both of us paused when a booming bass vibrated the walls of the hall. "Get off her."

Barrett barely twisted his head to say, "Fuck off, man." But then, he was gone.

The massive titan I saw earlier had pulled the mayor's son off my body by the collar of his blazer, holding him out of reach of me. Barrett tried to get away from the creature, but to no avail. I took the opportunity to run and dashed for the back exit.

CHAPTER
TWO
GEORGE

THE DWARF TWISTED under my grasp as Snow White rushed out of the bar. Like a comic book villain, he bellowed, "Don't you know who I am?"

"No." I dropped him as soon as she was gone. He turned in a flash to look at me. Oh, wait, was that…

"Barrett Grant. Oh, hello. Who do we have here?" The twerp started laughing. "George Turner, Junior. Chief Turner's son. Well, well. I'm sure he will be proud to hear about your arrest for assault."

Clenching my jaw, I held my tongue. His green eyes relaxed as he smiled and brushed his fancy blazer back into place. Taking a step back, I leaned against the wall.

"Looks like you don't want that kind of trouble. Smart man. It appears you understand me." He pointed a finger towards the exit. "Now, tell your little girlfriend to back off, or she'll cause us both unwanted attention." I must have looked confused because he continued. "She's not yours? Well… for both of our families' sake, it's best to keep it that way." With the air of someone who would say the phrase "I have people for that", he strode off back to his drink.

I wasn't quite sure what he was implying, but knowing the Grants, I wanted to remain in the dark. Father's dealings were too deep; I didn't want to get involved. Tried to keep my nose clean and my head down, not say a word.

The twerp went towards the bar, and I headed out the way the princess did. The night was over; I didn't need any more excitement. At least I had *Serenity* to carry me home. I reached my black Ford F-150 and jumped in, cranking up the music. Being a member of TRZ had privileges, and the expansive garage at the manor was one of them. Only the best for my truck.

Not a fan of going out to the club, my shoulders eased their tension as I made my way to the safety of my room. Neptune was in opposition, and I wanted to catch the little blue light with my telescope before going to bed.

While searching the skies for it, I received a text from Dan. Opening the message revealed a picture of my youngest brother, Aaron, passed out on the floor of my mom's apartment. On the coffee table in front of him was various drug paraphernalia and empty liquor bottles. The words beneath the picture said:

DAN
Visited mom tonight...

It was too late in the night to deal with it. Sighing, I flopped on my bed and tried to shut out the thoughts that flooded my mind every night. If I could have just...

If only I had… Maybe if I… So many alternate universes I could have created if I'd done things differently. Suppose I had kept my mouth shut. If I took better care of them all. If I hadn't been born…

☽ ☽ ☽ ● ☾ ☾ ☾

My alarm blared, and I sluggishly rolled over to turn it off. We had a gym in the manor, but I had access to the university's sports facility from the football coach who heavily recruited me. My brother, Dan, was a superstar baseball player for the Nighthawks and would let me in, even if my ID didn't work there.

Football was a passion, but I always knew I would have to give it up to care for my family. A division one school would be too far away. And I didn't want to spend all the extra training time when my mother or brothers would need me. Theta Rho Zeta took up enough of my time.

When I pulled open the locker room door, Dan was already changed for our workout. "Sup. Get my text?"

I nodded. "I'll stop by." Right after my gym therapy session.

It was back and biceps day, and I hit the weights hard until my muscles shook, and my T-shirt was soaked with sweat. Half the football team was in there, slapping me on the back or saying hello as they passed. Given my talents, I could have been a walk-on with the team anytime I chose. Some days I thought about it. But I couldn't. I needed to be available to nurse Aaron back to some sort of shape of a living person again.

Hitting the showers, I changed into fresh clothes as Dan stepped into the locker room. "So, what are you going to do with that bitch today?" My eyes narrowed at him. "G, our mother's a cunt. You know this. Probably chopped up the pills for Aaron herself." As a threat, I moved closer to him. "G, come on. You can't get mad. You know it's the truth. Dad was right to ditch her sorry ass."

With a palm on each of his shoulders, I shoved him against the locker. A few guys in the room were afraid to approach us, but came over to try to help. I let Dan slide from my grip. Hurriedly, I finished dressing and grabbed my bag, darting out of the room before I did something stupid.

It was the same shit, and I didn't want to hear it. Dan never took our mother's side, and he never stood up for Aaron. Whenever their names were mentioned, he blamed them for all their own problems. Dan didn't understand. Our mother's and brother's issues were because of me. I was responsible for what had happened to them, and I tried every day to make amends for my mistakes.

Jumping into *Serenity*, I drove toward the factories on the outskirts of town. Rows of studio apartments had been constructed in the mid-century for the industrial workers. No one had updated them since. Surrounding a rectangular pool filled with rainwater were balconies leading up four stories high. Inside one of the doors on the second story, lived my mother.

Parking far away from the other vehicles so no one would touch mine, I grabbed a bag from the backseat of my truck and headed up the rusted metal stairs. Using my spare key, I opened the door to the smell of pungent human waste, stale cigarettes, and liquor. Marijuana smoke billowed from the room as soon as I stepped inside. It appeared someone was awake already.

Walking straight to the one window, I opened the blinds fully, then let air inside after opening it. My mother was smoking a joint in her chair, staring at the little TV's squiggly image. Her pink robe was now a faded cream color and more matted than fuzzy. She scowled and cried out when the sunlight streamed over her pale blue eyes. Grabbing her spliff, I stubbed it on the metal window frame, and then tossed it through the open window.

"Hey! I was smoking that!"

"Not anymore." My brother was passed out on the couch when I leaned over his face, checking for any breathing. Digging around in my bag, I found a naloxone nasal spray. Just in case. I shook Aaron's shoulders, then rolled him on his back. His chest was rising and falling normally. Watching the steady rhythm flooded me with relief.

Scooping his scant body up in my arms, I carried him to the dirty bathtub and laid him inside. Turning on the cold shower water, he screamed and sat up. "What the fuck, G?!" His hands frantically wiped his face of the wet droplets pouring off his shaggy blond hair.

"Take a shower. You reek."

Closing the door to the bathroom, I went into the kitchen and washed the dishes in the sink. Going through the cabinets and refrigerator, I saw Aaron had already gone through the groceries I purchased a few days prior, except for a few eggs. A cardboard silo of oatmeal still sat in the back of a cabinet, and the mice hadn't gotten to it. Two lonely brown bananas sat on the counter. I started on breakfast.

"George. I don't like you coming here. It's a waste of time. I don't need your help. Aaron helps me plenty. Where's your brother? Dan, that traitor. Probably with his father now, huh? Isn't that where you should be, too? You're just like him. Always nosing into other people's business. Where you don't belong." My mother kept talking as she pulled out a cigarette. "Aaron's all I need. I don't want you here. What are you doing over there? You messing with my stuff?"

"Here. Eat." Thrusting a bowl of oatmeal and some eggs at her, she scrunched her face up in disgust.

"I'm not eating that. You probably poisoned it. Just like your father…" But she took it from me and dug in. It had probably been a few days since she ate actual food.

Moving to the coffee table, I scraped all the pipes, cards, razors, syringes (that was new), and pill crushers into a large black plastic bag. Using some disinfectant wipes, I cleaned up the mess. Holding up some pill bottles, I shook them at my mother. "Stop giving these to Aaron. Stop with this shit. I'm calling this doctor."

She laughed. "Ha! Try. It was from an emergency room. I'll go back. You have *no* idea the pain I'm in. I need those pills. Don't you dare throw them away, *Junior*." I popped my neck. She used the name she knew would get to me.

Aaron came out of the bathroom, rubbing his light blond hair with a towel as I brushed past him, dumped the rest of the pill bottles in the toilet, and flushed.

"Hey, man!" Aaron watched me from the door. Turning around, I snatched his naked arms, inspecting the undersides of each one. Spotting a couple of red dots on his forearms, I shook my head. He yanked out of my grip. "I just needed some help last night."

"Go eat." Pouring them both some water, I finished cleaning up the place. Aaron sat on the couch, slowly eating his oatmeal. His face was gaunt, with dark marks settling into each crevice beneath his cheekbones. "When did you start injecting?" His bloodshot eyes met mine briefly before he looked down.

"I just tried it once before."

"Leave him alone, George. Aaron is an adult. He can do what he wants—"

"He's not a fucking adult, Mom. He's *sixteen* years old! He should be in school right now. This is why you don't have custody."

My mom jumped up from her chair with a spryness I didn't know she still had. Despite her short stature, she was able to reach up to my face and slap me across the cheek. It didn't hurt… physically.

"Aaron can stay here if he wants. I'm his mother. He's better off with me than a piece of shit like your father… like *you*. And he doesn't need Dan's influence, either. We understand each other. You have no idea the kind of pain we deal with on a daily basis..."

She kept going until I tuned her out. Finding the few items on the floor that were clearly Aaron's, I thrust them into my bag. Grabbing the trash, I marched to the dumpster and tossed the bags inside, then returned to gather my brother. Mom was still talking as I walked out and back in. She never shut up. Despite her tirade of insults, I walked over and kissed her forehead.

"Move. Let's go." Aaron was still wearing a towel around his waist, but I didn't care. I needed to get him home.

"Fine! Go tell your father, you big fucking *traitor*! You fucking asshole! I hate you!" Mom was screaming at me as I walked out with my baby brother in front of me.

Before I closed the door, I turned and said, "I'll get some lightbulbs for your lamps, Mom. And buy more groceries."

She screamed, "Bring me back my pills!"

After we got in, Aaron let his head rest on the passenger seat of my pickup. The pressure built inside the cabin as we drove until he said, "I'm sorry. I shouldn't have done that. Please don't tell Dad. You know what he'll do."

"You're shooting that shit now, Aaron. What am I supposed to do?"

"I'm not like you and Dan. I'm not good at sports." Quietly, he turned to look out his window. "I'm not good at anything."

"No one's asking you to be good at sports." I sighed.

I had no desire to talk to our father, either, but maybe it was time to. He needed to know how bad things had gotten. As we reached my father's colonial, I pulled into the driveway and commanded, "Get dressed. Go to school."

Aaron gawked. "It's too late! I've already missed like two classes this morning." I stared at him until his skinny shoulders slumped and he slowly opened his car door. "Fine, fine. I'll go."

If I hurried, I could almost make my own mid-morning class before grabbing a quick takeout lunch in the cafeteria, but first I needed to stop by for my dreaded errand. Adding protein powder to my blender bottle, I downed it and drove to the town's central police station.

"George Turner, Junior. It's been too long since you've visited me!" My dad's assistant, Grace, was sitting at her desk when I ambled to his office after being greeted by several officers. Leaning over her desk, I kissed her on the cheek in greeting. "I think he's busy." She pointed to my father's half-closed door down a short hall. I shrugged and walked that way. This was too important to wait. Whichever officer was in there could step out while I spoke with the tyrant.

As I approached, a woman's seductive voice carried out of the half-opened door. Squinting my eyes closed, I pinched the bridge of my nose. Was he already fucking someone new? He started boning Clarissa a few months ago. The closer I got, the tighter the knot in my stomach twisted. I recognized the voice. No, no, no. Nausea hit me like an explosion in my belly.

"Thank you for the check, darling. Next time you cover up crimes, maybe you'll think about how much your actions (she laughed here), sorry, your *inaction* has cost you."

"Get lost, Gianna."

"Is that any way to treat your ex-wife? Any way to treat a *concerned citizen*?"

"You got your September check. Out." My father opened his door more, and Gianna Cunningham's svelte body slinked toward the exit in a bright green dress. She flipped her thick auburn hair as she sashayed past the threshold.

"See you next month!" Pressing my body against the wall, I hoped she wouldn't see me. No chance. "Oh! Wow! Lookie here. Georgie has grown up." Her eyes danced down my body and landed on my crotch. Leaning her body into mine, she said in a low, sultry voice, "Still have the same phone number, Georgie?" I didn't move. "I'll be in touch." Crawling her fingers down my stomach, she grasped my penis lightly with a growl before walking down the hall.

"George. What are you doing? Leave her alone." My father beckoned me into his office and closed the door tightly. I wandered in and sat in the plastic chair across from the nameplate on his desk that stated, "Chief George Turner, Senior." Dad sat in his office chair. "Don't touch that woman, George. She's trouble."

Like I had a choice. Like I ever had a choice. "Aaron's in trouble."

My father leaned forward, placing his uniformed arms on his desk pad calendar. "What is it now?"

WHITE HOLE

"You're not watching him. He's going to Mom's and—"

"I'm watching him fine. That woman has screwed him up. I cannot be held responsible for her actions when he is with her." His gray eyes glared at me down his long, straight nose. "If you'd show a little responsibility, hadn't quit your football career, maybe he'd have an older brother to look out for him."

My fist pounded on the arm of the chair, vibrating the entire seat. "I am looking out for him. I'm the only one!"

"Do we need to have a go?" My father stood, loosening the buttons on his jacket. I knew what he was doing. If I assaulted him, ten officers would be in here, and everyone would blame me, his unhinged son. "Just like your mother", he would say. Possibly stick me in an institution somewhere against my will. I settled back in my chair. "Fine. Military academy it is, then. I told him last time that's where he was heading."

"He needs rehab, Dad."

"He'll learn the discipline he needs to get off whatever he's into if he's in training." With a last cursory glance at me, he sat down and picked up his phone. "I'll make some calls."

I got up to leave, but before I could, he said, "Oh, Junior? Don't tell him. I don't want him running to *her* before the school picks him up."

It would be a challenge for me not to tell Aaron, but if I did, he would likely use "one last time" as he did anytime my dad threatened to send him somewhere. Dad was right. My mother would use it as an excuse to

51

"celebrate" with her youngest son until they were both blasted.

Walking past Grace, I waved a quick goodbye as she made a comment about stopping by more often. In the parking lot, a white note was tucked under the windshield wiper of my black truck. Ire rose within me, thinking someone had dared damage her in any way. When I opened the folded piece of paper, it contained a date and address written in curly cursive. At the bottom was a final warning message:

See you soon.

CHAPTER
THREE
KINSLEY

STEP THREE HAD GONE HORRIBLY wrong. I was short on attractive dates to outshine Cale. *And* I ran into the man who ruined my future. The mayor's son... Culpability had been written in his expression, but he feigned innocence. I wasn't sure how to force a confession from him.

Step one wasn't going so well, either. The last few years, I avoided my father as much as I avoided driving, and I had no desire to visit the tomb of my childhood. Not even for a revenge pawn of Cale's bracelet.

Step two was also a disappointment. The first astronomy quiz scores were posted, and I got a C. A C! I had never seen that letter on my grade reports. At first, I thought it was a mistake. So, I went to Dr. Torrad's office hours. She assured me the grade was correct, but referred me to tutoring sessions in the library. Me getting *tutored*! I was the one who usually helped students. After the initial shock, I knew I had to swallow a heaping spoonful of pride to get straight As again.

Tucking the paper with the session time and location into my backpack, I headed back to my apartment and changed into running tights and a tank top. It was a go-hard day. As I ran, I thought about Barrett Grant's shocked look from the night of the accident, which morphed into his smirking villain expression from the bar.

How was I supposed to prove he was the cause of the accident? Why had the police said no one else was there? Where would I even *start* to figure out what was going on? Maybe I could talk with a lawyer. Ugh, Barrett *was* a lawyer. Okay... I wouldn't use his law firm.

Jogging down the alley between the old science building and the new one, I had a skin-prickling sensation of eyes following my body. I didn't want to stop to check behind me. Shuffling footsteps approached, and I slowed to a walk. Coming to a stop, I flipped around, but no one was there. I paced back, deciding to turn around for the evening.

"Hey, Kins!" Cale was walking by on the sidewalk near the science building. Probably there for the research project, *my* research project. I tried to wave and jog off, but he stepped in front of me. "Did you have a chance to find that bracelet? I need that charm."

"Sorry. Not yet, Cale. I'll look for it this weekend." As I went to sidestep him, he moved with me to block my path.

"It's mine and Sydney's second anniversary soon. I, uh, was going to give her that charm. It's important."

"Okay. I'll search for it. Excuse me." I hurried off. How had I not noticed what a punchable face he had all those years we were in high school?

At home, Elle was almost ready to leave for dinner. Her blond hair was perfectly styled, and she wore a cute little dress showing off her extra cleavage and long legs. "Hurry up! I want to snag a good table before it's too busy."

"I have to shower, but I'll be quick." Tuesday nights, we always headed to Manny's Mexican restaurant for Taco Tuesday and half-priced margaritas. I topped my wide-legged sailor pants with a vintage flutter-sleeve keyhole blouse. My flats were neatly tucked in the rack at the bottom of my organized closet. After brushing my long, dark hair, I pulled it into a side ponytail before spritzing on my Chanel perfume. The final touch was a string of my grandmother's pearls.

I knocked on Marissa's door to beg her to come with us. She and Sharice had a knack for trying to skip out and stay home. She agreed to join only since Sharice was going. After gathering our purses, we strolled towards Main Street.

Elle and I lagged behind Sharice and Marissa on the walk to the restaurant. "Hey, sorry about the bad set-up the other night. I thought Barrett would be perfect. Who knew he'd be such a drunken louse?"

"It's okay." Elle didn't know about my accident. We were close enough to go out together and have a good time but had never really shared emotionally intense feelings before. Or much about each other's histories. I didn't think bringing up Barrett Grant as the man who ruined my future would be a good way to start.

"I'll find someone better. I'm usually good at these things!" Elle started to list off more boys that would be "just right" for me.

I didn't feel like anyone would believe me if I told them Barrett Grant was at the scene of my accident. No one had thus far. Keeping my mouth shut, I nodded along with Elle's suggested matches while devising a strategy for investigating how Barrett Grant got away with a hit-and-run.

"Sure, sure. Any of them sound fine. I trust you." It didn't matter who he was, as long as he wasn't Cale and was better than him.

As we entered the painted blue doors of Manny's, I glanced at our usual corner, but a crowd of rowdy Theta Rho Zeta occupied the space. Elle shrugged and said there was room enough for us, leading our group to the tables where a few seats were left unoccupied. I immediately spotted the stone titan that rescued me from Barrett. He was sitting quietly apart from his buddies. Wanting to thank him for his heroism, I slid into the wall booth next to him. Glancing at me with a furrowed brow, I stuck my hand out to him to introduce myself.

"Hey, I'm Kinsley. You saved me last Friday night from that asshole." The man turned his head away toward his fraternity brothers, sipping his pint glass of hoppy ale. I lowered my hand. "Um. You're Big G, right? I think Eric told me your name." I looked around the table at the crowd of TRZ boys. Spotting Eric, he waved from the far end of the row of tables, and I lifted my fingers in acknowledgment. Big G continued to drink.

The waiter came over to get more drink orders. I ordered an apple martini and snacked on a few chips but tried to control the amount, mindful of the upcoming marathon. "Well, anyway. Thank you. It was very kind of you." He wasn't speaking. Had I done something to piss him off? "Why do they call you Big G?"

Big G only snorted and downed the rest of his beer. The server put down another as he returned with a drink tray. I sipped my martini. Maybe he had social anxiety. I could help him feel more at ease, get him talking, and feel more comfortable.

"I like how they make their martinis here. Nice and dry, the way I like them. Have you had an apple martini?" Big G scanned the room. I followed where his eyes were looking. "Despite the chaos, I appreciate how Manny decorated the place after the renovation. Did you see it before they redecorated a couple of years ago? It wasn't nearly this nice. The tables didn't have this decoupage on top, and the floor tiles were not as colorful as this. Also, the walls now have this distressed look going on that makes it seem old-world charming—"

The TRZ in the wall booth next to me bumped my shoulder. I believed his name to be Tyson after seeing him at the Lounge or a party a few years back. "Sweetheart. If you're trying to talk to G, you may as well give up. The guy's the definition of the silent type." A few of his brothers sitting in chairs across the little tables from us laughed. "Isn't that right, horse cock?"

Big G looked down at his beer. I stuck up for him. "Maybe he's just *shy*. It's okay, Big G. Or," and I lowered my voice and head so only he could hear me, "horse cock." G rolled his eyes and sat back. "Oh, does that annoy you?"

He finally contemplated my face, and my entire body heated down to my core. We latched onto each other's gazes, tapping into them for a small eternity, pupils widening into black holes before he downed his second beer, never blinking away from my stare. I tried to swallow as my mouth went dry and my heart raced. Breaking our connection, he threw two ten-dollar bills on the table and stood up. Then he lumbered out the door while I scoffed. What an incredibly rude man.

I finished my martini and decided the night was over. Besides, the longer I sat there, the more appealing the food smells became. I needed to stick with my premade meals since I was training. Bidding goodbye to my friends, I planned to walk home and prepare one of Sharice's dinners.

As I left the restaurant, the giant was getting into an enormous, pristine black truck with a light rack on top of the cab. Below the shiny front grill was a custom vanity plate that lit up. It was a picture of the phases of the moon. He noticed me watching him start his truck. Once I reached it, I had to jump back from the exit as he rushed out of the parking lot. When he passed, his license plate read "J3DI KNT".

I arrived home annoyed and distracted. After eating, I performed my nightly routine and changed for bed. The frustration made my neck tense, my body yearning to relax. I pulled out my clit sucker from the bedside table.

Relaxing on my pillows, I tried not to picture Cale's face. Instead, I remembered my weekend with Matt. Matt on top of my body. But Matt's face morphed into a giant's with a squared jaw and long, blond hair. With a thick neck and broad shoulders. And corded muscles. And a cock as big as a horse's, long, fat, and veiny. Possibly uncut. He turned into Big G. I hated it, but I screamed in ecstasy as I reached orgasm, "G…" He didn't deserve any space in my fantasies.

I couldn't sleep. Irritation at my imagination lingered. Deciding I'd laid in bed long enough, I got up to study astronomy. Maybe something would stick. I attempted to memorize the pictures of the sky. When I looked out my window, I could see nothing that matched the pages in the book.

Slamming the text shut, I decided to watch more videos in preparation for my medical college admission test. It was coming up in a few weeks, and a near-perfect score was needed for the top schools in the country. Any time I hadn't been training for the marathon or studying for my college coursework was spent preparing for the important test. Eventually, I became drowsy enough to return to bed.

The following day, I trudged through morning classes after a fitful night. I had nightmares about my car wreck and Barrett's laughing face, blood streaming from his eyeballs. Enduring a Cale and Sydney make-out session almost made me lose my appetite for lunch. After grabbing a to-go meal from the cafeteria, I headed directly to the library to meet the astronomy tutor.

I pictured a lithe hippy girl who loved astrology—or a nerdy guy with a love of all things sci-fi. Perhaps I would luck out, and it would be an attractive professor type with a secret trust fund. Whoever it was, hopefully, I could absorb their knowledge by osmosis.

My note said to meet the tutor in section three of the dedicated open study alcoves. Rounding the corner at the prescribed location, I stopped short. The Goliath was sitting at the round wooden table, staring into a book. His body was so big that the table looked like dollhouse furniture. I checked the placard above the alcove. It stated, "Section 3". Big G peered at me. His behemoth shoulders slumped.

I pursed my lips. "Hello to you, too. I'm supposed to meet someone here. Would you mind?" I held up a hand, waving to the rest of the library for him to leave.

Big G huffed. "Astronomy tutoring?" His voice sent waves into my bloodstream, vibrating my bone marrow with the sound of his bass.

Ugh, I felt sick. "No way. *You're* the tutor?"

Big G kicked out a chair next to him with his foot.

I glanced around, seeing if anyone was filming my reaction as a prank or if anyone else was available to teach me. We were alone in this area of the library. Sighing, I plopped into the empty chair next to him. "Well. I didn't think you could speak." He didn't respond. "I'm going to make the best of this. I don't care if you don't like me." I arranged my stuff on the table. "I wouldn't have expected someone like you to be into astronomy. Or science. Or studying. How can you even tutor if you don't open your mouth?"

Big G flipped open a map of the stars and smoothed it out on the table. He silently wrote on a piece of blank, white paper. Speaking into his lap, he said, "Astronomy is a science. Science is—"

"Are you seriously going to explain to me what *science* is? Sir, I am in pre-medicine. A chemistry major. With a 4.0 grade point average. I think I have an enormous grasp on what *science* is."

"Then why are you failing?" He blinked at me. My jaw fell open. I was speechless. What a disrespectful prat. "Here." He shoved the paper he had been writing on at me. It contained some mnemonics to aid with my studies. "You'll need these."

"Shoving a piece of paper at me isn't going to do anything. I don't know how experienced you are with teaching, but I don't learn with rote memorization. I need to *understand* what I'm studying. And I need to pass this class with an A. Aren't there some tools… There!" I pointed to the wall. "Use the whiteboard over there and show me. Draw something. Unless you don't know what you're talking about." I glanced around the alcove. "Honestly, the whiteboard really should go over on that wall so one wouldn't have to crane their neck to see it while sitting at this table. And these chairs aren't conducive to long hours of study. Nevertheless, *instruct* me. Go on."

Big G snorted and mumbled under his breath.

"I'm sorry. What did you say?" My eyes blazed fire at the side of his face.

"Gabby. I said you're gabby. Loquacious. Garrulous. Voluble. It means you talk too much."

"And you're rude. Taciturn. Reticent. Laconic. It means you don't talk enough." I shut my notebook. "I can't learn from a meathead, anyway."

"I'm not the one who needs help studying *stars*, princess. Ms. Pre-med with a four-point oh."

"Oh? Really?" The anger rose within me. I wasn't about to hold back. "I think they call you 'horse cock' to cover up your bird brain."

"Maybe you'd be better off studying interior design." He sat back in his chair and put his arms behind his head.

I grabbed my bag and threw my notebook inside. "Screw you, asshole."

Big G smirked at me as I darted out of the library.

CHAPTER FOUR
GEORGE

PRINCESS LEIA GAVE me a free hour by dipping out of our tutoring session early. That gave me plenty of time to make it to Springfield. Using my navigation system in *Serenity*, I found the seedy motel Gianna picked. It was hidden behind an abandoned discount goods store, set in the same cracked asphalt lot.

Showing up earlier than the time she specified allowed me to check out my surroundings for an ambush. There were a few cars parked in front of the rooms, but overall, the place was abandoned. I was sure Gianna had planned it that way. Watching a green Mercedes pull up, I finished my protein shake and waited for her Jessica Rabbit figure to exit.

Gianna had no business wearing a red velvet dress to a place like this. Her dyed auburn hair fell long over her back as she glanced around to find me sitting in my truck. Painted red lips smiled seductively as I jumped out.

"Well, hello, handsome." Her long fingernails

scratched me as her hand grabbed my arm, rubbing her thumb gently over my irritated skin.

"Let's get this over with." With her hanging onto me, I marched to the room she had written on the note. Gianna pulled out a key with a plastic keychain attached and opened the thin wooden door.

Two queen beds with floral covers that had seen better days sat in the middle of the room. There was a small Formica table near the window with rolling wicker seats. The back of one had been popped out. A faux wood dresser was on one side of the room with a cracked mirror but held a new flat-screen TV.

Gianna sat on the edge of the bed, crossing her legs so her short dress rode up her thighs. I chose the wicker chair. Lifting my eyebrows, I waited for her to start. When she didn't and began sliding one of her high-heeled feet toward my lap, I spoke. "What do you want, Gianna?"

"Don't be so harsh. Is that any way to treat your old lover?"

Shaking my head, I looked down. She and her amber musk made me ill. *Lover*. I could spit at the word. "You're blackmailing my father. I don't know what it's about, and I don't want to. I'm not involved in his dealings. You can leave me out of whatever you're planning. I don't have any money." There. That was probably the most I'd ever spoken to her. And now I was done.

"Oh, baby boy. You're so innocent. I love it."

I wasn't. Not anymore. Not after her.

"Let me tell you a story," she said. "There once was

a young man who was so upset after losing several rounds of poker that he drank a fifth of vodka before leaving the casino on the river. After getting into his car, he realized he couldn't see straight, but didn't care. As he drove, he slid into a little car that had a high school girl in it. One with a bright future ahead of her. Poor thing wanted to be a surgeon and was a star tennis player. But the young man knew he would be in a lot of trouble for driving drunk, so instead of stopping to help the girl, he drove away and called his father… the mayor… Who called your father… the chief of police."

My neck started to sweat. "So?"

"Your father helped Mayor Grant take care of the problem. His policemen were ordered, *by him*, to destroy the evidentiary videos from the traffic lights that night. And some smart cookie got that conversation on audio recording. Who was that?" She sat back. "Oh! That was *me*!"

"So why not blackmail Mayor Grant?"

"Because I only have your father's voice recorded." She shrugged, her shoulders coming up almost out of her dress, revealing more of her expensive cleavage.

"What does any of this have to do with me?"

"Well, you see, Georgie." She leaned forward and crept her fingers up my thigh as she smiled, bright ruby lips spreading across her white teeth. "I don't want money from you." Her hand latched onto my soft, thick cock, laying on my thigh. She squeezed. "I want something I've been missing."

"No." I stood up.

"Or else…"

I started to walk out, but paused. My shoulders dropped. "Or else, what?"

"Or else I reveal your father's secrets. The mayor would *love* to take him down. Your family name would be ruined, but that's not what would bother you, I know. Your father would cut off your mother. She is poor now, but she'd become destitute. You and Dan's tuition would evaporate. And," she faked a sniffle here, "Widdle Aaron would be sent to foster care because your mother can't get custody."

"*I* could take care of Aaron."

"Oh? Take care of an opioid addict? You home to watch him, or would you be off at that playboy mansion you call a fraternity house? Give up your useless degree to get a job at a fast-food restaurant? And what about Dan? Would he give up baseball? Would the three of you make a happy family?"

She smirked as I sat back down. Then she continued, "But that's not the kicker. I *know* Mayor Grant." I was sure her vagina knew him well. "And I *know* what he would do if it was revealed that your father covered up this crime. He would make your father take the blame, and he would frame your family. Where were you that night, Georgie?"

I shook my head, not understanding her meaning.

"Were you at home with your friends, raping your poor stepmother and stepsister with your fat cock? Or were you out driving drunk?"

"Are you fucking kidding me?"

The villain laughed. "No. Alenna will file charges

WHITE HOLE

against you for rape. On your friends. On your father. And I plan to back her up."

"What do you want, Gianna?"

"I want you. I want you to meet me and fuck me whenever I call. I want you to fuck me raw."

I thought I had escaped my prison, but I was just in a holding cell. The metal door just clanged shut. "Can I have a week to think this through?"

Gianna got up and sat in my lap, grinding her round ass on my crotch. "Sure, sweetie. But you'll say yes." She leaned forward so she pushed her butt more into me and grabbed her phone from the bed. "I have your number. I'll text you this new one. You have one week. Otherwise, I'd wait for the police to knock on your door."

She slid off me as I moved to a standing position. Turning around, she whispered close to my neck while grabbing my cock. "I've missed you, Georgie."

I didn't want her to see how sick she made me. Darting out of the room, I made it to the truck before hurling my protein shake onto the ground near the tailgate. There was no way out. I was trapped. She knew exactly what to say in order to get me to comply. Freedom was an illusion.

☽ ☽ ☾ ● ☾ ☾ ☾

The next week brought on the autumn rains. I pulled my hoodie closer over my head and darted through the Northview University library lot. Figured I would get some early studying out of the way while waiting to see if the princess would return for tutoring. Though I wasn't in the mood for her snark, something inside me anticipated her arrival.

After an hour of going over notes, a smell of cinnamon and coffee wafted to my nose. Glancing up from the table, Ms. Priss was standing across from me with a travel mug in her hand. She looked as if she were debating whether to stay or not. I leaned back in the little wooden chair.

"Are you going to be nice to me today?" Her small mouth pursed as she raised one eyebrow.

"Are you going to be nice *to me* today?"

She scoffed. "I've always been nice to you." She sat in the seat next to me, throwing her bag into the empty chair beside her.

"Bird brain?"

Kinsley chuckled. "Oh, that one bothered you, huh?" She suddenly grimaced and flexed her fingers, and straightened her legs, propping them up on the empty seat.

"You okay?"

"Yeah, sorry. A drunk driver hit my car a few years ago, and sometimes things hurt. Like when it rains, or the weather is changing."

The memory of Barrett Grant's drunk face from the bar flashed into my mind. He said something about this girl causing "both" of our families problems. The mayor's son had been involved in a hit-and-run a few years ago.

"Oh? Bad accident?"

"Yeah. You saved me from the other driver last Friday night."

I must have grunted.

She flared her nostrils. "You don't believe me?"

The problem was, I did believe her. If she kept pressing Barrett for the truth, the mayor was likely to harm her. She could be in over her head without realizing what danger she was in. Even my father could try to silence her. What were the chances that this girl would be assigned to me for tutoring? Northview really was too small for me.

Kinsley never shut her mouth. I knew she could never stop talking about the incident, especially if *I* was the one telling her to shut up about it. She had no idea the kind of danger she'd put herself in if she spoke about it so openly.

"Well, I guess the answer is no. You've returned to your mute state. Do I need to press a button to turn you on or something?"

Fuck. This girl was cute. She was definitely turning me on; my dick twitched in my pants. She was the type that had no idea how sexy she actually was. Her brown hair was in a messy side ponytail. I wanted to grab it. Despite her oversized sweatshirt, I could tell she had a nice figure. I'd checked out her ass in leggings the other day. Her perky tits were almost jumping out at me the other night at the club.

"Earth to Mr. Astronomer. Are you going to teach me, or should I find someone else? I'm sure YouTube has someone better than you."

I cleared my throat. "You actually want to learn today, or are you going to run off?"

"Seriously? You insulted me. You were an asshole."

I shrugged. "How did I insult you?"

"You said I should study interior design."

"And? How is that an insult? You keep talking about how to improve areas. Figured you'd be good at it."

She snorted. "I just notice things. I'm very observant. It's a necessary skill for my future career. I'm going to be a doctor... What, you can't imagine a female doctor? Am I not smart enough, in your opinion? Because I didn't get an A in stupid astronomy or whatever?" I pulled out the star map and prepared some notes for the lesson. My mind needed to get off how mesmerizing her eyes were. Hazel? Green? Some light shade of brown?. "What are you majoring in? The outer space? Rocket ships and aliens?"

"Physics and math."

Kinsley shrunk in her chair. "Oh." She seemed to reconsider what she was going to say. "Like double major?"

I stared at her. "Yep."

"Huh. What are you planning to do with that? You're a senior, aren't you? What will you do next year?"

"Get a masters in aerospace engineering. Hopefully, work for NASA."

"Really." She got out her notebook and placed it on the table, finally quiet.

"What? You think 'meatheads' can't be engineers? Am I not smart enough to become an engineer, in your opinion?" Mocking her voice, I knew I had never been provoked enough to talk like this to anyone. Even Mason, and he pissed me off more than anyone. What was she doing to me? Some of her words were rubbing off on me.

When I arrived, I wanted peace and quiet for the day after the stress of dealing with Gianna's proposal. Now, I was itching for a good fight. "Oh, did I finally make princess quiet?"

She gasped. "I am *not* a princess. I was just surprised, that's all." Her face flushed. "How are you qualified to teach me astronomy when you aren't even majoring in it?"

"It's my minor. And I've gotten all As in it. You're not the only one with a four-point oh, *princess*." I smoothed out my notes and the map. "Now, are you going to shut up and learn, or get intimidated and run away again?"

"I was not intimidated." She sighed heavily. "Fine. Teach me. But first, tell me your name. I'm not calling you 'Big G'. It's so asinine." I started to say my name, but she raised her eyebrows and interrupted. "Nor 'horse cock', so don't even say it."

"George."

"*George*? Your name is *George*?" Her eyes blazed and locked on mine.

"Yes, do you have something asinine to say about my name?"

"No! I just... I don't know what I expected. Maybe Giovanni. Or Gage. Or Grayson. Something less classic than George."

"What can I say? I'm a classy guy. Can we get started? I've got plans tonight."

"Hey, I'm not the motormouth today. I really didn't think you talked. You're the one dragging us into a conversation. I'd just assume we didn't talk and just worked on each other. With! *With* each other. Not on each other. I mean, with tutoring..." Staring into my eyes, she blushed deeply, and my cock started to stretch against my jeans. I smirked. She stammered, "S-start your teaching."

I wanted to teach her something, but it wasn't astronomy.

How was I supposed to concentrate now? She was distracting me with her little pink lips and flushed cheeks. She must have felt the temperature rising between us because she lifted her sweatshirt over her head and wrapped it on the back of the chair. She was only wearing a tight tank top with the NU Nighthawks logo on the front. I dared a peek at her cleavage.

The next hour was tough. I tried to teach her the basics, but every time she would flip her ponytail, I wanted to touch it. When she leaned in to see one of the constellations, her hand almost brushed my thigh and we both quickly straightened up. The back of her neck was right near my mouth. I must have breathed on it because her skin erupted with goosebumps. She pulled her sweatshirt back on.

I should not have thought about spreading her on the table like my star map and studying her folds with my tongue. Or about how she would tear up if I pushed inside her. She was petite. She wouldn't be able to handle the rocket in my pants.

Although he was a twat, Barrett Grant was right. She would cause problems for my family, especially if Gianna saw me with her. I was a threat to Kinsley, and she didn't even know it.

"That was surprisingly helpful. You are a good teacher. I didn't expect that."

"You were quiet; I didn't expect that."

"And... there it is. Just can't help yourself. It's just your nature to be rude, isn't it? I think you don't know what to do around an intelligent woman. You're intimidated. You're trying to bully me into feeling inferior. News for you, *George*, I don't. I am smart and proud of it."

"I know exactly where you can put that smart mouth of yours." It slipped out loudly before I had the chance to stuff the words back into my mouth. I let them hang there, in the open air.

Kinsley dropped her jaw wide open, and my libido shot through the roof, thinking about stuffing my thick cock inside her tiny mouth. I didn't normally feel this way about girls. Usually, pussy came up to me, begging for the 'horse cock'. I'd fuck them or show them the goods and they'd leave in fear. Then, I'd get over it. I was never turned on by banter. Perhaps it was because no other girls turned this shade of violet when I made crude remarks. It was rather enjoyable for me.

I lifted my thumb and touched her bottom lip before I could stop myself. While pulling her lip down, she stuck the tip of her tongue out to lick me, and the sensation went straight to the head of my cock. Her eyes met mine, and she blinked rapidly, inhaling quickly. I started to lean in so I could capture her breath with my mouth, but just as I did, she grabbed her bag and fled the library.

What was I thinking? *Thank fuck* she left before I did something. This girl was trouble for my family. If Gianna or Barrett caught sight of me with her, that would bring even more cause for concern for her safety. People like the mayor, like my father, didn't let problems just exist. They'd take her out.

Maybe I just needed to get laid. It had been a few weeks since I'd been with anyone. I'd have to think about what to do with Gianna. I needed to think. Try to come up with a strategy.

I headed to my sanctuary, the observatory in Springfield. It was still two hours from closing, which would give me plenty of time to sit under the stars and ponder.

If I didn't do what Gianna asked, she would come after Dan and Aaron. Ultimately it would hurt my mother. I knew how she operated. There was little escape. She always knew how to gain the upper hand.

I remembered a freshly fifteen-year-old George. One whose only sexual experiences were fingering Katie Lane in the back of the gym and getting a sloppy blowjob from Nadia Burke in my garage. I may have not even kissed a girl then.

Gianna flirted with me even before she married my father. At first, I didn't pick up on it, too naïve at fourteen. Her hugs would last slightly longer than usual. Her fingers crawled slower up my arm.

When my father announced that she and Alenna were moving in, I was so anxious that I started vomiting every morning before school. Then before every football game. Everyone thought it was just nerves about player performance. Coach picked up on it and sent me to the counselor, but I didn't talk. She told the coach that if I wouldn't speak, then therapy wouldn't help.

Gianna would "accidentally" walk in on me in the shower or when I was getting dressed. Her towel would "unintentionally" slip off when she had just bathed. I hated that I got boners from it. It was so confusing to hate my own body that way.

Then, she started to get friskier. Cornering me and pressing her lips to mine. I wasn't sure what to do. She was my father's wife. She was much older than me. It felt very wrong, and I didn't like it. But my body betrayed me, and she would take that as confirmation that I was into it.

The first time she kissed me, she made me cum in my sweatpants by writhing on my crotch. She was so satisfied with herself. I pushed her off and ran to the toilet to lose my lunch.

I tried to find ways to avoid her, always having Dan with me or Aaron. Always trying to visit my mother or be at school. Hoping my dad would be home more. She would find me whenever I was alone and then visited in the middle of the night, creeping into my bed when my father was out at "work".

"You ever eat pussy, Georgie?" she asked me the first time she sneaked under my covers. I shook my head. She pulled down her panties and laid back on my bed, curling her finger at me.

"I don't think I should."

"Oh, you don't? Well, I'll tell your father you've been messing around with me, Georgie. Who do you think he'll believe?"

She was right. I was a guy. I was supposed to *like* it. I was supposed to brag about my first time making out and getting touched by a seductive older woman. Instead, I felt confused. Like, what was *wrong* with me that I was so anxious about it? I felt like I'd failed everyone in some way for not being able to stop it. For not getting off on it. Wasn't I *supposed* to be into this?

Things continued with Gianna shoving her pussy in my face any chance she got. She'd give me blowjobs, laughing at me when I'd blow my load and moan. The first time I had sex was with Gianna. She acted like a stern school teacher through the entire two minutes it lasted, especially when I rolled her off me so I could vomit on my rug. I was hoping she'd go away after that. But her predation continued. On and on… for years.

I tried locking my door. She just used the key to open it. When I put a chair in front of it, she waited until I was by myself, then jumped me. If I threatened to tell my father, she'd say she knew he would believe her over me. I couldn't tell anyone. She was the shame etched into my soul.

Anytime some girl at school would come forward

about a male teacher or older man abusing her, I would be filled with jealousy and outrage. Why couldn't I do the same? I knew what would happen if I did. I'd be seen as a "lucky guy" and get comments like "what's his problem" and "if only I'd had a stepmom like that when I was his age".

I was too naïve to think Gianna would leave after they divorced and never come back. Now, I knew I had to return to my prison once again to save my family.

CHAPTER
FIVE
KINSLEY

DRIVING over to my childhood home, I hadn't decided what exactly I would do with the charm bracelet when I found it. Gripping the steering wheel tighter as I approached, I hoped my father wouldn't be there. I was luckless, though. Since his youngest, Sarah, was born, he worked from home to help *Bethany*.

Parking in the driveway, I sat in my car breathing deeply for a long minute before stepping out. Driving was already stressful enough for me. I was too reactive whenever a car horn blared or when the traffic lights changed colors. Regulating my breathing, I approached the front door.

It felt odd to ring the doorbell of a place that was my own. Staring at *my* front door from the guest side made the ire within me rise to the outer edges of my scalp. The fact that it was my own fault for being on the wrong side of the door made me want to run. I'd need to do sixteen—no, twenty miles later.

Bethany answered the door. Not Beth.

"Oh… Hi, Kinsley. Um, did you call your father?" Her curvy figure stood in front of the doorway, blocking my entrance.

"Should I have?" Was I supposed to schedule appointments to see my dad now?

"No. It's just…" She sighed and flipped her dirty blond hair over one shoulder. "Come in, but be quiet. Sarah is finally down for a nap. Junior and I are doing our tactile activity for the day." Bethany opened the door a little wider, enough for me to have to ease past her. "He's in his office, busy on a meeting call. Better wait in the kitchen, and I'll text him to let him know you're here." She followed me through the house. My father's son sat at a little kid's table near the breakfast area, smearing paint on paper. He glanced up at me, then looked away. I felt the same.

"Actually, I just wanted to get something from my old room."

"What is it? I can get it for you." Bethany stood like a mama bear in front of her child, blocking him from my view.

"It's personal."

"Well, we have been doing some remodeling, and I moved your things into storage."

"Remodeling?" I turned for the stairs and she tailed me, the intruder in her home.

"Yes. I moved your things downstairs." As I sped my pace to try to ditch her, she hustled to keep up. I wanted to see how far she would go to be obnoxious about trailing me.

"Downstairs? Like the basement?" I paused, and she

seemed relieved I wouldn't disturb her precious baby's naptime.

"Yes. That's where we store things, Kinsley."

"With the cat pee?"

A few years ago, she took it upon herself to move my prom dresses and childhood Halloween costumes there. Her cats "accidentally" shredded the fabric and urinated on everything. That smell never left.

When she didn't respond to me, I sprinted the rest of the way to my room. Opening the door, I gasped. The entire thing was decorated differently. All the walls were a pale blue gingham wallpaper. A white rocking chair sat in the corner and a baby's crib was set up against the wall where the bed, *my* bed, had been.

"You're fucking pregnant *again*?"

"This is what happens to married couples, Kinsley. Do I need to explain this to you?"

"Please. We went to high school together, *Bethany*. I think I know very well how it's supposed to work. But normally, women don't have *three fucking children* before the age of twenty-four, *prom queen*."

"How dare you judge me! And don't use that crass language in this house. Junior could hear you."

I snorted. "This was my house before it was yours."

She softened. "Kinsley, your father and I love each other very much. I know that it is hard for you to accept, but we do. He's always wanted more children—"

"He's always wanted *sons*."

"He loves you, Kinsley." Shoving my shoulder into hers, I tried to move past her to go to the basement.

"Your siblings would love to have their big sister in their lives."

"Fuck you. Those cretins aren't my siblings." She smacked me across the face. I almost punched her, but remembered she was pregnant. Despite my hatred of my father's chosen spouse, I wouldn't hurt her that way. Instead, I walked quietly down the stairs.

My father was waiting at the bottom, his eyes narrowed behind his glasses. "What in the world is happening? Did you just come over to upset my wife?"

"Hello to you, too, Jeff."

"Kinsley. I'm your Dad. Call me that."

"Sure, *Dad*. Tell your *wife* not to slap me." Dad raised his eyebrows and looked up the stairs at Bethany behind me. Putting a hand on my shoulder, he led me into his office on the first floor.

"Maybe you should call before you come over. We run a tight ship over here. Not like your mother's place."

"At least Mom isn't a bitch."

"Kinsley!" He pointed to a chair near his desk. "I can't have you coming over and yelling and cussing in front of your brothers and sister." As he sat, he undid another button on his shirt and stretched his neck.

"Brothers now, is it? When were you going to tell me about your next spawn?" I sat with a huff into the winged back chair.

My father sighed heavily. "I know you get jealous, but—"

"I'm not jealous. I'm neglected. Ever since my accident, you gave up on me. You thought you could have some boys to be your progenies instead of your broken, second-rate *girl*."

"That is absolutely untrue, Kinsley. I love you. Your mom just couldn't handle things after the accident. We've been over this."

We had. He left my mother for *Bethany*, who was two years ahead of me in high school. She was eighteen and the prom queen. She gave birth to Jeff Junior nine months to the day after their wedding. How she and Dad got together was a story I never wanted to know.

"I just need to grab something from the basement. Is that okay with you?"

My father's brown eyebrows lowered with concern. "How are you? I haven't heard from you in a while."

Oh. Now he was going to play Dad. "Fine. Just wanted to get something of mine if I have your permission."

"Yes, Kinsley. Of course. You're welcome anytime." I got up from my seat and walked down the hall. Like his wife, he followed me. "How's school? You're getting straight As, right? Been studying for the MCAT?"

"Yes, father. Of course. I've been perfect."

"And your marathon training? It's going well? Beating your times?"

Making my way into the storage room off the finished basement, I found the plastic bin of memories from high school and opened it. It smelled like cat piss. "Yes, yes."

"You could get the top women's result if you tried."

"Could I? Could I, Dad? If I only *tried*?"

Placing his hands on his hips, he said, "Kinsley,

what is wrong? I just know you can be the best. What's wrong with encouraging you?"

As soon as I found the charm bracelet, I shoved past him and flew up the stairs while he told me to wait. I wasn't stopping. I made it to my car, and he came out onto the porch to watch me drive off.

Feeling the urge to run, I quickly went home to change into my running gear, then drove back to the park. It was going to be a full marathon run today, no matter how late it took me. I *would* beat my times, but I'd do it for me.

I knew it was a vast disappointment to my father when I couldn't play tennis again. He kept trying to push me into it after physical therapy. Finally, the doctor had to step in and explain in basic terms that I couldn't hold a racket. Despite that, Dad tried to force me to for weeks after, hitting balls at me as hard as he could. I didn't have the grip strength to return them. When he yelled, "You're just not trying hard enough!" I threw the racket at him and didn't speak to him for weeks.

The farther I ran, the better I felt. I hadn't eaten all day, but I kept pushing, ignoring the groans from my stomach. I'd eat after. The night was settling into the sky and stars started peeking out. I was able to spot Venus, then Ursa Major, and smiled.

Dirty George thought I wasn't clever enough to learn stars. I'd show him. The next time I showed up for tutoring, I was going to blow him away. I slowed my run to a jog, trying to catch my breath.

George's face came to my mind at the thought of

blowing him in other ways, and I felt my cheeks get hot. Why did he have to be so fucking attractive? Worse, why did he have to be so fucking smart? I could ignore his attractiveness if his brain wasn't so big.

I wondered if the other parts of him were just as big as they all said... *No, Kinsley!* He was a rude, arrogant prick. I should not have been so flustered by him.

As I jogged back, light footsteps crunched behind me on the paved trail. Glancing over my shoulder, I saw nothing. I stopped hearing the steps after a few minutes and pressed on. When I rounded a corner of the trees in the park, a dark figure jumped out from behind the oak tree and tried to grab me. The person was wearing a fully black outfit with a black mask covering their face.

I screamed and sped up, sprinting as fast as I could. No one was around at this time of evening. I had been foolish to run alone in the dark forest at night. Heading towards the lights of the parking lot, I dashed in a weaving pattern in case the figure was close behind, but the running thuds grew farther from my ears.

A small stone fence bordered the area for cars. Only mine was parked in the lot and I set my eyes directly on it. I vaulted over the rocks as quickly as I could without tripping. A thump and groan of pain came from a man behind me when I jumped over the wall. He must have stumbled, but I was not going to turn to look. Scrambling to pull out my car key, I ran over to the driver's door, and quickly pulled it open and jumped inside.

Flicking on my bright headlights, I shined the light on the fallen figure. When I turned on the engine, I drove straight at him, but he darted towards the forest again and ran off. Digging through my center console, I found an old can of mace I usually took with me on these types of runs. It was still charged. For next time.

After arriving at my apartment, I found it empty. Marissa seemed to be spending a lot of time with her new boyfriend. Elle was probably at a party somewhere, and Sharice was probably practicing her music. I was alone. I used the opportunity to heat up one of the dinners in the fridge and catch up on trashy TV.

A few hours later, I took a shower and decided to end the evening by studying astronomy to slay George away during the next tutoring session. His notes were coming in handy, even if his mnemonics were dirty. He wrote "I Eat George's Cock" for the Galilean moons of Jupiter.

The day of our next tutoring session arrived. I dressed in a short plaid skirt (with black tights to hide the scars) and a black sweater that happened to have shrunk in the wash. It wasn't for *George* at all. I just happened to put on makeup: a little blush and lip gloss, and some eyeliner. Highlighter and contour. Just that. And some of my favorite Chanel perfume. Nothing else. And my grandmother's pearl earrings.

Okay, so maybe I wanted to really show him up and see what would come out of his mouth. Part of me couldn't wait to blush between my legs if he spoke dirty to me again, and the other part of me wanted to smack him if he did.

Rounding the corner of the library to our section, the sight of the big man made my palms sweat. He stared at me intensely, then I saw his Adam's apple bob in a slow swallow. Hmm, maybe I'd already shown him up without even speaking.

Sliding into the wooden chair next to him, I pulled out my notebook with a sly grin.

"What perfume are you wearing?" he asked.

"Chanel. Why?"

He didn't answer me, just nodded and clenched his jaw. "Let's get started. Now, the next step to the—"

"I know what you're going to say. I have it all right here. The last quiz," I showed off my test results, "I got an A. I've been studying."

His eyelids narrowed as he stared at me. "No thanks to me? Your tutor?"

"Well, I mean, you were here." I shrugged. "Not that you did much. *I* was the one who put in the work."

"Seriously, Kinsley? Why do you have to be a bitch all the time? There's no reason for it. I've been nice and—"

"Nice? You've been *nice*? How about telling me to put my smart mouth…" I bit my lip.

George sat back and a small smile crept over his lips. "Put your smart mouth where?"

My cheeks got hot, and that made me more embarrassed than anything. I whispered, "You know what you implied."

"No, I don't know. Tell me." The blue of his eyes seemed to sparkle like the sun on the ocean as he spoke.

"Will you guys shut up?" Someone from the next section over was clearly annoyed.

"I'm not going to repeat such—such crass words. Especially ones coming from an ogre like you."

"Shh!" The other student said.

"Oh, shush yourself!" I yelled back, but before I could turn, my body was yanked from the chair I was sitting in.

George ushered me forcefully down some rows of books to a deserted corner of eighteenth-century poetry. His huge chest shoved me against the stacks and I had to look up to breathe. His face was close to mine. "What the fuck did you call me?" he whisper yelled. I couldn't answer. His breath smelled like spearmint and his body like a warrior: a mixture of sweat and steel. I blinked. "Princess, you turned on right now?" I was. I so was.

George leaned down and captured my lips with his as his hands threaded through my hair and mine through his. I loosened the tie holding back his long hair, letting it fall over our faces. He growled and lifted me up easily, grasping under my skirt. Each of his gigantic palms held an ass cheek. His thick fingers delved into my crack, with only the fabric of my tights separating our skin.

His kisses were unexpectedly sweet, his lips soft and caressing, as if they were tenderly caring for my own. My body was craving more. As his tongue danced with mine inside my mouth, I imagined what it would feel like to be tangled up together elsewhere.

George's body moved in such a way that his lower half pressed against mine, and I felt it. The horse cock. They were not joking. It. Was. Massive. Like a Clydesdale. The heat rolling off the thing could have supported its own living solar system. Even through his jeans.

I think I made a loud moan because he pulled his lips away from my suction and put his mouth over my ear, whispering, "Shh. I know you're a naughty girl, but try to keep quiet. For once." He sucked on my ear, and I whimpered behind my closed mouth. Writhing on his cock, I knew I could come just from the weight of it on my clit.

Locking my legs around his waist, I humped him like a rabid dog while he pushed into me. Chuckling a breath into my neck, I heard him say, "Not such a pristine princess, are you? You think you can handle something this big? I'll break you in half, little girl."

I clenched my teeth as my orgasm started to rise, but I yanked his hair, so we were face to face. "I can. I will."

"Oh, you will? You want me to give it to you raw right now? Watch you bleed on me? It would make good lube." His fingers dug into the crotch of my tights as if he might tear them.

"You-you don't s-scare me, George."

He pushed into me harder, his face buried in the crook of my neck. "You want this thick cock that bad, huh, princess? I knew you were a sneaky freak. Dirty fucking whore." He let go of one of my cheeks, only to smack it.

Then he dug inside my tights, ripping them so he could fill my hole with one of his fingers. Adding a second one, I almost screamed. "Princess, if you can't even handle this, I'm going to enjoy ripping you wide open."

With a last wave of my hips, I came so hard he had to thrust his tongue into my mouth again so I would be quiet. Once we pulled away, he held me for a moment as our eyes searched each other's. He let my legs slide down his body, the baseball bat in his pants catching on my stomach as I did. He hovered his massive body over mine completely, putting his arms above me against the bookshelf.

"Don't wear those stupid tights again," he commanded. Then, he left.

My panties were disgustingly doused. I wasn't sure what to do. Was he waiting back at the table to continue our lesson? I didn't know if I could face him, feeling too embarrassed that I allowed myself to do *that* in the library. With my tutor.

Fixing my hair and clothes, I took a deep breath and walked back to our stuff, but George was gone. So were his things. Gathering my items, I wondered if he'd gone somewhere to jerk off. My body involuntarily shivered all over, picturing what that would look like. I hustled out of the library.

George made it sound like this was to become a thing. That he was going to give me his gigantic cock. It was a test. He was trying to scare me off, and I wasn't going to let him. I would pass with an A.

I knew what I had to do. Once I made it home, I showered and changed into fresh clothing. Opening my laptop, I searched out a sex toy store and ordered the girthiest dildo they had. It wasn't nearly as big as he felt, but it would do. I'd show up 'Big G' and be ready for him when he would put it inside me.

CHAPTER SIX
GEORGE

WALKING through the university campus with a huge boner was awkward. Not to mention painful. I kept telling my cock to wait just a little longer until I reached *Serenity* and jumped inside. Quickly undoing my jeans, relief flooded my body from the release of some tension. My dick jumped out of my boxer briefs and I wanked it furiously. Little pants from princess' pert mouth came back to my ears. Lifting my fingers to my nose, I sniffed. Fuck, she smelled amazing. I stuck the fingers I'd had in her cunt in my mouth, licking them clean. Her flavor made me cum all over myself.

Reaching behind the seat, I grabbed my gym bag and pulled out a towel to wipe myself up. It was a massive load and all I could think was that I wished I'd put it inside Kinsley's tiny cunt.

Leaning my head against the seat, I considered what had just happened. Did I tell Kinsley I'd fuck her? When she couldn't even handle my fingers? I'd break her. "I can. I will," she'd said. No girl had ever talked like that to me. Usually, a chick saw my member and ran the other way. Or wanted "just the tip" or couldn't open their mouths wide enough to give me a proper blow job. One girl told me she wouldn't have sex with me because she didn't want to be "permanently stretched out" for other guys.

Thoughts of Kinsley and what her face would look like taking my cock were ruining my orgasm afterglow. I shouldn't fuck her. She pissed me off. Couldn't stop talking and was so pretentious. A true princess. Not my type. I thought about fucking her just to get her out of my mind. The image started getting me hard again, but before I could enjoy the fantasy, I got a text.

GIANNA

Meet me at the spot in 30.

I banged back against the headrest a few times. Thinking about Gianna made my dick instantly soft. It was getting out of hand. She'd made me eat her pussy for the last few days. Right after, I would vomit in the motel toilet every time while she laughed.

Putting the truck into drive, I headed towards the seedy motel she'd booked for our trysts. I popped a mint in my mouth as I knocked on the door to her room. She opened it wearing a little black negligee, her auburn hair set in perfect loose curls.

"Come on in, handsome." Opening the door wider, I brushed past her to the bed. The place smelled of mildew, and the worn patterned carpet crunched beneath my boots.

"Let's get this over with."

"Oh, Georgie. You're not enjoying being with me? I thought you loved the taste of my cunt." I stood still like a statue. Nothing I could say or do would get me out of this trap. "Well, it's your lucky day. I don't want cunnilingus today. I want to ride your dick."

"What?" Shit. I didn't bring condoms.

"Yep. I want that big dick inside me." Swaying her hips, she walked over to me and rubbed her hand on my crotch. "Hmm, why is he not waking up?" She undid my jeans and fished out my flaccid, sticky cock. "Did you just jerk off before you got here?"

"Yes."

"Oh, Georgie. Were you thinking of me?"

"No."

She cackled. "Well, let's see if I can get him back in working order." Dropping to her knees at the side of the bed, she started to lick the tip of my dick. I wasn't going to get hard and fuck her. No way. Not without protection. Who knew what she had? She wasn't going to let up once she set her mind to something. Why the fuck didn't I bring condoms?

I stroked a finger under her jaw to force her to look up at me. Then, I picked her up under her arms and threw her back on the bed. Ripping off her panties, I spread her legs and ate her snatch, sticking two fingers inside the way she liked it. The mint helped to hide her taste.

"I want—I want your dick, Georgie."

Shaking my head into her pussy, I moaned a no as she gasped. If I could just hit... Yep, there it was. I hit her spot with my fingers curled inside her and she came. Leaning over her, she thought I was about to kiss her. Instead, I spit her juices back into her face.

"We good now?" The nausea rolled through my throat. I didn't want to throw up again in front of her. I couldn't stand to hear her laugh at me.

"You ungrateful child. Men kill to fuck me. What's wrong with you?"

Crossing my arms, I said, "I'm just not into you, Gianna. I know no one's ever said that to you, but there it is."

She reached up and slapped me across the face, her long red fingernails scratching the skin as she did. "You should be more careful with your words. I'd hate to release that tape."

I cracked my jaw and rolled my neck. "I have to be somewhere."

"Are you seeing someone? Is there someone else in Georgie's life?"

"No," I said a little too quickly.

"Hmm… I'm not so sure. Who is she?"

"Gianna, there's no one."

She tilted her head and considered me for a moment. "Good." I turned to leave, hoping she wouldn't make me stay and perform. When I put my hand on the doorknob, she said, "And there better not be."

Motoring to the nearest gas station to fill up (premium only for my baby), I bought two boxes of condoms, stuffing them into the glove box. I shoved a few into my wallet as well. If I continued to jerk off before our rendezvous, maybe I could get out of sticking my dick in crazy.

By the time I was done, I barely made it to the Theta Rho Zeta meeting. Sitting in the uncomfortable little chair, I stared straight ahead to give the impression that I was paying attention. All I could focus on was ways to get out of fucking my ex-stepmother. Then, my thoughts got invaded by images of Kinsley and being inside her.

Her fucking fragrance and pussy scent lingered in my nose. It was pissing me off. The need to taste her fully, the desire to impale her on my cock… As soon as the meeting concluded, I stood up and marched straight to my room. Flopping on my bed, I grabbed my dick out of my jeans and beat it. I was mad at it for betraying me.

Afterwards, I was able to focus enough to get my studies done. Finishing up, I showered and set up some ground rules for myself. No more Kinsley fantasies. I'd avoid Chanel perfumes and any princess reminders. It would be strictly business. Before bed, I scribbled out some lesson plans for the next three tutoring sessions to get her to midterms with an A. Hopefully, by then, she'd be good to study on her own.

The next couple of days, the plan worked. I didn't see her. We didn't have tutoring until the following week, so I was able to relax a little, pushing any lingering thoughts of her from my mind.

Over the weekend, Dan and I helped Aaron move into his military academy dorm room. Aaron didn't want Dad to come, and I had convinced the chief to let us take him. The school was a few hours away, but any time I got to spend with *Serenity* was quality time well spent.

As we pulled up on the state route, a large, gray concrete conglomeration of gothic buildings beheld us. The place looked like an abandoned prison, complete with bars on some windows.

"What the fuck? He can't be serious!" Aaron yelled from the backseat of my truck, peering through the side window. He had me pull over three times on the way so he could shit on the side of the road. His nose was dripping like a faucet. I'd told him to withdraw well before he got in my truck, but he couldn't resist using the day before.

"Yeah, there doesn't look to be pussy for miles around here." Dan smirked. "Not that you could get it up anymore, anyway."

I punched Dan in the arm and shook my head.

"Fuck you, Dan. I still get hard," Aaron said quietly.

"Better not say that around all these *boys*."

"Daniel. Stop." I warned him. Despite him being the star short-stop athlete for the Nighthawks, I was still much bigger and could put him in his place.

As we pulled into the facility, my phone vibrated in my pocket. I tensed, knowing who it would be. Once we jumped out of the truck, I checked the message. Gianna was requesting my dick, but I responded with a picture of the outside gate of the facility, explaining that I was out of town. At least I got one day off from the job.

We unloaded the truck. Once inside, we checked in

with the front desk. A buzzcut-headed guide led us to Aaron's assigned room. It was tiny and depressing, made of yellowed painted cinder blocks. His roommate wasn't there when we showed up. The director arrived to give us a small tour of the place. Aaron had to keep darting to the bathroom every time we passed one.

The three of us were able to eat with the other students for lunch in the mess hall. Aaron didn't touch his burger or fries and Dan grabbed both without asking, happily munching away. Aaron looked around the large cafeteria like a lost puppy.

"Man, you're going to be fine. This could be good for you. Figure out what you want and go for it." Aaron didn't look convinced by my pep talk. "I'll be graduating next semester and can take you with me wherever I get into graduate school. Even if you gotta finish school online."

Aaron's head made a motion of a nod, but his eyes were fixed and wide. It was more like a fear reaction to the scenes around him. The other boys were fit, stoic. Aaron looked gaunt and scrawny compared to them.

"Just keep your head down and do what they tell you. If you need me, I can get back here quick." Eyeing one big guy, I nodded to let him know who my little brother was. Maybe it was good I had come and not my father.

Before we left, I embraced my little brother in a tight hold. Dan went out to the truck before Aaron even said goodbye. "I'm here for you." He sniffed and wiped his nose with the back of his hand and watched us leave as the director came up to escort him back inside.

When I got into the driver's seat, Dan had already started the vehicle and was blaring music. I turned it off. "Dan, I know you and Aaron don't get along, but you could try to be more supportive."

"Not you, too." Dan scoffed.

"Me, too, what?"

"Everyone babies him. He's *not* a fucking baby. He's a fuck-up that makes bad decisions."

"Even if he were, show some fucking sympathy!" I turned up the music and started down the road. Dan was quiet, probably reeling from my outburst. I hadn't raised my voice in years. All the words I had, everything I wanted say, it was all bubbling inside, just on the surface, yearning to get out.

Dan had Dad. Aaron had Mom. I had no one.

))) ● (((

The following Monday, I showed up at the gym for my morning workout. Dan tapped his buddies on the shoulders, and they all headed toward the locker room. Dan paused on his way out near my bench. "I don't think you're going to be welcome in this gym any longer."

"What do you mean?"

Shrugging one shoulder, he put a hand through his short blond hair as he spoke. "I mean, you're not on a university team. This gym is for student-athletes only. Coach is revoking your access."

"Are you fucking kidding me, Dan? Because you wouldn't show any compassion to our little brother?"

"I think it's time you went to workout with the regular students on campus. It'll teach you some humility, which is *compassionate* of me." He breezed through the door as I stared at the exit. Dan had been spending too much time around Chief George Turner, Senior.

After showering, I headed to my morning classes, but had a difficult time concentrating. When my quantum physics professor called on me, I spaced out, unable to answer the question. Dr. Schumacher seemed disappointed and moved on to the next student.

By lunch, I was looking forward to shoveling in a large meal before my one afternoon class, then heading home. I'd had enough human interaction for one day already and wanted to be alone in my hole. Maybe I would go to the planetarium for some thinking time.

Grabbing a lunch tray, I filled it with my usual: proteins and some vegetables. The menu showed mac & cheese, which the kitchen made pretty decently. My mouth watered. At least there was mac & cheese... When I got to the dish in the line, the pan was empty.

"Miss? Any chance there's more mac & cheese coming out?" The cook shook her head and walked to the other end of the serving line. My shoulders slumped.

Shuffling to my regular table where Xavier and some other TRZ guys usually sat, I stopped short. Xavier was sitting with his new girlfriend on his lap. And Kinsley was next to them. Fuck. I did not have the energy to listen to her.

Sliding in, I sat at the table across from Xavier, next to Mason. Xavier gave me a small smile and Kinsley looked away. Good. Maybe she would ignore me.

"'Sup, big guy. George, you need to teach me your ways. I feel like your biceps have grown another two inches since the last time I saw you," Mason said. If it wasn't Kinsley running her mouth, it would be Mason.

"Yeah, those must have migrated from his brain," Kinsley said, and everyone at the table chuckled except Xavier, whose eyes darted from hers to mine. "George here is intimidated by strong, smart women," she announced to some of the girls at the table. "He isn't quite sure what to do with himself when he's around one, right, George?"

Shaking my head, I mumbled under my breath.

"What was that?" She narrowed her eyes at me.

"You're a white hole."

The table fell quiet. "What's that supposed to mean?"

"If you'd studied your astronomy notes, you'd know. It's the opposite of a black hole. Nothing gets in your brain. You spew out whatever comes to your mind without a thought."

Roars of laughter peeled from the table. Everyone said they agreed.

"Dude, she *is* a white hole."

"Kinsley, you never shut up."

"Ha! It's funny 'cause it's true!"

Kinsley's face darkened to crimson as she glared at me. She gathered her bag and ran out of the cafeteria, which just made everyone laugh harder. Even tables nearby heard me speak and joined in. That was the thing about being quiet. When you chose to say something, everyone listened.

Finally got her to shut up, at least, but I did start to feel a little guilty. I glanced at her best friend in Xavier's lap, but the two were busy. Probably fucking under the table.

Throwing away my trash, I walked to my next class early to find some peace. Sitting in the small study area of the science building, I pulled out my senior physics thesis notebook and read over the previous day's work. While adding to it, my phone vibrated in my pocket. The call came from an unknown number. Thinking it could be Aaron, I answered.

"Hello?"

"You the guy with the Ford F-150 for sale?"

"Uh, no."

"Oh. Sorry. I saw your sign. That's not your black Ford F-150 for three thousand?"

I guffawed. "Uh, no. That's way too low. No, I don't have a truck for sale."

"Sorry to bother you."

The man hung up. That was weird. As I started to slide my phone back into my pocket, it vibrated again. Another unknown number. Now, I was very curious.

"Yes?"

"Hey, I'd like to make an offer on your truck for sale."

"I don't have a truck for sale."

"That's not your black truck with the license plate that says Jedi Knight?"

"Where did you see it was for sale?"

"The sign on it. In Northview's parking lot, right?"

What. The. Fuck. My body moved like a meteor. Fuck physics class. *Serenity* needed me. "She's not for sale." I hung up and sprinted the rest of the way to find a group of guys hanging around my girl.

"Hey, man. This is your truck, right? Did you put her up for sale? That's a steal."

There was indeed a large for sale sign with my number listed on it and a $3k price tag. I ripped it out from under the windshield wiper. "Show's over. Not for sale." When I flipped over the sign, it read:

From: your favorite princess

That bitch would get what was coming to her... *and* her white hole.

CHAPTER SEVEN
KINSLEY

I RAN. The marathon was approaching, and I was ready. I was prepared for anything George threw my way, too. The troll didn't understand... I never backed down. If he wanted to start a war with me, try to bully me, I'd give it back to him tenfold.

It was early evening, not yet dark. I ran the commonly traveled paved main trail. The leaves on the trees boasted all the colors of autumn, and the smell of rain hung in the air. I passed a few couples, hikers, and some people with dogs. I was alone but felt safe with others around me. Since the incident, I quit listening to audiobooks or music, opting for the security of my hearing. And didn't forget my mace.

Making it to the final stretch, I pushed my legs to go faster. Around a thick cluster of Junipers, one long U-turn was left before reaching the parking lot. As I sprinted, I heard footsteps behind me. I stopped and whipped around, but no one was there. Maybe I was too paranoid now.

Mad that I had to quit suddenly, I turned and raced off again. Almost near the small stone wall of the lot, a large rock was thrown into the path from the thicket, and I had to leap over it at the last second. My legs could not handle the quick change of movements. The jarring caused my knees to wobble. I fell to the ground, scraping my shins and palms on the asphalt.

"Ouch!" I looked around, but couldn't see anyone. "George, you motherfucker! Is that *you*?" No one answered. Gingerly rising to a stand, I hobbled over to my car and got in. I'd need ice, but couldn't wait too long. My MCAT practice test was that evening. It was the last before the actual exam.

Pissed that George would follow me and try to hurt me, I gunned the engine and headed home. After shoveling dinner into my mouth, I quickly showered and changed. At least I wasn't too badly injured aside from the cuts.

When I emerged, prepared to jog over to the science building for my test, Marissa entered the apartment with her boyfriend, Xavier.

"Oh, hey, Kins!"

"Hey! I gotta head out."

"Okay, wait." Marissa eyed Xavier, who kissed her on the cheek, then headed into their room. "Their" room because they had practically moved in together. She was at the Theta Rho Zeta manor if he wasn't at our place. I didn't mind. Xavier was cool. I just didn't want him to share anything about my personal life with his friend, George.

"What's up?"

"Are you okay?" Marissa asked.

"Yes, why?"

"Today at lunch, you seemed upset. You left after George…" She scrunched her face as if she didn't want to continue.

"I'm fine. The ogre never talks, so when anyone speaks, he thinks they talk too much. Meathead's a total douchenozzle."

Marissa gave a slight nod as if she didn't believe me. "Are you two involved?"

"*Please*. I only date smart guys." I spoke loudly enough that I hoped Xavier heard me through the bedroom door.

She chuckled. "Okay. Well, if you want to talk boys, don't be a stranger. I know I've been busy with Xavier, but I don't want to neglect our friendship."

"Thanks. I'll see you." I quickly made it across campus to the testing location. When I arrived, I tugged on the doors, but they were locked. Confused, I tried again. They didn't budge. A handwritten note was posted on the glass that stated the location for the MCAT had changed and listed a room number somewhere near the art building.

As I read the paper, Maurice, a TRZ member, came up behind me. "Oh, hey, Kinsley." Maurice had been sitting at our lunch table earlier that day. I shirked at his approach, embarrassed at running out of the cafeteria so dramatically.

"Do you know about this?" I asked, pointing to the sign.

"Yeah. Heard some of my brothers say the location changed to the fine arts building."

"Oh. That's weird." I turned, but paused to see if Maurice was able to open the doors or not.

He tried, but the doors would not open. "Huh. These doors locked?"

"Yeah, I guess. Well, I'll see you." I ran off towards the fine arts building.

I was late. I'd never been late for anything. My heart raced and sweat poured from my forehead. Would they still let me in to take the exam? I had already paid for the course, so hopefully, they would. It would be horrible to have less time than everyone else.

When I threw open the doors of the fine arts building, I scanned the directory to find the room listed on the note. It was in the basement. What a weird place for the MCAT. As I approached the windowed door of the classroom, however, the lights were off, and no one was inside.

I panicked, not knowing where to head from there. Digging through my emails on my phone, there was nothing from the test prep company about a location change. Strolling in a daze, I made it back to the quad. As I wandered, I spotted Maurice, Jackson Riley, and another guy in a TRZ hoodie standing near the science building. They were laughing loudly.

I sauntered again towards the building, and a new notice was stuck to the door. In block letters, it read:

From: your favorite ogre

Infuriated, I pulled on the door's handle, and it opened. I ripped the note from the door, and the TRZ guys howled with laughter. My face flushed, and every muscle in my body tightened. I ran as quickly as I could to the original testing locale. The moderator narrowed his brow as I opened the back door. He held a finger up to his lips to tell me to quiet down.

Filled with rage, I was unable to concentrate on the exam. My mind kept racing with ways to annihilate my enemy. It was my worst practice test to date.

George would pay.

I turned in my test booklet early. There was no use trying to figure out the answers when my brain was fried with fury. Marching back to my apartment, I almost made it inside the glass entry doors when I felt extremely woozy. Before I knew what was happening, the world faded to black.

"Kinsley?"

Mary, one of the night resident advisors, was standing over me. I felt clammy and nauseated.

"Wha-what happened?"

"I don't know. I think you fainted. You were coming in the door, then just sort of sunk to your knees and fell over."

I started to get up.

"No, I had to call the campus emergency service. They'll send the paramedics."

"No, I'm fine. I just probably need to eat something."

"Well, I'm not getting in trouble for you. I already got in enough trouble over Elle's visitors."

I didn't know what that meant, but Elle liked to party. Maybe she'd had some late-night guests over.

Mary made me lie there until the emergency services arrived. As I suspected, my blood sugar was low when they checked. They gave me some nasty glucose syrup, but I assured them I would go upstairs and eat.

Sharice was in the dining room, painting her nails, when I got in.

"Hey, you look like shit."

"I'm sure I do. I need one of your meals." I grabbed two from the fridge to heat up. Kicking myself for not taking the time to eat properly, I shoveled food in while Sharice sat next to me at the table.

"I'm glad to see you. I never get to anymore. I've been working on my concerto and it's taking all my time."

"Yeah, it has been a while. What's been going on with you?" She finished her polish, and I stretched my legs out on the chair next to me, inhaling the reheated chicken and rice, then reached for an apple in the fruit bowl in the center of the table.

"I actually want to know what's going on *with you*." Her dark brown eyes danced with playfulness.

"What do you mean?"

"Oh, uh, Maurice was telling me about lunch today. I heard him and some of the Theta guys talking about Big G messing with you."

I sighed. Why was I the big news of the day? "That oaf is an asshole. That's all that's going on." God, could I not escape him for one moment?

Sharice laughed, her voice like a song. "Okay."

"What?"

"He's a hot oaf. Maurice is well endowed," she said, and I scrunched my face. "But Big G apparently outweighs even him. I'd give that a spin."

"He probably leaks his brain cells through his cum. Not interested." I knew I was lying to her and to myself. Of course, I wanted to try out his big cock and I hated that I did.

After I finished my dinner and loaded the dishwasher, I spotted a package on the kitchen counter. As casually as I could, I wandered over to check the label. It was mine. I yawned loudly. "I'm heading to bed. Goodnight."

"Goodnight," Sharice said.

Once I got into my bedroom, I locked the door, then ripped open the cardboard. It was my oversized dildo. After cleaning it, I pulled off my clothes and got into bed. I poured lube all over it and tried to insert it, but got scared. It was huge.

"Come on, Kinsley. You got this." I could imagine George saying, "See, told you you couldn't handle it." Fuck him.

Carefully, I slid the plastic in and out until I felt I could push it in further. "Oh my god!" I had to clamp a hand over my mouth. The sensation was amazing. I felt so full, like it was supposed to be there. Using my vibrator on my clit, I got myself off thinking of George fucking me against the stacks in the library. The ire I felt towards him made me come so hard that tears leaked from my eyes.

If George was bigger than this, it would be a miracle

to fit him inside. But I would do it. I would show him I could handle it. He would not scare me.

The next day, we received our graded papers in Russian literature. I got a ninety-three percent and sighed. It could have been better. Glancing in front of me where Cale and Sydney sat, I saw her red mark, and she got an eighty-eight. Ha! Then I saw Cale's. He got a perfect grade. Puke.

Opening my phone, I checked to see if my latest astronomy quiz scores were posted yet. I got a C again! What the fuck? I had studied using George's notes and mnemonics. I thought I had a grasp on it! This was his fault. What if he had given me false information to try to mess with me? That would be something he would do.

That afternoon, I stomped to the library for my astronomy tutoring session. George was peacefully reading at our table. Holding up my phone, I thrust it in his face, showing off my quiz score.

"Did you do this?" He narrowed his blue eyes and set his square jaw. "George, let *me* tutor *you* on something right now. I am not one you want to mess with. I will end you. You have no idea what—"

"SHH!" The same shusher as the previous session was in the opposing alcove. I whipped around.

"Find someplace else, fucker!" I screamed.

The guy got up to come over to me. I was ready to punch someone. Granted, I couldn't really make a fist, but I'd hit him with my bag. Just as I was about to sling it, George grabbed my arms and shuffled me down the aisle.

"No. Where are you—"

"We're leaving." The bass of his voice rumbled through my chest as George continued to direct me toward the library exit. Once we got outside, I tugged my jacket tighter around me. The wind was biting.

George let go of my body, but marched in the direction of the parking lot. He glanced briefly over his shoulder at me. "Come on."

"Where are we going?" I had to jog to keep up with his pace.

"To study."

"Study where? I need more of a description, George. Don't turn so stolid on me now. You made me fail my quiz!"

He paused his steps, lowering his head toward me. Then he kept going at his frantic pace.

"You're just not going to say anything?" He led us to his large, black truck.

"No."

"You're just going to say 'no'?"

"No." He held up his key fob, and the truck beeped. He got in. I stood next to the passenger door. He lowered the window. "Get in." I hesitated. "Do you need help getting in, your highness?"

I bit my tongue and threw open the door, jumping in using the chrome step bar. The cab was roomy, with plenty of space for my bag at my feet. It smelled of George's cologne, like citrus and leather. The scent made my heart beat faster.

"So, are you going to talk?" I asked as he backed out of the lot.

"Why, when you talk enough for the both of us?"

"If you're kidnapping me, I'd like to know where you're taking me."

George snorted. "Always the fucking victim."

I gasped. How dare he? "I am not a victim! I'm a survivor. You don't even know what I've been through."

"I'm sure it's a real good story, princess." My mouth fell open at his audacity. "Does it have anything to do with those scars on your hands?"

Tears sprung to my eyes. I didn't want to talk about it with him. I wished I had not even brought up my accident. I looked out at the passing scenery, turning my head so he couldn't see me wipe my face.

"Quiet now? So I guess I was right." George cleared his throat. I watched his Adam's apple bob as he swallowed. "I'm taking you to the planetarium in Springfield."

Gathering my composure, I responded, "Oh. I've never been."

"Hopefully, it will help. I can show you the stars instead of just looking at a piece of paper." His large hand turned up on the center console and he extended his fingers toward me. "Kinsley, I'm sorry you got a C. We'll get you that A, don't worry."

"Thanks." I nodded. We rode in silence, and I took the opportunity to capture views of the rolling hills of the countryside. George turned on some heavy rock music. "You ruined my MCAT practice exam," I yelled.

"Well, you ruined my truck."

I giggled. But the giggle turned into laughter. Then, I

couldn't stop and was cackling so hard that I started to cry. George's normally stoic face smiled broadly. "What?"

"I didn't *ruin* your truck. You're so dramatic."

"That, princess, is something I've never been called before." We pulled into the parking lot of the giant dome-covered building.

We went inside and George spoke with the attendant at the reception desk as if he knew them.

"Let's go." He slid his large hand down my arm and grabbed mine. We were holding hands. Well, more like my tiny fist was balled into his gorilla paw. It wasn't the worst thing that ever happened to me.

"How much is it? Don't we need to pay for tickets?"

"No, we'll use the B studio. I know the manager; it's cool."

"Huh. I could have known a guy that got me into the hottest clubs or restaurants, but I can brag I know the man that can get you into the planetarium for free."

George turned and put a large finger to the end of my nose and tapped it. "Nerdy princess."

"George, your license plate says Jedi Knight. I'd be careful about who you call nerdy."

"Oh, I'm proudly nerdy. You should be, too."

He pulled us into an expansive auditorium. There was a glowing light overhead, illuminating the white fabric sky. The acoustics made my ears feel as if there were muffs covering them. George tugged me to a seat near the middle. We were the only ones in the room.

"Just a sec. Gotta start the program." He disappeared into a small tower in the middle of the room and the lights darkened overhead.

Suddenly, the white screen was replaced by the black night sky. Slowly, it sparkled with twinkling stars. I gasped at its beauty. An announcer's voice introduced the program as George returned to sit next to me.

"This is better than anything I could teach you." George had to talk close to my ear so I could hear him over the video. Tingles went down my spine. George's body was so large he had to put his arm around the back of my seat to fit.

I tried to concentrate on the stars. I did. It was educational. The program would help with a better grade. *Focus*. But a cosmic wave of energy traveled from George's aura down to my core, causing an explosion in my belly. My clit thumped once as if it could sense the nearness of a giant cock nearby.

As if he felt something, too, George leaned in more to whisper, "That's Cassiopeia." I had turned my head to hear him more, and our mouths were close. George was looking at my lips, and I at his. They were smooth, surrounded by a fuzz of blond hair. I involuntarily licked my bottom one.

George lifted his free hand and threaded it through my dark hair. "Princess, you're making it hard for me to think." I sucked in a breath. He dove in and dragged my lips into his, tongue slicking through to part them. He groaned inside my mouth as he grasped the back of my head to bring me closer.

I reached down to feel his hardness and squirmed at

the size of it. George pumped his hips up into my palm once. Moving to his lap, I straddled him.

"Don't wear jeans again, either."

"Oh? What *is* okay for me to wear, George?"

"Something I can easily fuck you in." That made my pussy pulsate. I writhed on his lap.

"Who says you can fuck me?"

"No one's gonna stop me. Not even you, princess." Before I could say anything back, he plunged his mouth onto mine. I wasn't going to say no.

George lifted me off his lap and set me between his legs on the floor. I knelt in front of him, his legs spread wide, hand on his crotch. "I'm not jean jamming you. I'm not a teenager."

I started to protest, but he undid his jeans and pulled out his enormous cock. It was as large as my forearm, hard as steel, and sticking straight out at me. A thing of beauty. George pumped it a few times with his hand as I gazed at it in awe.

"I don't know—" *How* was I supposed to fit it *in my mouth*? I'd prepared below, but not orally.

George shoved my face onto his waiting cock. "Shut up and suck."

I did. I had to spread my lips as wide as they would go just to get the tip in. George yelled, "Fuck!"

If he wanted me to suck him, I'd give him the best blowjob of his life. Despite his hand on the back of my head, I pulled back enough so I could lick and spit on it, lubing it for my face.

When I put him back in my mouth, it hit my throat and I swallowed, ignoring my gag reflex. It was near impossible, but George seemed to be enjoying it, anyway. His eyes were half closed and he thrust his hips into my face. I worked him as much as I could, but my jaw quickly grew tired and sore. His jeans were prohibiting me from reaching his balls to massage, but I felt his cock throb in my throat, knowing he must be close.

"This is what your mouth is good for. Next time you try to smart off to me, remember this is what you get. You're gonna be a quiet girl with my dick shoved down your throat." He grasped my hair and pushed in as far as he could go. "Drink some of my cum, princess. Then I'm going to cover your pretty face."

George spurted some of his load down my throat, loudly groaning and lifting his hips while holding my hair. Then, he pulled me off his cock and spurted the rest all over my lips, cheeks, forehead, hair... I had to close my eyes so his cum didn't burn my eyeballs and used my fingers to wipe my lids off.

"Taste it."

I stuck my fingers in my mouth, then I swabbed my face, gathering all his sticky cum, and licked it off my fingers. It tasted like salt and Big G. I liked it. My face must have shown it because George's post-ecstasy face turned into a sly smile.

"Mmm, you like my flavor. Good, 'cause you'll get more where that came from. Plus, you look so perfect covered with my cum." He fixed himself back into his pants and then pulled me into his lap. "Now, let's learn."

"George!"

He nuzzled my neck. "Hmm?"

"I can't focus!"

"Why not?"

"I have your cum all over my face and I—" How was I going to say it?

"You want me to get you off, is that it?"

I nodded.

"Then you shouldn't have worn jeans."

I gasped, exasperated. I stood and ran to the bathroom while he chuckled. Once I got cleaned up, I returned.

George hadn't budged, though, and when I went to take my seat, he grabbed me by the waist and hoisted me into his lap.

"Okay, back to it," he said. He pointed out some constellations. I wriggled on his lap, but he spanked the side of my ass. In his deep bass, he said, "Kinsley...," but that only made me wetter between my legs.

He loosened the button on my jeans casually with one hand. I leaned back against him, so he'd unzip them, but he didn't. "And which one is that?"

"Um... *Ursa Minor*."

"Correct." He unzipped my jeans.

On my ear, his voice vibrated, "And that one?"

"Uh... *Aquila*?"

His hands stopped moving. "Wrong."

I whimpered. "*Aquarius*?"

"Is that a question?"

"No. It's *Aquarius*."

He pulled my fly open. "That's my girl."

The way he said it made my stomach do back flips. I

wanted to be his girl. I didn't know why. He pissed me off most of the time.

It went on like this: me correctly identifying constellations or formations, and him slowly digging his hand under my panties. By the time he had a finger on my clit, I was gasping for air.

"You want me to play with your pussy?"

I made some noise that seemed affirmative.

"Then tell me each of the constellations you see right there."

As I named some breathlessly, almost unable to even see them, he began to forcefully fuck me with his thick finger.

"I can't… I can't name them all," I cried out as I came on his hand, as he sucked on my neck.

"You get a B. Next time, be more prepared."

He slipped his hand out of my jeans.

"Next time, *you* be more prepared and *tutor* me!" I stood up and straightened myself.

"That's exactly what I just did."

"Take me home."

"Gladly."

He turned up the heavy rock on the way back to our town and neither of us spoke.

CHAPTER EIGHT
GEORGE

GOD, she pissed me off. And yet, as soon as she jumped out of my truck, I sucked my fingers so I could savor her flavor again. I'd wanted to rip off those tight-ass jeans of hers and munch on her pussy for lunch. I was afraid Jim would come in and I'd never get full reign of the planetarium again.

If she didn't infuriate me so much, I would have followed her up to her apartment and fucked the shit out of her. Maybe I would do it, anyway. Maybe it would shut her up. Just as I put my hand on the door to jump out after her, I got a text.

> GIANNA
> Meet me at the spot.

Fuck. I just left Springfield. Now, I had to turn around and go to the shitty motel. Good thing I'd just gotten off and didn't have any cum left for Gianna.

Fuck my father. Why couldn't he be a decent human being? Why couldn't the mayor? I couldn't take having to taste Gianna juice on my tongue any longer.

By the time I arrived, I was ready to slash Gianna's throat and throw her body into a river. My fist pounded on the door and she threw it open wearing only purple underwear and red lipstick.

"Well, hello to you, too, handsome."

Using my body, I pushed her toward the bed and ripped off her panties until they were shredded.

"I appreciate the enthusiasm, young man, but you need to wait a moment."

"Gianna, just lay the fuck back and let me hurry out of here. I don't got all day for this shit."

Her mouth fell open in mock offense. "Now, now, now. What did I say about making me *feel* good? You're not. I also called you here in order to talk."

"I don't want to talk to you."

"You don't have to. You can just listen." Perching in the nasty chair near the window, I raised my eyebrows at her, waiting. Crawling over to me on the bed, she swung her legs around to face me and spoke. "Good. Remember when I asked you if there was someone else?" I remained silent. "Let me ask again. Who is she?"

Inhaling deeply through my nose, I responded. "I don't know what the fuck you're on about."

Gianna stood and faked a laugh, pacing in front of me, her big fake tits bouncing with every step. "Oh, Georgie. I'm not as dumb as I look. I saw you with her."

"With who?" I shook my head.

"Kinsley Alice Whittemore."

Making my face appear bored, I responded, "Yeah. So? I'm tutoring her in astronomy."

"You usually fraternize with the woman who could end your father's career?"

I sighed. "What are you talking about? Spit it out."

"Kinsley, your little girlfriend, is the one from the accident. The one the mayor's son hit."

I had already figured this out. But now Gianna knew, and that was a problem. My face remained stoic.

"Did you know?" Gianna asked, staring me down while pausing her movements. "Do you think she's trying to get close to you to find out information about your father? Because that could ruin my income. And I don't appreciate someone else touching my property." She ran her finger along my cheek as I looked at the ground.

Would Kinsley do something like that? Use me like that?

Yes. Yes, she would.

Fuck. I'd been played. She got to me through my cock. I needed to avoid the little princess or... I could play along until I got her to confess. Get her to give up her game first.

"So, now. What are you going to do about her?" Gianna interrupted my schemes by lifting my jaw to look her in the face.

"I'll handle it. Stay out of it."

Pursing her injected lips, she said, "Okay. But if you don't, I'd hate to have to visit Aaron and start fucking the youngest Turner."

My stomach twisted. "You wouldn't." As soon as I

said the words, though, I knew she would. She'd done it to me.

Sensing my realization, Gianna chuckled. "I think you know that's exactly what I would do. Do you think he's a virgin? Should I show him the same lessons I taught you? You've become a very good pussy muncher, George. Dynamite in the sack, too. You just needed an older woman's education."

She bent over in front me and ran her hand up the crotch of my jeans. My dick didn't move even a little.

"Let's play."

"It's not going to work, Gianna."

"Oh, I think I know exactly how to get it to work." Unzipping my jeans, she pulled out my flaccid cock. With her full lips, she sucked the tip of my cock, flicking her tongue around the edges. All I could think of was Kinsley's pert mouth. Imagining her face with my cum all over it, I hardened. "That's it. See, Momma knows how to take care of you."

Grabbing Gianna's auburn locks, I shoved my dick in her mouth so she'd stop talking. She smiled around my shaft, and I hated her even more. I didn't think I could come again, but I'd use my dick as a weapon. Maybe then she'd stop calling me.

Gianna pulled back and walked to the bed, laid back, and beckoned me with her long fingernail. "Come fuck me."

Getting up, I took the two steps towards her. "Turn over. I don't want to have to look at you." She laughed, but did, sticking her ass in the air with a wiggle. Fishing my wallet from my back pocket, I found a condom and rolled it on.

"Oh, you won't need that. I want your cum inside me. I'm ovulating. I want your baby."

Instantly I got soft. "I'm sorry, what? You can't be serious."

She tossed her long hair as she looked over her shoulder. "I'm dead serious. Give me that cum. I want a George Turner the third."

"Fuck you, Gianna. No way." My feet took two steps back.

"Yes, fuck me. That's what I'm talking about."

"Gianna, I'm not impregnating you. You can go ahead and release the tapes. I'm not doing it." And most of me was serious. I couldn't have a baby with the wicked witch. Even if it did save Aaron. Fuck, what if she—

"Should I use Dan's sperm? Or Aaron's? His military academy is all boys, isn't it? I'm sure he's *dying* for pussy."

"No. Dan wouldn't fuck you. I'll talk with Aaron. Please, don't do that to him. He's still a kid. He's got problems. Please, Gianna. Don't."

She turned around and narrowed one green eye at my floppy cock hanging from my open jeans. "The next time you come here, you better *come* here." She pointed to her twat.

Tugging off the condom, I tucked my dick back in my pants and quickly got the fuck out of the room. Did they make birth control for men, yet? Fuck! Why didn't they? Could I get snipped before I had to have sex with her again?

Jumping in my truck, I called the number for Aaron's school while jetting back to the manor for the TRZ meeting. "Hi, yes, this is George Turner calling for Aaron Turner."

"Sorry, Mr. Turner, but Aaron is in class currently. He can take calls after dinner at seven."

"This is an emergency."

"Oh, sorry, sir. Right away."

I waited for my little brother to come to the phone and almost made it home.

"Hello?"

"Hey, bro! How are you?"

Aaron's voice cracked. "George. I-I'm. I'm not okay."

"Shit, what's wrong?"

"It's really tough, man. Is there any way I can get out of here?"

"I'll talk with Dad. Hey, I need to tell you something. If Gianna tries to contact you, stay away from her. Okay?"

"Gianna? Gianna Cunningham? Our ex-stepmother?" he asked.

"Yes. If she reaches out to you in any way, make sure to let me know. Immediately."

"Why? What's happening?" He sounded suspicious.

"Nothing you need to worry about. Hang in there. Are you doing what they tell you? Is anyone bothering you?"

"It's just... it's *hard*, man. I'm doing what they say. No, no one's bothering me. Not really."

"Not really?"

Aaron sighed. "Nothing *you* need to worry about. I'll stay away from Gianna, but *please* talk to Dad. Try to get me out. I want to come home. I won't use anymore, I swear."

"I will. Love you, bro."

"Love you, too, George."

When I pulled into the manor, Xavier was getting out of his Maserati in the stable garage. Our TRZ meeting was in an hour, and he was early, for once. He'd been spending all his time with his new girlfriend.

"Hey, man," he said with a smile.

I gave him a head nod.

"What's going on with you? Do you want to talk about it?"

He always knew when I was on tilt. "Nah."

"Is it Kinsley?"

Grabbing my gym bag from *Serenity's* backseat, I slung it over my shoulder as we walked to the house. "Maybe." Sort of. I mean, was she fucking with me? Xavier knew about Gianna. After the incident in high school, I knew he'd kept fucking her for a while. He ended it once I confessed to him what she had done to me. "Gianna's back."

Xavier's eyebrows raised. "Oh? Whatever for?"

"She's trying to—she wants me to impregnate her."

Xavier snorted and held the front door for me. "And why would you be dumb enough to do that?"

I shook my head.

"You're not considering it?"

"No way."

"So what's the issue?" Xavier furrowed his brow and we headed upstairs to the bedrooms.

If there was anyone who could keep things on the down low, it was Xavier Cardell. Our secrets were deep. I clenched my jaw and pointed to my room as we passed my hall on the second floor. We entered, and I tossed my bags on the bed. "She's threatening to squeeze out Dan's or Aaron's sperm if not me."

Xavier huffed. "No way Dan would fuck her. Aaron… he may be an issue." He paused and his eyes darted up and to the left. Xavier would figure this out. "She's blackmailing you?"

He was always smart as a whip. I took a deep breath in. "Yeah, well, my father."

Xavier nodded. "Has she been hurting Aaron like…" Neither of us spoke for a minute. He cleared his throat to try again. "Has she been hurting Aaron like she did with you?"

Someone said it out loud. It was strange to hear it that way. "No, I don't think so. It was just me."

"I can have my people—"

"No. She'll hurt him."

"Okay." Xavier's brow lowered. He smirked. "If you change your mind, I got you."

I knew he wasn't going to let it go. I trusted him, though, even if he was a sneaky fucking bastard. He patted my shoulder once and walked out of my room. My shoulders relaxed, and I hit the shower.

))) ● (((

The following morning, I went to the student gym for leg day. Glancing around, my lips tightened into a grimace. I missed the athlete gym's superior equipment. When I went into the locker room to change, I pulled out my weight-lifting gloves and slid them on. As I did, red ink smeared across my hands. *What the…*

I ripped off the gloves. My palms, the backs of my hand, and fingers were covered in bright red dye. Running to the sink, I tried to wash as much off as I could, but the stains remained. My skin looked less red after the scrubbing and more salmon pink.

Shuffling through my gym bag, I sighed in relief, finding everything else untouched. At the bottom of the bag was a note.

> *Looks like you've been caught red-handed.*
> *Stop trying to follow me.*
> *- White Hole*

Follow her? I wasn't trying to follow her. Although I probably should for my own safety. Fine. If she wanted to play with my stuff, I'd play with hers.

The notion of leaving her alone and being professional was quickly abandoned. This was war. Changing the testing location hadn't been enough to make her stop? I'd go harder.

In order to accomplish my plan, I needed to get

close to her. That was the opposite of what I should do, given what I knew about her accident. But maybe I could keep an eye on her to prevent her from pranking me *and* see if she was trying to get to my father through me.

If I could just get to her apartment, I could set my plans into motion. I could tag along with Xavier when he visited his girlfriend... I could pick a time when Kinsley would be out.

The perfect opportunity arose two days later. It was a Friday, which meant I had no classes. I texted Xavier, and he was with Marissa. Excellent. Making up an excuse to drop something off to him, I wandered casually into the girls' apartment. Xavier and Marissa left me alone once I returned his computer mouse, heading to her room to fuck. No one else was home. Once I was done with my task, I dipped out without Kinsley or her roommates aware of anything.

After that, I stopped by my father's office.

"Have you spoken with Aaron?" I asked.

"Yes. Well, I checked with his teachers and the principal. Why?" He busied himself with the stack of papers in front of him.

"But have you spoken with your son?"

"No." Father straightened his tie and faced his computer.

"He told me he's having a rough time."

Without looking at me, he said, "I would expect so. Coming off drugs and having to do what you're told or facing severe consequences is no easy matter."

I took a deep breath. "He's trying. He's done his best. Don't you think he's learned his lesson?"

Finally, he stared at me with his light blue eyes. "No."

"Are you punishing him or our mother?"

He sighed. "Junior, I'm not *punishing* anyone. I'm helping your brother. If you can't see that, it's because you're not a father."

"Yeah, well, neither are you." I got up before he could throw me out. I already knew he wouldn't change his mind about Aaron, but I had to try.

After stopping by the grocery, I headed over to my mother's. It had been two weeks since I visited. When I walked in, the smell of rotten food hit me in the face like running into a brick wall. One day, I expected to find her dead body decaying along with the bananas.

She was still alive, though, sitting in her usual chair. Wearing the same clothes as two weeks before. The meal I'd prepared for her last sat moldy on the counter in the kitchen. There was an open gallon of spoilt milk next to it.

"Hey, Mom."

"I don't want you here."

"Yeah, well, too bad." I grabbed trash bags and cleaned up. Opening a window, I let the fresh fall air do its work.

"Shut that window! It's freezing!"

"No. It reeks of death in here."

"Good."

I reached into my bag and pulled out a novel. Mom

used to love to read. Tossing the book on her lap, I went back to work. She flinched.

"What's this?"

"*Great Expectations*. You'll like it."

She harrumphed at me.

Usually, she cascaded me with insults. Today, she was being stoic.

"Anything wrong?" I asked.

"I told you I don't want you here."

"Who will take care of you?"

"George, I do that myself. Besides, you can't even take care of yourself. Aaron was helpful. You're useless. All you're good for is running to tell your father about everything I do. He doesn't need to know about me."

There she was. I nodded, finished up my work, and made sure her groceries were put away. Then I left to a barrage of insults.

XAVIER

Warehouse at 11

Looks like I was heading to the club again. I was *not* going to see if Kinsley would show. But if she did, I could keep an eye on her. Maybe get a read on if she was trying to use me.

Would definitely not have sex with her. Probably not. Most likely. Maybe not have sex with her. Who was I kidding? I was going to fuck her into the next year.

I may have spent a little extra time getting ready. Not that I was expecting anything. But I did put on a white button-down with my black dress pants. And sprayed my cologne. That was a normal thing for Friday night club nights. Really.

Somehow, I got stuck driving Mason to the club. Levi had been missing in action and Xavier was taking his girl. If I was hoping for silence on the trip, Mason always disappointed me.

"Get any good lays lately?" Mason asked me when he jumped into my truck. He wasn't in TRZ. Not sure why he didn't drive himself and meet us there.

I turned up the volume on the radio.

"Fine, fine. You don't want to talk." He looked out his window, and I thought that was the end of it. "Man, I hooked up with this one chick with the mayor's son. Barrett Grant? Yep. Both of us fucked her at the same time." He made some weird seal laugh.

Didn't surprise me that Barrett Grant was into that kind of thing, but I wondered how close Mason was with him. "You friends?"

"With Barrett? Nah. Just happened to be at his parents' party with my parents and the Cardells." Mason was Xavier's cousin. Mason's mother was Malcolm Cardell's sister. Cardell Enterprises owned the town and everyone in it. My father had probably been invited, as well. I stopped being a showcase son in middle school.

"And?"

"And we hooked up with this girl... Layla, I think her name was. She wanted to fuck the mayor's son. I tagged along."

"Good for you." I hoped to God Almighty that was the end of the story.

"You ever do DVP?"

Of course, it wasn't. "Nope."

"Man, it was wild. They were making me watch forever, but then they said I could join in."

"Are you a cuck, Mason?"

"I don't know. I like to watch girls get fucked. Maybe."

I nodded. That meant yes. To each their own. I just didn't want to picture Mason's dick in any way. Finally, he shut up enough that we made it to the club in some peace.

Once I arrived, I strolled in and quickly found the other guys at a table. Xavier had his girl at his side... and right next to her was Kinsley.

Before I sat down, I ordered two old-fashioned doubles from the bar. Downing one, I took my time with the other, meandering to our group in the corner booth. I'd need to wait awhile before driving again.

Kinsley looked fucking amazing, and I hated that my dick rose in my dress pants at the sight of her. Never in my life had I wanted to fuck and fight someone at the same time. Little Snow White was wearing a cream-colored dress with thigh-high boots. No tights... which meant she had paid attention to what I said. And that she expected me to show. I licked my lips.

Sipping my bourbon, I leaned against the wall near their booth, which was almost full. Certainly not enough room for a big guy like me.

"Scrunch in for Big G." One of Marissa's roommates said to the group, and everyone moved around the circular booth with Xavier's girlfriend ending up on his lap, as usual.

The only available seat was right next to Miss Priss herself. When I sat down, she was squished between me and Xavier, and she fidgeted to try to make some room. I set my drink on the table and picked her up around the waist, plopping her onto my crotch. May as well just get it done and over with. If I fucked her, I could get over her.

I didn't give a shit that she felt my erection in my pants. She needed to understand exactly what she was dealing with. Kinsley made it seem like she could handle it. I wasn't so sure. Although the blow job she had given me was impressive. She'd taken me farther than anyone had dared.

"Excuse me!" She wiggled in my lap, only making the blood pump faster into my dick.

"Pipe down and sit," I said so only she could hear. She settled at the sound of my voice. "I see you wore exactly what I asked. Hopefully, your pussy is exposed. Otherwise, I'm going to rip your panties off your body." I placed my hand on her thigh and slowly glided my thumb up her leg to her core. She froze.

Then she slowly parted her thighs enough so my large hand could slip to her core. She was wearing some thin and skinny fabric. Pushing it aside, I fingered my way around, then gently caressed her nub. She gasped and turned into me.

"George. They could see."

"I don't give a shit." Her wetness soaked my fingers. After playing with her pussy slowly for a while, I placed my lips on her ear and said, "I want to fuck you." The skin on her neck erupted in those goosebumps I'd seen before in the library. "Do you think you can get prepared for this?" Thrusting my hips up into her, she leaned back into me.

"I'm already prepared."

So she thought. Reaching around her, I grabbed my glass, downed the drink, then slammed it back on the table. Sliding out of the booth, I grabbed her hand and led her through the club and to the parking lot.

CHAPTER NINE
KINSLEY

WAS THIS IT? Were we finally going to have sex now? I had been practicing with my dildo, but I had seen George. He was bigger.

I had been hoping to have sex in a bed, but George led us to his truck. It reminded me of nights in Cale's Honda, and it lessened my excitement.

"Um, you want to fuck here? In your truck?"

George stopped us. He turned me so my body was back against the front grill of his large pickup.

"Not *in* the truck, princess."

"Wh-where?"

Grasping my waist in his large hands, he plopped me onto the hood. My core was just beneath his head. I had never gone without tights. If he lifted my dress, he would see some scars. That would probably turn him off.

Fortunately, there were no streetlights near where he parked. It was dark and shaded from view. George slid my dress up my thighs, exposing my black thong. I sat up on my elbows on the hard metal.

"No, I'm going to snack here first. Dying to eat you." He didn't seem to notice my scars that had been exposed in the moonlight. Maybe he couldn't see them properly. Before I could even think more about it, he ripped my thong straight off my body and stuffed it in his pocket.

Then he dove in. I arched into his face.

Oh. My. God.

If there were awards for cunnilingus, George would win. I clasped his large head between my thighs; he didn't seem to mind. He spent *time* on me. I didn't want to orgasm too soon because it was the best feeling of my life. My fingers crawled through his long blond hair as he flicked his tongue, sucked, then bit my clit.

If it were possible to hear beautiful music while getting eaten out, I did. Perhaps actual angels visited me because by the time I orgasmed, I saw heaven. Was I dying? If so, I was reborn and breathing for the first time by the time my pussy stopped pulsing. I must have been panting with my eyes closed because when I opened them I stared into the night sky for some time before I sat up.

"Holy shit. What was that?"

His blond stubble gleamed with my wetness. Spreading his thumb and forefinger, he used his hand to wipe his mouth clean, then sucked his fingers. The intense stare of his eyes never left my face. "I can't fuck you here. I don't want that, princess. I want to take my time with you."

"Then let's get out of here."

George nodded. His large, thick cock was visible through his pants. No one would miss it. It was its own homing beacon. A flagpole standing erect for the world to see. I wanted it all inside me.

He unlocked his truck and lifted me into the passenger seat. Moving around to the driver's side, he jumped in and grabbed my hand. The cab was big, but he forced my arm and hand onto his dick.

"Keep it company until we get home."

I stroked him through the ride, leaning over the console. He didn't make much noise until we reached the iron gate at the manor, when he moaned and sighed, letting his head fall against the headrest. His long hair fell around his shoulders.

When we got to the garage, the place was empty, given it was Friday night and most of the boys would be out partying. As we headed towards the manor, I must have been walking too slowly for him because George lifted me up and threw me over his shoulder, my short dress exposing my thighs. I tried to reach down and tuck it down as much as possible, but he just carried on.

George was on a mission to make it to his room. When we arrived, he threw open his bedroom door and slammed it shut with a kick of his heel while simultaneously dropping me on his bed.

"Fuck!" The wild gaze in his blue eyes had my core heating with need as I lay back on the mattress. "You look so appetizing. I want to fucking rip you apart and devour you."

"Do it."

He locked his door, then came over to me and almost ripped my outfit, but I stopped him with a gentle touch of my hands to his. Pulling the sweater dress over my head, I exposed my body in just a bra and no underwear. Along with my thigh-high boots.

"Leave those on," George commanded, pointing to my shoes. His voice made me tingle. He did rip my bra off like it was nothing, not even working the clasp.

His lips latched onto one of my nipples like a starving child. I almost came again when he bit down and ate hungrily while rubbing my clit with a large thumb. Unbuttoning his shirt, he undid his pants for me and let his lead pipe lay out. It was massive. I understood the name 'Big G'. His cock had its own gravitational pull. My pussy was certainly drawn straight to it.

He reached into his pocket and grabbed a condom out of his wallet and rolled it on. It wouldn't even fit close to the base.

"I'm going to put it all inside you. You're going to take it all if I have to shove every inch in while you cry. Do you understand me?"

"Yes." If my wetness was any indicator, I wasn't lying. I was ready.

George slid me up on the bed with one arm wrapped around my waist, so he could climb his enormous body over me. *Come on, Kinsley. You got this. Relax.* His gigantic cock was like a tree trunk sprouting from his body. I spread my legs wide, so I could try to fit him in.

George held my hips open and lined himself up with my entrance. I focused on breathing deeply. He slid the tip of his tennis ball-sized head through my cream, then started to puncture my hole.

Nothing prepared me for how large he was. "Ugh!" I gasped, losing a breath.

George wasn't stopping. He kept pushing in like he said he would. It would feel less pressure if he were fully inside me. Every inch felt like a new experience. I forced myself to relax through each one.

"*Fuck*, princess. You're insanely tight. Pussy has a chokehold on me." He couldn't go any further. I leaned up to look down between us. His cock was almost all the way in. When he shoved in more, he grunted. "Spread your lips for me so I can fit in more." Reaching between us, I spread my labia as wide as it would go so he could stretch me out.

George lifted my chin and kissed me as he dragged his dick back and then plunged in again.

"George!" I screamed into his mouth.

"Yeah, princess. I'm going to fuck you hard now. Try not to cry too loud."

Tears were already forming in my eyes from *pleasure*, not pain. I wanted whatever he was going to give me and laid back to show him how much I would take. Even if I cried.

George pounded me roughly, holding the back of my neck. My eyes latched onto his crystal blue ones. He rested his forehead to mine for a moment before he sucked on my neck roughly. He spread my legs so wide he was at a 90-degree angle with his hips pumping inside me.

"Oh my god! So big!" I cried out.

His fullness made me feel whole, and each time his hips met mine, my clit tingled with the anticipation of another orgasm. Combined with his hot breath on my neck, the stretch in my core made my legs quiver.

Backing up, he grabbed my waist and flipped me over to my stomach. "You're gonna take it like a big girl." A sharp smack landed on my ass, and I jolted.

George stood at the foot of the bed and yanked me to him. One of my bent legs was up and resting on the mattress. The other was standing on the ground. My back was against his sculpted chest. He dipped down and entered me. He had almost full control of my body and pulled my hips into his.

I moaned at how deep he got. When I turned my head to look behind me, he captured my lips with his, and we kissed deeply, tonguing each other in the madness of lust.

"No one else will ever do it for you after this, Sins." He railed into me. "This is it for you. The best sex you'll ever have."

George was right. No one else could measure up. Literally.

"Sins?"

"That's what you are. My Sins. Only your body can save me. Your wetness is cleansing me." He panted, strokes growing deeper. Reaching between us, he thumbed my clit in pressured circles. Ecstasy ripped through my body. Twisting, I laced my arm around his neck, trying to grab him however I could, while everything tightened within me. My toes curled inside my boots at the height of my orgasm. All my muscles melted into jelly coming down off my high as I puddled in his arms.

"How long has it been for you?" George asked.

"A-a long time." I panted.

"You clean?"

"Yes. Why?"

George pulled out and tore off his condom. "These things don't fucking fit me. I'm clean. You okay?"

"Yeah." I noticed he didn't ask about birth control.

As soon as I answered, he pushed back inside me. The sensation I felt before was nothing compared to the velvety goodness that encapsulated my insides.

George's head rolled back. "Fucking hell. Princess, every wet, hot, tight inch of you feels amazing." He gripped my neck and pummeled into me. "Fuck, I want to shoot all my cum inside you. You ready?"

"Yes!" Thinking about his balls emptying into me made me so hot that I was ready to climax again.

He punched his hips a few more times and reached forward to rub my clit. When he did, I came so hard my legs gave out. He wrapped his arms around me and used my pussy as a toy, plunging deeply inside while my inner muscles contracted around his massive pole.

"Fuck!" George groaned loudly and filled me so much I thought I would explode. When he pulled back, the full load squirted out from between my thighs and ran down into my thigh-high faux suede boots. Ugh, cleaning them would be a bitch.

George lifted me and threw my body like a ragdoll onto his bed.

He collapsed on top of me in the blankets. "You're staying here." His voice was muffled while his face was buried into the bed.

"Okay." I was sleeping over at George's. Weird. It was like sleeping with an enemy. I unzipped my boots and tossed them to the side of the bed. "I have to leave early. I'm running a marathon tomorrow." Although I was unsure how I would run when I knew I couldn't walk after tonight.

"Oh, yeah," he said like he already knew.

"I can leave if you want me to since I have—"

"You're not fucking leaving. Can a guy enjoy his high?"

"Sorry, I just—"

Lifting his head from the mattress to stare me down, he said, "Do I need to fuck you again already to shut you the fuck up? If so, give me ten minutes." George grabbed me into a giant bear hug and sucked on my neck. His skin was sweaty, and his chest rose and fell rapidly. I snuggled further into him. It was peaceful. "That's it, princess. Just relax." The wall of his chest vibrated as he spoke, lulling me into a trance.

He tossed his blankets over us. Within one minute, his breathing was steady and deep. Wow. George *would* be one to sleep like a rock. In the comforting weight of his arms, and under his hot breath landing on my skin, I was able to sleep soundly.

George's cock woke me up. The pole was laying

between my legs and prodding my pussy apart. "Shh, go back to sleep. I'm just going to fuck you again."

A whimper escaped my lips.

"I like you better while asleep, Sins." He thrust inside. "You're quiet."

I smirked and enjoyed the ride, still half-asleep. For someone so reticent, he was quite talkative during sex. His ragged breaths filled my ears. Rocking forward, I could lift my hip and get more of him inside. I used to require my clit to be touched during sex, but he was so huge that his thickness was enough to make me detonate. Gripping the pillow, I screamed into it.

"That's a good girl. That's my princess." His cock pulsed and erupted inside me. The waves of his pleasure were one of the best feelings my pussy had ever experienced. "Fuck, what time do you need to leave? Cause I want to do that again before you go."

I chuckled. "What time is it?"

He rolled back, and his semi-erect penis slid slightly out, but most was still sheathed within me. Looking at his phone, he said, "Five. I can take you home if you need to go now. You need breakfast first?"

"No, I'll get something at the apartment, but I don't like to eat before my marathons."

"That's ridiculous." As he sat up, his cock spilled out of me.

"What would you know? You ever run a marathon?"

"Princess, I've been training longer than you. Not running, but I know the proper way to fuel a body. Look at mine."

Snorting, I couldn't come up with an argument against him. He *was* a perfect beast of a man.

"Come on. Get dressed, and we'll get you something to eat before I drop you off."

"No way."

"Sins, I am not taking no for an answer. Put your clothes on. I expect you to be ready to go in five." He got up and started to dress. "Use the bathroom two doors down the hall." He snapped his fingers and pointed like a drill sergeant.

I needed him to take me home, so I did as he said. If he was going to try to make me eat, it was fine, but I wouldn't eat much.

After using the nasty bathroom down the hall, George made us protein shakes for breakfast. I sipped mine carefully as we loaded into his truck.

He eyed me and the fullness of my protein shake. "You need to eat some oatmeal or some complex carbs when you get home."

Now he was mansplaining nutrition to me. I sipped my shake, not wanting to get into it.

Sensing my irritation, he changed the subjects. "Do you have a good luck charm?"

I thought of Cale's bracelet, still sitting in my backpack. "No. Not anymore."

"What's that mean?"

"I mean, I had something, but it's no longer lucky. Had it on when I got hit by that drunk driver."

"Ah." George nodded.

"Do you have something?"

"Yeah. My letterman's patch from my jacket in high

school. We only lost two football games, and both those times I didn't have my jacket with me."

I snorted.

"What?" he asked.

"I just didn't expect you to be superstitious."

George huffed. "Fine. I won't wish you luck today, then." We reached my apartment building. The sun was just starting to break into the sky. "Don't trip."

"Thanks." I leaned into the passenger door, ready to open it and make my walk-of-shame back to my room.

"Sins, wait." George jumped out and came around to open my door, lifted me out of the truck, and kissed me. Flushing with desire, I was ready to forget the marathon and go back to bed with him.

George broke our kiss and pulled out his phone. "Text me your number." He showed his number on the screen. I texted him mine. "See ya, princess."

He jumped back in his truck and eyed me as he drove away. I fiddled with my lips, remembering his George taste and wanting more. But first, I had a race to run.

Darting upstairs, I made some instant oatmeal (I wasn't going to tell him that) and downed a half bowl. I quickly threw on my race tights and sports bra. Covering myself with an NU hoodie, I had just enough time to make it to the start of the race. When I got out of my car, I heard a rip. Feeling my butt, a large hole had formed in the crotch of my tights. I always went commando under them.

"No, no, no, no!" I cried. What was I supposed to do? I had no alternative outfit, and the race would start

WHITE HOLE

too soon. Kicking myself for not packing an extra bag like normal, I decided to try to run, anyway. Maybe no one would notice.

After approaching the check-in table, I felt a breeze hitting my backside. I was worried, but kept going. I didn't want to reach down to feel how large the hole was in case other people took notice.

The start of the race was fine. I was able to ignore the rip. By the end, the hole had grown so large that almost my entire bum was exposed. My face wasn't just flushed from the exercise, I was going to die of humiliation. I didn't stop, determined to make it to the end.

It was my worst time ever.

When I crossed the finish line, I hurried to my car and jumped in without even stopping at the water table. I should have checked my clothes before I went! Looking at my phone, I saw a text waiting from George.

GEORGE

Text me when you're done with your race.

I'm done.

Was it a holy experience?

?

I'm sure you RIPPED down the street as fast as you could.

Did you do this?

shh emoji

> You fucking asshole! Never speak to me again.

> *laughing emoji* Sins, you get what you deserve. Don't fuck with my workout gear, and I won't fuck with yours.

That wasn't going to happen. Not after this. I needed to up the stakes. He thought he could embarrass me like this? Ugh, just when I was starting to crave his cock, too. I had been thinking I would meet up with him after the race for some fun time in his bed. Now, the thought disgusted me. He just ruined it.

GEORGE
> Meet me.

> No fucking way. Go to hell.

> Meet me or I will come get you.

> Nope. I'm disappearing.

I started my car and pulled out of the back parking lot designated for the participants. Once I reached the road, my car wouldn't turn. It shook and made a loud screeching noise. Flashbacks from my accident flooded my mind. My chest tightened, and my fingers ached on the steering wheel. Air would not get into my lungs. I froze.

Someone honked behind me. I tried to pull the car to the side to let everyone go around. Once I did, I jumped out of the car, bent over, and hurled.

Feeling lightheaded, I sat on the curb with my head

in my hands. My car tire had busted. The others looked low as well. Inspecting them closer, I saw giant slash marks in each of them. George had tried to kill me! He'd tried to slash my tires! He had gone too far.

I picked up my phone and called his number.

"Where are you? I'm coming for you," he answered.

"Go fuck yourself, George. You trying to *kill* me now?"

"What are you talking about? Where are you?" he asked more firmly.

I wailed, "You-you fucker! You slashed my tires! You will *pay*, George!" I was sobbing.

"Sins, stop. Where are you? I am coming to get you."

A large black truck pulled up on the other side of the street on the opposite curb. George climbed down, still holding his phone to his head, then ended the call and slid it into his back pocket when he spotted me.

Trying to wipe tears from my eyes, I wouldn't look at him. I didn't want him to know how much his prank affected me.

It didn't matter. Large arms swept me into his warm body like I weighed nothing. I wrapped my legs around his waist and buried my head into his neck, sniffling.

"I did not fucking do this, Sins. I *wouldn't* do this." I was clinging to him like a koala. He bent down to inspect my tires. Tugging back on my ponytail, he made me face him. "Let's get something straight, princess. You annoy the fuck out of me, but I don't want to hurt you. Except when I fuck you."

Despite my tears and snotty nose, he kissed me,

sucking my lips into his. I moaned and then broke the kiss to nuzzle his neck more. He smelled like safety.

"I hate to put you down, I like you tucked into me like this, but I need to turn off your car." He set my legs on the ground and turned off the engine. Then he picked me back up and walked us to his truck.

George waited with me until help arrived, drumming his fingers on the center console and darting his eyes around, scanning the scene. I sat on his lap, straddling him, feeling his heartbeat against my chest. My fingers slowly stroked his long hair. Once the tow truck arrived, the driver pulled my car to the nearest shop as we followed. Since it was so late, the mechanic couldn't fit new tires on it until the weekend was over.

"You need food," George said after placing me back in his truck. I hadn't even thought of food the entire day. Now that he said it, I was faint.

"Sharice has my food at home. Will you take me?"

"Of course, Sins. But would you rather go to a restaurant?"

"With you?"

"Yeah. With me," he said with annoyance.

"I'd like that." I would. I didn't really want to leave him.

"Okay. What do—" Before he finished his sentence, he glanced at his phone after receiving a text. "Fuck!"

"What?"

George sighed deeply and let his head drop back. "I have to drop you off. Something's come up. I do want to take you out, though."

When we arrived at my building, I made a move to

get out of the truck, but he grabbed my waist and pulled me onto his lap again. "Where you going, princess?" He brushed pieces of my dark hair out of my eyes that had escaped my elastic band. He tucked each side behind an ear. His lips held mine, and he moaned, not wanting to let go. "I want to stay and fuck you all night."

"Okay," I said breathlessly into his mouth.

"But I can't. I'll text you later." I slid off him and got out. "Eat," George yelled before I shut his door.

I went promptly upstairs and devoured two meals.

CHAPTER TEN
GEORGE

THERE WASN'T time to devise a solution to the Gianna problem before she texted me. Right when I was going to get some princess pussy, too. The wicked witch was ruining my life. Like always.

What worried me more than the Gianna situation was Kinsley's car. Someone was indeed trying to kill her. She had an entire league of undesired enemies and had no clue. She suspected me immediately. I wondered if that meant she knew who I was, who my father was. If she knew the police covered up her accident. I still couldn't be sure.

If Kinsley knew the police covered it up, she could go to internal affairs. She was smart; she'd figure out immediately that the mayor was involved. With how stubborn she was, I knew she wouldn't let it go until everyone burned. And that included my brothers and me. My mother would suffer without me around and it was my fault she was in the state she was in.

Motoring the familiar highway toward Springfield,

I turned up Metallica. The drums and guitar lines helped me focus on the task at hand. I had my blackmailer to consider before stressing about Kinsley. My anger rose within me each mile I drove towards the motel.

Once I parked in the lot, I quickly jumped out of the truck and marched to the room on a mission. Knocking on the faded red door, I checked my back pocket for a condom. Feeling the plastic wrapper, my shoulders relaxed slightly.

Gianna opened the door in another lingerie getup, this one green. I brushed past her into the room and slammed the door, locking it. Turning to her, I stuck my finger straight in her face.

"Let's get something straight, Gianna. I could hurt you. I could fucking kill you. You don't want that, do you?" I was walking her body backward until she hit the wall by the far bed.

"Ooh, I like when you're rough with me, Georgie." She lifted a finger and dragged it down my cheek. "But if I die, the audio will be released. You, your brothers, *and* your mother will suffer. I know you don't give a shit about the Chief."

I cracked my jaw.

"I'm not impregnating you." I grabbed her arms and slung her around, throwing her on the bed. She landed with a thud. I wondered how difficult it would be to twist someone's neck until they died.

"George!"

Grasping her red hair, I dragged her over to the edge. "Take my cock out." She unzipped my jeans and pulled it out. "Get me hard. Suck. If you bite, I'll make sure you don't have any teeth left."

Gianna was a good cocksucker, but not as good as Kinsley. I tried to focus on Sin's face and lips, letting my head drop back and watching the ceiling instead of my ex-stepmother.

Grabbing the back of her head, I shoved into her stretched mouth repeatedly. She gagged and tried to back up. I grasped her neck with my other hand and tried to cut her air off. She turned bright red. Could I do this? Could I fucking kill her? At the last moment, I let go and pulled back.

"George, this isn't how this works." She spat, gasping for a breath. "You need—"

"Don't finish that sentence." Wrenching her waist with my hands, I flipped her over to her stomach and spread her legs. After rolling on my condom, I let my jeans drop to the floor.

Clutching a handful of her auburn locks, I pulled until her head was at an awkward angle. Hocking up some saliva, I spit in her open mouth while I shoved my cock all the way inside her. She screamed, and I clamped my other hand over her mouth. "Shut the fuck up, bitch."

She wailed around the skin of my palm. Using her head as leverage, I ripped into her with my full length over and over, pounding into her with every bit of rage and hurt and pain I'd ever had. It was the definition of *hate fuck*.

When she came all over my dick, I yanked myself out of her. Ripping off the condom, I stroked myself to completion. I spunked jizz all over her back and in her hair.

"There's your hush money. How's it feel to constantly get fucked by men that can't stand you?" She rolled over to look at me with a face full of tears. Her black mascara had run down each cheek. "You feel powerful? You feel *in control*?"

She sniffed and tried to sit up, narrowing her eyes at me.

"Finally! That shut you up. My cock seems to do that to a lot of women... I'm done here." Reaching down to pull up my pants, I bolted out the door and to my truck. I made it to the diner about two miles down the road before pulling over and banging my head against the steering wheel.

I was a piece of shit. Why was it that this woman hurt me since I was fourteen, and *I* was ashamed for pummeling her, for treating her like garbage? Not to mention feeling like I'd just cheated on Kinsley. Just like my father…

Throwing open my truck door, I jumped out in time to vomit all over the gravel of the lot. I clasped my hands together and put them on my forehead, leaning back for a breath. Wiping my mouth, I got back into my truck and headed home.

Kinsley and I weren't together. I was pretty sure I annoyed her as much as she annoyed me. I was planning to fuck Sins all night long in her bed. Now, I felt like a big asshole for having sex with my ex-stepmom. Even if it wasn't consensual.

Fortunately, when I entered the manor, no one was

around to irritate me more. I went directly to the telescope in my room. I wanted to fade into outer space.

No sound.

No gravity.

Freedom.

Maybe being an automaton wouldn't be so bad. I could just shut everything off and perform. Do what was required of me. Be a drone. Drones didn't feel ashamed, and they weren't assholes that cheated on their non-girlfriends.

For the next few days, I avoided Sins. I should not have been involved in her life. I'd only bring her problems she didn't need. I already had, she just didn't know. It was wrong of me to use her body like I had. She was my ultimate sin.

Sitting on a bench at the gym, I couldn't stop thinking of her. Why couldn't I? Mulling over my shame for cheating on someone who wasn't mine was ridiculous. I felt guilt, like I owed her something.

A white towel was shoved in my face, breaking my thought loop. Xavier smirked, and I took the towel from him with a nod.

"What are you thinking about? You have a look that is a million miles away." Xavier was chipper. He was always chipper these days. In love. I was happy for my friend to finally *be* happy, but it pissed me off to be around him.

I shrugged my shoulders, unsure if I could even put my thoughts into words.

"You bringing Kins to the Halloween party?" He knew. He knew I was thinking about her, the arrogant bastard. Xavier was so much more observant than people gave him credit for. I didn't say anything. "Well, you should."

I sighed, then grunted. "Can't."

"Fuck, Gianna." Bending to pick up a weight, he lowered his voice. "My people can—"

"No. I have to think of my family." I stood, grabbing my dumbbells.

"If you're going to keep fucking them both, may as well do them together." Xavier lifted his eyebrows quickly up and down, then walked towards the locker room. Smartass. He sounded just like Levi sometimes.

Perhaps Gianna was pissed at the way I'd treated her. Maybe she was hurt and wouldn't call again. No, the bitch probably just wanted it more.

After morning classes, I had an hour to work on my thesis in the campus cafe before eating lunch with my TRZ brothers. Grabbing my to-go cup of black coffee, I sat at a corner table and reached into my bag for my thesis notes. When I opened it, the entire thing was blank. It was an identical, but empty, notebook.

My chest tightened, and my breath hitched in my lungs. *Where the fuck was it?* The thing contained all my observations for my final project. *Fuck!* The last page of the blank book had something written in permanent marker:

Ripped my leggings, I ripped your notebook.
– Your friendly neighborhood princess.

Quickly, my feeling of panic turned to rage. What was I thinking? Her pussy had me getting weak around her. Yeah, I had messed with her practice test, but things had gone too far. Now she was messing with my career, with my dreams. She was trying to fuck up my future out of here.

Sins would never stop. She was too obstinate. I wanted a truce. If I waved a white flag, I could cut her out of my life once the semester was over. No more tutoring, and she'd go her way while I went mine. It was the best for both of us. I'd be washed clean of my sins.

In the cafeteria, I snagged my tray of steak and potatoes. When I turned to our normal table, I spotted Kinsley sitting next to Mason. Levi was across from her, next to Xavier and Marissa. My neck tensed.

Sliding my tray on to the table, I sat on the other side of Levi, careful to avoid eye contact with Sins.

"Yo, G. Big man loading up on your proteins there." Levi pointed at my food. "You on for the airsoft game Saturday?"

I nodded.

Mason was talking in a low voice with Kinsley. Their conversation almost unheard. I couldn't help but stare at them.

"Mason!" Levi snapped while rubbing his face with his hand. Mason jerked his head up, breaking his intimate conversation with Kinsley. "You doing the airsoft thing again this year?"

"Of course. You fuckers would be lost without me.

You going to be able to make the Halloween party, Lev?"

"One hundred and ten thousand percent."

Mason laughed. A knot formed in my stomach at what I *knew* would happen next. Mason turned to Kinsley and quietly said, "Hey, you going to the Halloween party?"

Xavier coughed, and Levi shoved an empty chocolate milk bottle at Mason. It rolled, then fell into his lap. Kinsley looked at me, and Mason yelled at Levi.

"What the fuck?"

Levi smirked, "Oh, sorry. Can you hand that back?"

So Levi knew.

I held Kinsley's golden eyes for a moment. After blinking a few times, she turned to answer Mason. "Um, I hadn't been invited, so…" She gave me a brief glance.

"Well, I'll invite you!" Mason said excitedly.

I banged both fists on the table causing the lunch trays to jump. Then, like the ogre I was, I marched over to where she was sitting and plopped down next to her while everyone watched me. Picking her up, I placed her on my lap before sliding my food over to myself. Stabbing a potato, I took a large bite, quietly chewing.

Mason's jaw was wide open. "Uh, well, I—"

"She's coming with me," I said with my mouth full. Like a pirate guarding his booty, I gripped her waist tighter with my arm. Staring straight ahead, my body radiated back off energy.

"I think she's going with Big G, Mason." Levi laughed. Xavier and his girlfriend joined in.

"Yeah, not a problem. No problem at all. You take her." Mason didn't move an inch.

"Are you *asking* me?" Kinsley finally perked up, twisting her torso to look at me.

"No," I said, then took a bite of my steak.

She gasped. "Fine, then I'm going with Mason."

"No, no, no. You should go with Big G. I gotta run to my next class." Mason grabbed his stuff and bolted. Levi laughed harder.

Kinsley placed her face close to mine so only I could hear her. "George, I'm not going just because you tell me I am."

"Kinsley?"

"Yeah?"

"Darling? Sweetheart? Apple of my eye?"

"What is it, George?"

"Will you do me the honor of accompanying me to the Halloween party?"

Her pert little pink lips spread into a broad smile. "Yes, George, I will." Then she paused a moment and furrowed her brow. "Hey, what's your last name?"

I took my time to chew my food and swallow before responding. Did she really not know who I was? "I thought you knew."

"No." Her cheeks flushed to match the color of her lips. Quietly, she said, "I've never slept with someone I didn't know their full name."

"That embarrasses you?"

"A little."

"Come on. You know my name," I said.

"Big G? George? What is it? A huge secret?"

"It's Turner." I waited for her to throw a fit, to show some recognition, or slap me. Something, anything.

Instead, she said, "Oh." She shrugged. "Why was that so hard for you to say? It's quite a common name. Many people have the name Turner. I think I knew at least three people or more in elementary school alone with the name. Cousins, I presume?"

"Sins, we need to go to tutoring." In a lower voice with my lips on her earlobe, I said, "And, obviously, you need my dick in your mouth to shut the fuck up."

It seemed she had not put the two together, whose son I was. Her reaction was enough for me to know that she wasn't trying to trick me. Kinsley wasn't good at hiding anything she was thinking or feeling. I just hoped she didn't figure it out.

When we got to the library, I twisted her around by the shoulders before she could sit. Her face was a mixture of anger and shock when I did.

"What are you doing?"

"Let's get something straight between us. No more pranks. Give me my notebook. Now."

"George, you ripped my leggings to shreds. I had to run a *marathon* with my ass crack exposed to everyone!"

I tried not to laugh. "Yeah. But that wasn't taking your whole future away. Everything is in that notebook."

"You tried to ruin mine by messing with my practice exam!"

"Hence, the name *'practice'*. It wasn't fucking up your future. Seriously, give it back."

She smirked. "Or else, what?"

"No 'or else'. We're done with this shit."

"Maybe I'm not."

Stepping into her tiny body, I grasped her thick brown hair, pulling her face up to meet mine. "Sins, I'm not playing. Give me the notebook." She held her breath and didn't speak. Watching her chest rise and fall so fast, her puckered little mouth, her insolence… it all made my dick raging hard. Narrowing my eyes, I lowered my lips to touch hers lightly. "Princess, if you don't give me that notebook back right now, I'm going to fuck you in front of that nerd group sitting in the next alcove." I nodded my head in the direction.

She gasped and I had the urge to stick my finger between her parted lips. "You wouldn't."

"You going to give me the notebook?"

She grimaced. Twisting her by her hair, I turned her body so she was bent over the study table. She hit it with a thud and tried to squirm away. "Ow!"

"I guess I need to make you give it up." I pushed an arm into her back to hold her and with my free hand, reached down to lift her skirt. She wanted this. It's why she'd listened to me and wore one today. When I slid it up her thighs, my breath hitched. First at her naughty schoolgirl thigh-high stockings. The tops revealed some old surgery scars, but that was not what made me hard as a fucking rock. Kinsley, Miss Priss, had forgone underwear.

"No panties, princess?"

She whimpered and shook her head.

"*Fuck*. You really needed this cock today, didn't you, dirty slut?" I ran a finger down her pussy lips. She jolted. My hand was coated in her sopping wetness. "Mmm. Tasty." I sucked on my fingers.

I was calling her out, but I needed to fuck her just as much as she needed me. I'd been trying to avoid it, but her fucking Chanel perfume. Her infuriating mind. That dark hair knotted between my fingers. Little sassy lip. She was maddening. And I had to expel the feeling with my ejaculation.

Pulling my arm back fully, I smacked her bare ass cheek with a giant swat. She made some weird noise of pain, surprise, and pleasure while shifting from foot to foot and trying to look behind her.

"Shh!" Came from the alcove next to us.

Leaning over her back while unzipping my jeans, relief flooding me as my dick got more room to breath. "You better be quiet, princess, or that guy will come over here and see you getting it hard." I spanked her again, and she yelled behind her closed mouth.

Pulling out my cock, I ran it through her dripping pussy lips before lining up and plunging in. Sins was a trooper. She held it together, though I knew it was a lot for her to take.

To make room for my thickness, she climbed up on the table and spread her legs wide. I let go of her hair and grabbed her hips. She stretched her arms in front of her, gripping the opposite side of the table for leverage while humping my long dick. Like a fucking pro. I watched her go for a full minute.

Leaning over her back, I slid a hand up to her throat. Her quiet grunts while she worked me were making my balls tingle. "Princess, I think you've just received your coronation to size queen. You're taking this big dick so good." I kept my voice low. I didn't give a shit if the twerp next to us came over or not. As soon as he saw me, he'd turn the other way. Or I'd make him, not wanting him to see my girl like this.

Kinsley grabbed my hand around her neck and pulled it up to her mouth. I put my other around her chest, twisting her nipple through her shirt. Her moans were muffled under my skin. She opened her mouth enough to bite my finger. I pushed in harder.

"Milk the cum out of me. Take it." I sucked her neck and could feel her pussy clench and pulse on my cock while she screamed behind the wall of my hand. Fuck, I was waiting for that. I thrust rapidly and exploded, shooting off ropes of cum deep inside her while her hot interior squeezed me dry. Leaning on my elbow, I held there until the last pulse of our orgasms faded.

Panting, I breathed in her ear. "Now, you going to be a good girl and give me that notebook, or do I need to spank you more, brat?"

I moved my hand as she whispered, "I'll get it. Truce." She melted onto the table as I pulled out of her, cum dripping onto the surface. Pursing my lips, I thought about the next sorry soul that had to sit there. Oh, well. Worth it.

She slid off the table and pulled down her skirt. Then, she waddled wide legged to her bag and pulled out my notebook, handing it to me.

"That wasn't so hard, was it?"

Kinsley lifted one side of her mouth. "Actually, that was *very* hard."

I snorted. "Sit. We have studying to do. You have an A to earn."

"Didn't I just earn it?"

"Not until I fuck you in the A."

Brown eyes turned into round saucers as her jaw dropped along with her chin. "You can't be serious. There's no way, George!"

"Shh!" Came from the alcove next to us.

She whispered, "No way!"

"Sit."

Still shocked, she eased into her seat next to the one I had taken, but I couldn't stand it. Grabbing her waist before her butt hit the chair, I moved her to my lap again. "Nah, this is your seat now." Wrapping my arms around her, I tilted her head to mine to kiss her. Then, I started to teach.

CHAPTER
ELEVEN
KINSLEY

I WAS HAPPY. George got me an A on my astronomy midterm. The marathon was over. All I had left to focus on was my medical college admission test before the Halloween party the following evening.

Despite my mind continually fantasizing about George's cock throughout my days and nights, I pushed him aside to focus on the exam. The butterflies in my stomach turned to birds, then screeching pterodactyls, as the week progressed. By Friday morning, I felt like I had two heart attacks before getting dressed to walk over to the testing site.

Slinging my bag over my shoulder, I noticed the zipper pocket was open. Something was stuck in it, so I couldn't close it. When I went to stuff the items back in, I pulled out George's patch from high school. His lucky letter. I smiled, my nerves easing.

ME
Thank you.

> **GEORGE**
>
> For what?

> For the luck.

> You don't need it. You're ready.

> And don't wake me up again this fucking early.

So George was grouchy in the mornings. Good to know.

Bouncing to the building, my shoulders relaxed. I took a deep breath and entered. He was right. I was ready.

That night, Elle arranged that we all head to the club to celebrate. She said it was because my exam was over, but, really, she just wanted any excuse to party. I'd have weeks to wait before hearing my test results and needed to blow off steam, so I was grateful for the outing. No boys were invited, but I thought that might have to do with her irritation over a *certain* boy.

"Come on, and I'll buy you a drink, Kins." She led us all to the bar. Marissa lingered in the back and I grabbed her hand, tugging her with me.

"You've been MIA too much. Stop looking around for him." Her dark brown hair was bouncing as her head swiveled around, looking for her boyfriend, Xavier.

"But I *feel* like he's here."

Sharice snorted. "Probably because he's hiding in the shadows somewhere. Dude's creepy."

Marissa's jaw dropped. Then she closed it and smiled. "Yeah, he is."

Elle handed us each a martini and led us over to a U-shaped booth filled with Deltas. She made them scoot over so we could sit. The fraternity brothers didn't mind seeing four hot women wanting to sidle up to them.

"Hello, *ladies*," said one guy with thick glasses and a lip ring.

"We aren't here to talk to you. We just wanted your seats," I said.

"Well, maybe I wanted to talk to *her*," the guy said, pointing at Elle. She was a bombshell. I didn't blame him. Elle turned to flirt with the other guys, and Marissa nudged me.

"So, you and George, huh? How's that going?"

"How did you—did he say something to Xavier?"

"It's pretty obvious you two are a thing, honey," Sharice said.

"Oddly, I think it's going well."

"Why 'oddly'?" Sharice asked.

Squirming in my seat, I replied, "'Cause I don't think we like each other. Or maybe he's just always annoyed with me, and I with him."

The girls grinned at me. "And... how's the horse cock?" Marissa giggled.

"It's, um. It's *good*." My pussy tingled just thinking about our last encounter in the library. Halloween was the next evening, and I couldn't wait to play with him again.

WHITE HOLE

"I'm sure it is," Sharice laughed. "What are you guys going to dress up as for the party tomorrow?"

"Oh. Damn, I hadn't even thought about that. I've been focused on my test."

The girls started talking about their costumes as I pulled out my phone.

> ME
>
> What are we wearing for the party tomorrow?
>
> GEORGE
>
> *We* are wearing something?
>
> Yes, George. You invited me as your date. You forced me to sit in your lap all week like your property. That means we need to coordinate.
>
> Princess Leia and Han
>
> Sure. Do you have the stuff to make up a costume like that?

George didn't respond. Disappointment rose within me the longer I stared at the blank phone screen. Everyone at the table was talking, laughing. I sipped my drink and tried to casually glance at my phone for any notifications.

"What's wrong?" Marissa picked up on my mood shift.

What *was* wrong? I shouldn't like him. He infuriated me. His very presence set my teeth on edge. So why did I want him to text me back?

"Nothing," was my chosen response. My eyes scanned the club. I wasn't looking for *him*, per se.

My throat constricted when I spotted Barrett Grant at a table across the club. His face triggered my memories: flashing red lights sparkling in the falling ice glitter and blood drizzling into my eye. The rest of my martini went straight down my throat as I tossed my long brown hair over my shoulder and stood.

Slinking through the shadows along the walls, I crept close enough to watch my nemesis with a pretty brunette woman. The two were making out near a table. I'd figured it out: if Barrett got away with a hit-and-run, that meant the mayor was involved. Which meant the mayor told the police to destroy the video evidence. So those who *protect and serve* were in on it, too. What if this went all the way to the chief of police?

How was I supposed to *prove* anything? Even my own parents didn't believe me when I told them about the man who hit me. If the store on the corner still had their footage, I could start there. Go up and down Main Street to get Mr. Mayor's son on video.

My legs motored to where Barrett was sitting. No plan had formulated in my mind, only rage and bitterness. Vague images of snatching the woman off his waist and punching him in the face flashed through the screens in my head. Advancing towards the table, my flowy top snagged on something, and my fury turned to the object holding the hem.

"George!"

"Where you going, princess? Trying to get yourself killed?" My body was moving towards the hallway near the bathrooms as George directed my shoulders with his gorilla paws.

"*Please*. He's not even that big."

"He's got security, Sins."

Peering around George's ginormous body, a few men in black suits stood at the ready near Barrett's table. My focus had been on taking him out, not on the others surrounding him.

"Oh. Well, I didn't see them."

George gently pushed me to the back of the club with a large hand pressed to my lower back. I turned my face to his as he opened the back club door leading to the parking lot. We stopped short before walking out as a couple were making their way inside.

It was Cale and Sydney.

"Oh! Hey, Kinsley." Cale was behind his girlfriend and eyed George suspiciously. It was the first time I'd noticed how very tiny Cale seemed compared to the lumbering giant at my back. George's arm slipped from my back around my waist possessively.

"Hey."

Sydney smirked her painted red lips and raised one eyebrow almost imperceptibly.

"Uh, Kinsley. You have that bracelet?"

"Yeah, I found it. I'll, um, I'll give it to you in class."

"He's been asking for *weeks* now. It's *his*, you know." Sydney had never spoken to me, and I winced at the shrill soprano of her voice. Could Cale stand to listen to that all day?

"Yes, and he *gave* it to *me*. Well before he even knew you. So, run along and—"

"Listen, bitch—" Sydney said. Cale pushed her further into the club while the grip on my waist tightened.

George almost carried me outside while Sydney was tugged onto the dance floor.

"Stop! Stop! What are you doing?"

"What are *you* doing, princess? Looking for a fight?"

"Maybe I am."

"Then fight me." We reached his truck and he let me go. I spun around and he pinned me against the metal with an arm on either side of my body. "Come on, Sins. Fight me."

"You're infuriating."

"So are you."

"I hope I'm never as stubborn as you when I grow up."

George's lips pressed together, and one side lifted. As if the muscles could not control themselves, his mouth moved apart until I could see his white teeth, then his open mouth, and he let out a roaring laugh. The sound was so earth shattering, it shook my bones.

"It's not funny," I said.

He threw his head back and laughed more, adding to his expression a full body shake.

"It's not." I giggled. His laughter made me vibrate inside.

When his head came back from its vacation, he lowered his eyelids, and his mouth went soft. His sparkling eyes stared at my lips until they tingled. George lowered his head slowly and moved his arms to embrace my waist and neck. Our lips touched gently before he licked mine and dove his tongue inside. I ran my fingers through his hair, untying his ponytail, letting the strands fall loose to tickle my face.

It left me breathless, wet, and hungry when he pulled back, blue eyes glowing red in the neon lights from the club's exit sign. "Wha-what are you doing here, George?"

"Came to see if you wanted to craft our costumes tonight?"

"How did you know I was here?"

"Where else do you guys go if there's no party on campus?"

I nodded. "True." Looking at his lips, I wondered if he was going to kiss me again. When I lifted my eyes, he lifted his from peering at my mouth. Holding each other's gaze, my core tightened. I wanted more of him. Never breaking eye contact, he lifted me up by my backside until my legs encircled him, hands still stroking his golden locks.

"You wore jeans."

"Yeah, I did," I said with disappointment.

"That's unfortunate." His waist pressed into me until his massive pipe rammed between my legs. Our pants the barrier to ecstasy.

"I can't be out here with you."

George nipped my bottom lip that was sticking out. "Why?" He breathed hot air into my mouth. It tasted like mint.

"It's girl's night. No men allowed."

He dropped my legs and backed away with his hands up. "Okay. See ya."

"Wait, wait!" I grabbed his arm and tugged. "I guess I could ask if... We were going to make costumes?"

He gripped the truck door handle. "I was. But you're busy."

"No, no. It's an emergency. We need to get our outfits sorted before tomorrow night. They'll understand."

George tried hard not to smile, and his handsome face made my pulse stutter, wetness pooling in my panties. "An emergency. Yep. Better hurry, princess. Ship's leaving in ten. Don't get into any bar fights."

Running back inside the club, all my brain could think about was the massive cock inside his pants prison. Like an addict, I needed another hit as soon as possible. I skated past Cale and Sydney, who were too busy grinding on each other (*Yuck!*) to notice me. At our table, I snatched my purse, and the girls snapped their heads to me.

"Where do you think you're going?" Marissa had no right to sound accusatory as she sat on Xavier's lap. So he *was* there.

"I need to make my costume for tomorrow night's party." Before anyone could protest further, I darted out.

"Say hello to George for me!" Marissa yelled, and everyone at the table laughed.

Heart beating fast, my skin sweating and flushed, I hurried back to George. Spotting him sitting in the driver's seat, my belly flipped, and heat rose between my legs in anticipation of being near him. What was happening to me? Every moment I wasn't with him, he was all I could think about. George was consuming me. It wasn't right. I had other things, my future, to be thinking about.

Plus, I wanted to get started on tearing apart Barrett Grant and his escape from justice.

Using the step rail, I jumped in the passenger seat of his truck. His citrus and steel scent filled the cab, forcing my thighs to quiver with expectation. I wanted to jump in his lap and hump him. But without our clothes harboring us.

"Fucking Chanel." George muttered almost so I could barely hear.

"What?"

"Nothing."

I smirked. He must have been feeling the same as I. Putting the truck into drive, he pointed us toward Main Street with a flick of his blinker.

"Where are we going?"

"Thought we'd stop by Wal-Mart. Only place open right now."

Sinking back into the cozy seat, I crossed my arms. George glanced over and turned on the heat. "You cold?"

No, I was burning hot. For him. For George. And I wanted him to consume me again like he did at the library and in his bed.

"Uh, I'm good. Are we, um, going to your place after?"

George's normally stoic expression changed to amusement. "What are you asking, princess?"

"Um. Just wondering is all. It's late."

"You want me to take you home—"

"No! I mean, no. I mean, not if you don't want me to… What do you want, George?" I huffed.

"I want to take you out to Wal-mart."

"Oh. Okay. Great." Frustrated, I turned to look at the night sky out my window. "Cassiopeia."

George dipped his head to peek out at the sky. "Yep. That's why you aced your test." He grabbed my hand from my lap and held it on the large center console of the truck. An earthquake exploded in my chest with the heavy thuds of my heart. If he didn't touch more of me soon, I would explode like a dying star. Like a white hole.

"Thank you for your lucky patch. I need to give it back."

"You keep it until the MCAT results come in. That's how it works." He squeezed my hand, and I breathed deeply. "Who was that scrawny tool in the bar?"

"High school ex. Wants his cheap bracelet back to give to his new girlfriend." Involuntarily, my eyes rolled.

"Get rid of it and be done with it."

"I'm thinking of flushing it down the toilet. Or melting it into scrap. Or running it through dog poop and giving it back."

George grunted.

"What?"

"I should have known you'd be vindictive." He glanced at me. "What, did he leave you for her?"

"No."

We pulled into the parking lot of the store.

"But he broke up with you."

"Yes." I didn't want to confess the reason. It was too humiliating. If I mentioned them, George could see me differently. He hadn't said anything about my skin, yet, but I hadn't been completely nude in the light for him. I wanted to be. Almost imperceptibly, I said, "He didn't like my scars."

"What?!" George's brow furrowed and his eyes got dark. He jumped out of his side of the truck and before I could undo my belt and get out, he was there, pulling me to him. In our position, he backed me against the back window, putting himself between my legs. His erection was still palpable.

"He broke up with me because of the scars from my accident," I said more boldly this time.

"Toss that shitty bracelet and be done with him. Fuck that guy." He leaned into me, so his mouth was over my ear. His deep bass rolled straight to my core and made my clit vibrate. "I'm going to take my time and lick your scars. Every. Single. One. Bathe them with my tongue and suture them with my sucks. Then I'm going to kiss them to make it all better. I love them. They're *you*, Sins. And you're a fucking survivor."

I didn't know I needed to, but tears escaped my eyes and rolled down my cheeks as I cried. A tiny whimper and shaky breath escaped my mouth at his words, and he backed up to stare at my face which flushed with embarrassment.

Knotting his hands through my hair, he dipped into me and suctioned his mouth to mine. We were as close as we could be with our clothes on. He groaned, thrusting his hips to show his need.

He mumbled on my lips, "We gotta hurry with this and get the fuck back to the manor." I nodded in emphatic agreement.

Wait, did George just say 'love'? That he 'loves' my scars?

He let me slide down his body, but I got hung up on his pole in a momentary bump. He slammed my door shut, locked the truck, and grabbed my hand as we ambled to the store. Like a couple.

"Why were you trying to go after Barrett Grant again?"

"Barrett Grant? The mayor's son? He's the one that hit me with his car while drunk. And the police covered it up, and no one believes me."

"I believe you." His blue eyes were intense in their gaze.

"Really?"

"Yeah, Sins. Really."

I clutched his large, firm bicep and waltzed into the store by his side. One person believed me. And that was enough. Beating the system, I couldn't do it alone… Now, I had backup. I'd never felt so free.

George tugged me to the Halloween section first.

Perusing the stock costumes, I asked, "So, Princess Leia in the gold bikini situation?" I wasn't sure I'd feel comfortable showing my scars.

"Overrated."

My mouth dropped. "Oh?"

"I prefer her in the ceremonial dress."

"The white one?"

He placed me so I was walking in front of him as we perused down the aisle, probably hiding his erection. "Yeah, Snow White. Got a problem with that?"

"No. Just unexpected. You surprise me."

The store didn't have many good costumes left, but I was able to find a silky white top and flowy skirt that could work with a bangle belt. My hair would be just long enough for a large bun. I'd have to find a cape to make sleeves for the dress, but I thought I had something in my closet that could work.

George found his necessary items, but before we checked out, he grabbed a basket and carted me towards the grocery. He filled the plastic basket with chips, popcorn, candy bars, and gummy bears. Once we made it to the freezer section, he asked, "Which ice cream do you prefer?" He held his hand to the row of frozen goods like a game show host. I giggled.

"Cherries and chocolate."

"Wrong answer." He pulled a pint out for me anyway and dropped it in with the other snacks. He reached in, then pulled out another pint and held up his choice. "Moose Tracks was the answer I was looking for."

Once we made it to the self-checkout, George put his arms around me as we scanned our items together. He leaned in to put his face next to mine. "I'll feed you later."

Was this a date? A date to Wal-Mart? It was difficult to breathe when he was this close: timber and man and sweat and iron all dancing in my nose. His blond hair tickled my collarbone. My body stretched and he stuttered a laughing breath into my ear, knowing exactly what he was doing to me.

"Fuck, let's get out of here," he said.

Snatching his bag in one hand and mine in his other, he led us out of the store. His hurried, long strides made me shuffle to stay caught up with him. Throwing the bags in his back seat, he grabbed my waist and hoisted me inside the cab. When he leaned over me, he put his face in mine and growled, "I'm going to fuck you until you're raw tonight. Tenderize you with my meat. Squeeze those juices out of your pussy. Then eat it all up."

CHAPTER TWELVE
GEORGE

THE TRUCK WOULDN'T DRIVE to the manor fast enough. *Fuck!* I couldn't wait to rip her clothes off her body. Why did she have to wear jeans?

"When I told you not to wear your tights, I should have been more specific. Don't wear pants. Or panties. Or jeans." I could just reach her thigh across the cab and squeezed it with my palm. She put her hand on top of mine. "I get free use of all your holes, princess."

"Oh? I'm to be at *your* beck and call?"

"Yes."

"What about me?"

"Huh?" I asked.

"What if I need your cock? Do I get to use it when I need it?"

"Yep."

"Oh, okay." She settled back in the seat. "I'm good."

I smiled. Was Kinsley becoming quieter around me? Or was I becoming more talkative around her? The peace I'd reached for in the stars was coming closer to earth. Like right in the truck. With her. It was terrifying. More so than space.

We reached the manor garage, and I pulled in, trying to figure out a plan to get her naked as quickly as possible. "Sins. Look at me." I threw the truck into park while gathering all our bags from the store.

"Yeah?" She started to help, but I snatched all the bags as fast as possible.

"You better fucking run up to my room as fast as your marathon-trained legs will carry you. Ditch your fucking clothes and be waiting on all fours on my bed."

She put her hand on the handle slowly, checked my eyes to see what was there. The heat let her know how serious this was. "Run," I said.

I was going to devour her. Her throat bobbed in a thick swallow, and she jumped out, sprinting towards the house.

Like Darth Vader, I strolled behind her with all our stuff. When I reached the stairs to the second floor, right on her heels, she squealed, sprinting faster. I took two at a time. She screamed. If my hands weren't full, I'd take her there on the floor, but I didn't want these lowlife bros to see her.

Once we both entered my bedroom, I slammed the door with my foot and dropped the bags, then locked the door. Facing it, I said, "By the time I turn around, you better be in position."

Her clothes rustled, and I smirked at her hurry. When I spun to face her, only her top and bra were off.

"Sins…" I warned her.

"No, no. Wait! Give me a minute. Just—"

I grabbed her around the waist before she could move. She yelped when I ripped her jeans down her legs forcefully along with her thong, then sat on the edge of the bed and threw her over my lap like a bad girl.

"You didn't make it in time. I told you to hurry."

"But I tried—Ouch!"

I swatted the shit out of her ass. "That's one. How many times you gonna sass me, brat?"

"George!" She jolted when I smacked her again.

"How many?"

"I'm not sass—George! Fuck that's…"

Slicking a finger through her folds, I gathered all her wetness and rubbed her nub slowly. She started to grind her pelvis against my thigh.

"Do you need another?"

"Please."

Squeezing my mouth together so I wouldn't smile, I rubbed one ass cheek gently. She was a filthy fucking freak and I loved it… Loved it. Hmm.

Spanking her one more time, I threw her on the bed, so she was on all fours. Kneeling on the floor, I consumed her cunt for dinner. I was a big guy with a healthy appetite.

"You're amazing at that." She panted out in short, stabbing breaths. "Did you know that?"

Moving my tongue up from her clit to her hole, I hummed in response and her legs shook with her orgasm, the first of the night. But I kept moving on up until I hit her tight back entrance and she shrieked. Spreading her cheeks apart, I dug in and began fucking her there with my tongue, punching, then licking. She made animal noises and bowed her back when I stuck a large finger inside her wet pussy while fucking her ass with my mouth.

Once it was wet enough, I replaced my tongue with my damp finger and slowly pushed inside.

"George!" She jerked, but I stood and steadied her with a hand to her hip. She stilled and sank back, fucking herself on my finger. "Oh, my god. That actually feels so good."

"Wait." I walked to grab one of the sacks from the store and opened my ice cream. Drizzling the melting chocolate over her backside, she flinched, but I quickly stuck my warm tongue in to lick up whatever dribbled.

"Fuck! That's—that's…" She trailed off in heavy huffs of breath.

I'd train her up right. Get her to like it in the ass. Sticking my thumb in her tight hole, she squawked while I commanded her, "Take it." I lined up at her pussy and pushed in slowly while she tried to scramble towards the bed. I gripped her hip tighter. "Whoa, girl. Steady." Then, I swatted her behind until her cunt clenched me. She had a vice grip on my dick.

Her body relaxed into me, and I fucked her with my thumb in her ass and my cock in her pussy until she laid her breasts on the bed, giving me full rein to use her as a toy. The night was just starting, and I was going to fuck her body as much as she fucked with my mind.

Pounding into her from behind, I found myself missing the expression on her face while she mewled. Pulling out, I flipped her over on her back and her body bounced with the impact on the mattress. She was bendable, and I liked it.

Before I jammed in, I slid her to the edge of the bed and kissed down first one leg, then the other, suckling each gash and cut and bruise and scar I found. I licked her until my tongue ran dry, swallowed and did it again, then found her toe and sucked while I pushed my dick inside her once again. I fucked her like that, sucking on an old wound near her foot. Letting go, I crawled on top of her, dragging her with me while still inside, so we were in the middle of the mattress.

I met her face with a deep kiss. Dropping my head next to hers, I said, "You're fucking beautiful, princess. Every inch of you is perfection." She turned her head to gaze into my eyes and sucked my lips into hers while I plunged, our bodies fully connected. I held her arms above our heads with one of my hands.

"George, I..." she breathed in my mouth.

"What is it, princess?"

We held each other's gazes until her eyes squinted, face contorting and flushing with ecstasy. I scooped my hips, and she creamed my cock. It filled me with awe to be this close to her burning brightness, sucking me in until my particles were strung together in single atoms. The pull so strong, I couldn't stop the eruption as my cum exploded within her black hole, tangled up with her as we collided. Indistinguishable. We emerged through the portal together as one to a new galaxy filled with light.

Something happened. Something was exchanged, and I wasn't the same.

We stared at each other while I was on top, inside her, my elbows now on either side of her head. Our air mingled until it was the same breath. Her carbon was filling my lungs.

"What was that?" Her eyes were wide, taking in my face as much as I was hers. My thumbs stroked her forehead.

I knew what it was. It was something I had been feeling over the last few weeks. It was dangerous. If she found out who I was, who my family was, that I knew about the cover-up…

"That was round one," I said, schooling my face into its well-worn stoic expression.

Her eyes narrowed. I lost her. Just like that. Boom. It was for her own good, though.

Kinsley said she was tired and needed to use the restroom. I put away our snacks, the melted ice cream in my mini-fridge freezer tray. When she returned, she stood near the door, twisting her fingers and legs. I patted the comforter next to me. "Come on, get some rest." She slowly walked to the bed and climbed in, sliding under the covers.

Fuck, I'd made things awkward. Kinsley was so confident in her own knowledge, but she had no idea how much danger she could be in if she started looking into her accident. I didn't want that.

Despite the reluctance I sensed, I tucked her completely into my body. Whenever I found her pulling away in the night, I did it again. She wasn't escaping my embrace. It was her only protection. And her destruction.

Her gold eyes were staring into mine when I awoke in the morning.

"I need to go home."

I lifted my head. "What time is it?"

"It's early. But I need to go. I have stuff to do, George. Can you take me?" She was already dressed and laying on top of the covers.

My phone read 6 a.m. "What the fuck, Sins. It's six. Go back to sleep. We can hang here before I gotta go do airsoft. We got that party tonight."

"I can't stay here all day. I have studies and stuff. I need to go. Should I call a ride? Walk? Steal a bike? Can I have your key—"

"Fuck! Alright, just shut up. I'll take you."

I was hoping I'd get to fuck her again before she left me. Make up for the distance I'd put between us after whatever happened last night. That event horizon.

Throwing on some sweats, I grabbed my keys, wallet, and phone while Kinsley stood at the door. She was shifting from foot to foot like she couldn't wait to escape me.

I stayed silent on the drive. There was nothing I could say. It was better if I didn't say anything. Maybe she'd get fed up and stay away.

"Thanks for the ride," she muttered as I dropped her off without a glance back.

I felt like shit.

Kinsley, I'm sorry. I felt it, too. And I never have before.

The afternoon was filled with my annual airsoft game with Levi, Xavier, and Mason. We lost, and it was just another blow to my already shitty day. By the time I showered and dressed for the party, I was ready to down some shots. By my third, I was worried Kinsley wouldn't show. Checking my phone like my neck was a metronome, I was finally able to relax when Marissa arrived. Not far behind her was Kinsley.

When she arrived, I leaned to kiss her temple and she let me, but just barely. Once we were all in the kitchen drinking shots, she loosened up some. At one point, Levi hit on her and I about ended his life, especially when Mason brought up Gianna and Alenna.

Bolting out of the kitchen, I left Kinsley, but she followed me to the dance floor. Grabbing a cup of beer from the keg before I reached the DJ, I downed it, then threw the cup into the trash. Kinsley tugged on my sleeve. It was too loud and crowded for a conversation, and I didn't want to talk.

Watching the crowd in the room, Kinsley moved to stand in front of me, saying something I couldn't hear. Instead of leaving me be, she put her hands around my neck and jumped. If I didn't want her to fall, I had to catch her by her butt. She wrapped her arms around my neck, so we were face to face.

"What happened?" she asked.

I shook my head.

"Seriously, George. Tell me. Mason said something about your ex-stepmother? That must have been awkward."

"Don't talk about her." The further away from Gianna she was, the safer she was.

"I'm just saying you can talk to me about it if you need." Pressing her little lips against my ear she spoke.

"G, something happened last night. And now you're being weird."

"I'm not being weird. You're the one that took off this morning."

"That's because you treated me like... like a hookup."

"That's because you are."

She reeled back in my arms and the pain in her eyes was almost too much for me to take. It was necessary. Squirming so I'd release her, she stepped back and narrowed her eyes.

"Who are you?"

I shrugged a shoulder.

"What did you do with my George?" she asked.

My phone buzzed in my pocket. I knew who it was. Fucking cunt. I checked anyway and, sure enough, Gianna demanded my dick.

"I'm not your George. I gotta go," I said.

"Asshole!" she screamed at me as I walked out.

She wasn't wrong.

Jumping in my truck, I wiped a hand down my face before starting her up. All I wanted was to run back in there and tell her. Explain. Talk to her. And I never wanted to talk to anyone. *Fuck*. My phone buzzed again.

GIANNA

better hurry

Each minute that passed on the hour drive to the motel made my anger at her bubble into a fury. I didn't want to be my father, but the closer I was to Gianna, the more I felt myself turning into him. I wanted to *hurt* her.

Bursting through the door, I strode directly over to her. Grabbing her throat, I threw her body against the wall and pinned her there. "Let's get something straight, Gianna. I don't want to be here. I'm not rushing here just because you text me to do so. I've got shit to do."

"Oh, like *Kinsley*?" Her voice was barely audible because of my grip around her neck.

Releasing my grip on her neck, I dropped her. "Don't fucking say her name."

"Georgie." She slid down the wall and shook her head. "You're still fooled by her? She must have you wrapped around her tiny pussy."

Turning around, I threw off my Han Solo vest and my shirt. "And I'm not impregnating you. No way. Get undressed. I want this done and over with."

"Oh, I'll forgo the pregnancy… for now." Her fingers crawled up my bare back. I loosened my belt, and she wrapped her arms around my waist from behind. "I want something else now."

My heart rate climbed. "What?"

"I think your girlfriend should join us."

"What?" Whipping around, she stumbled back when I threatened her with my gaze.

"If you're so into her, why don't you bring her along?"

"No, Gianna. Shut the fuck up. Get on the bed."

"No. I want you to bring your girlfriend. The three of us are going to have a great time."

"It's not going to happen. Drop it." I put my hands on my hips.

"Either you impregnate me, or you bring your girlfriend. Which one will it be, Georgie?" She tickled me under my chin with her long, painted nail.

"She's not my girlfriend. I don't even know her that well."

Gianna laughed. Her curvy body slipped by me and went to her expensive tote bag, and pulled out a folder. Handing it to me, she stood back with her arms crossed. I opened the folder and pictures fell out and onto the floor. The photographs were of Kinsley and me fucking in the library, me eating her out on the hood of *Serenity*, us at the store holding hands.

"You've been following me."

"Of course. And you and your *girlfriend* look mighty cozy." Gianna's plump lips parted into a broad smile. "If she loves you, she'd do it."

"She wouldn't. And I don't want her involved."

"She's entirely involved. This entire *thing* is about her involvement."

Gripping the back of my neck, I sighed. "What's in this for you?"

She only smirked in reply.

I shook my head. "You just love the control."

"And young pussy as much as you, Georgie. And she looks young and fresh." She slinked closer. "We could all have a lot of fun together. You won't hate it." She placed her lips on my bare chest. "Or you can give me a little Georgie. I'm running out of time to get knocked up. Need as much sperm of yours as I can get."

"I am not impregnating you."

"So, there's your answer."

I clenched my jaw. "I need to talk with her."

"Of course, of course. I'm betting she'll say yes."

Unlikely. Kinsley was headstrong, and now I had ruined things between us this evening. How could I convince her to have a threesome with me and my ex-stepmother? Why would she ever agree?

The worst part was, I didn't want to share her with anyone, let alone the devil herself.

CHAPTER
THIRTEEN
KINSLEY

AS SOON AS I woke up after Halloween, I emailed Professor Torrad requesting a different tutor for astronomy. My midterm grade was perfect, but I needed an A for the final. George could go fuck himself.

I wouldn't be able to concentrate if he tutored me; especially when all I wanted to do was stab him with a pencil. George was a stone wall that I could never break through. And why would I want to? He was an asshole. I could do so much better.

Despite the frigid fall weather, I awoke early on Monday to begin my training. Since hanging out with George, I had slacked on my preparation for the next marathon. Ugh! I hated that I thought of him with every moment that passed. Like a virus, he infected every cell of my body.

When I returned to the apartment, I had a reply from Dr. Torrad. She requested that we "work it out" among ourselves and there was no one else available, even at the other times I had open. I thought about forgoing tutoring altogether, but remembered my poor grades prior to George's help and decided against it.

If he wanted things casual, wanted to treat me like a hook-up, he was cut off. I could use him for his astronomy skills, then we wouldn't have to speak again for the rest of our lives. Not that he spoke much, anyway. I could glean his knowledge, get an A on the final quiz and exam, then never see him again. Yep. That is exactly what I would do.

Fortifying my emotional reserves, I went in prepared for our tutoring session that week. My plan was to remain quiet, focused on the topic of astronomy only, and not deviate from it. If he tried to so much as glance at my body, I'd threaten him with sexual harassment. That's exactly what I would do.

Wearing jeans and a baggy T-shirt, I showed up early for the session, studying the notes from the previous lecture. I didn't bring coffee; my anxiety was already high enough. When he turned the corner, he appeared surprised to see me. I kept my head down.

George dropped a bag on the table with a thud and leaned over it, strong forearms flexing in my field of view.

"Dr. Torrad said you tried to find a different tutor."

I didn't respond.

"Kinsley."

Busying myself with shuffling my papers, I pretended to focus on my notes.

"Kinsley?" He paused. "Sins."

Keeping my eyes on the table, I ignored him.

"Princess," he said softly.

My entire body stiffened. His pet name made me rage. "Can we focus on the task at hand? Please teach me."

George slumped into the chair next to me and blocked me in with his arms, one resting on the table and the other on the back of my chair. "That's fine, Sins. But you're not getting another tutor."

"Dr. Torrad said there could be one in two weeks. If I miss my Russian Lit class, I can make the new time. I just need—"

George banged on the table with a large fist. My head snapped up. Staring at me with his intense blue eyes blazing, he roared, "You're not getting another fucking tutor."

Through gritted teeth, I said, "If I want another tutor, *Big G*, you can't stop me."

George grimaced. "Don't test me, princess."

"Don't call me that."

"I'll call you whatever I want to call you, *princess*."

"I am not your princess. If you call me that again, we will have a serious problem."

"Okay, *princess*."

"Are you sexually harassing me, George Turner?"

"Do you want me to?" His lips curled into a mischievous grin as he raised one eyebrow.

I gasped. "No! I just want to get tutored!"

"I'll tutor you good." Leaning closer to me, he almost placed his mouth on mine.

"G, I want to focus on work." My breath hit his cheek.

"I see that. You wore jeans." Backing away, he

motioned with his finger at my outfit. "Trying to stop yourself from jumping me, huh?"

Fury overtook me. "No! I'm trying to stop *you*, you filthy ogre! This isn't going to work. I need a new tutor." I gathered my stuff to take off, but he stood with me. Before I knew what was happening, George threw me over his shoulder as I squealed to a chorus of shushes coming from various parts of the library.

My body swayed as he carried me into a small bathroom on the third floor with one stall and a long sink. He dropped my butt on the counter and quickly locked the door before returning to me, spreading my legs and yanking my core to his. He slapped one hand on the mirror beside my head.

"You're *not* getting another tutor. I'm the only one who will tutor you. You got that, princess. You're *my* princess."

"I thought I was just a hook-up."

Running a hand down his face and rubbing his scruff, he looked up at the ceiling, then glared at me. "You're fucking not and you know it."

"No, I don't. You said—"

"What I said was stupid. I was being an asshole. You're mine, Sins, and no one else's." He shoved his lips to mine and his tongue inside my mouth. My anger fueled a frenzied passion, and I lost control. Clutching his hair, I pulled him closer to me. He picked me up off the counter enough to undo my jeans and tug them down along with my thong.

I quickly released his pole from his jeans. We connected violently. When he rammed inside me, I threw my head back, breaking the suction of our lips. At the same time, both of us yelled, "Fuck!" The sensation was unbelievable. It felt like he belonged inside me.

George didn't ease his strokes. He rampaged into me, one hand on my ass, cupping me into him, and the other pressed on the mirror. My legs wrapped around his waist as I ground on his pubic bone. Placing our foreheads together, I got a full view of his long cock plunging in and out of my pussy.

George licked my lips. "Only mine, Sins. Say it."

"Only yours."

"You're mine."

"I'm yours."

He kissed me deeply while fucking me harshly. An orgasm ripped through me before I knew what was happening. As if it surprised him how quickly I came, he pumped a few thrusts and exploded with me, grasping my hair and turning my neck so he could bury his growls of climax into it.

For a long while, he stayed there, cock pulsating within me. We were both panting, gasping for air. Finally, with a slow moan, he pulled out inch by inch. Grasping my face with both of his oversized hands, he gazed into my eyes before pressing his mouth to mine.

I thought I felt something between us the last time we had sex in his bed. Then, he acted so distant. The same thread was tying us tighter together now. I worried how he would act after a second time of whatever was happening with us.

"Do you have any more classes today?" George asked.

"No."

"Let me take you on a date."

My mouth spread into a little grin, but it broadened as the happiness overwhelmed me. "Okay."

He kissed me again and his lips widened until I felt his teeth with my tongue as he spoke in my mouth, "Okay."

Sliding off the counter, I flicked my hands at him to get out of the bathroom while I cleaned up. He adjusted himself and washed his hands before leaving. When I returned to the hall, George was waiting with both our bags around his shoulders. I opened my hand to take mine back, but he shook his head.

"I got it. Royalty doesn't carry their own stuff." He grabbed my hand, and we walked out to the parking lot. "How about we get some food? Then I want to take you someplace. A surprise."

"Sure. Can you drop me at my place first? I want to get ready."

"Yeah, Sins. Don't get dolled up, though. The surprise requires dressing warm."

When he dropped me at my apartment, he came upstairs with me while I changed my outfit. He waited silently in the living room as my roommates buzzed around him. Through the door, I heard Elle attempt to make small talk with him, but the conversation was mainly one sided.

"You ready?" he asked when I came out of my room with a fresh sweater on. I grabbed my heavier winter coat and gloves.

"Yeah, I am now."

"Where are you guys going?" Elle asked.

My eyes met George's light blue ones. "Uh, I don't know, actually. It's a surprise."

"Ooh, fun." She slapped George on the back. "Good job, big man."

George grabbed my hand and led me back to his truck.

"Where are we going for dinner?" I asked.

"I thought I'd take you to this little restaurant on the river in Leesville."

"That's almost an hour away!"

"Is that okay?" He put me in my seat and buckled my seatbelt before getting in the truck himself. "The second part of the date requires us to be out that way."

"Way out in the countryside?"

George snorted. "I'm not kidnapping you, Sins."

"It's fine. Never been there before." I settled back in my seat, which made George relax. "I'm game."

George turned on some music. "You like classic rock?" he asked.

"Yeah, I think I do."

"You *think*?" He pulled onto the state route, then briefly raised his eyebrows at me.

"Well, I've been listening to your music whenever I'm in this shuttle."

"So you like it because of me."

"Well, yeah."

George held his hand up on the console as an invitation for me to offer mine. I laid it in his big palm, and he gripped it. "Good." I saw the side of his lips lift. My body felt warm all over. I'd never felt so comfortable with someone in my life. Riding in the truck, listening to his music, it felt like home. Like it was where I was supposed to be. I belonged.

As we reached the outskirts of town, I lowered the music to talk.

"Is your family from here?" I asked.

George sat up straighter in his seat. "Yeah." He loosened the grip on my hand.

"Did you go to school with Xavier?"

"High school, yeah."

"So your parents must have been rich, huh? I went to public."

He nodded, focused on the road.

"Do you have siblings?"

"Two brothers. Do you?" he asked.

"No, I'm an only child."

"That makes sense."

I scowled and dropped my jaw open. "What do you mean by that?"

"You talk enough for three kids."

I laughed. "I guess so." A new song came on and I sang along with it.

"And you're tone deaf." He eyed me sideways.

"So? I'm not going to be a singer. If you think you can do better, go for it, songbird."

George belted out the tune with his deep bass and the reverberations made me tingle all over. Enraptured by his voice, I stared at him without realizing until he glanced over.

"What?" he asked.

"Wow. You can sing! I mean, you have a nice voice."

George focused on the road, but his shoulders straightened slightly as if he were proud of himself. "What do your parents do?"

His smile dropped. He paused looking into the rearview, then passed a car while remaining silent. I waited for his response. After a minute or so, he cleared his throat. "My mother's sick. Dad's a manager."

"Oh. Manager of what?"

"What's with all the fucking questions, Sins? Do I need to pull over and fuck you in the bed of the truck so you'll get quiet again?"

Snatching my hand back, I turned to face the road. His entire demeanor went grumpy again. "Sorry. I just wanted to get to know you," I said quietly.

George's jaw clenched. Reaching across the truck with his huge arm, he grabbed my hand and pulled it to him again. "My dad's a fucking asshole. I hate him. My mother's kind of wasted away Miss Havisham style. My youngest brother's a drug addict that was sent to military school. My middle brother has followed in my father's footsteps. Like the guys were saying on Halloween, yes, I had way too many stepmothers growing up. I've had to take care of my family because no one else would." He glanced over at me to make an impact of his last statement. "Again, my father's an asshole."

I watched the side of his face for a long time, thinking about everything he had relayed. George had been through a lot.

"You have an asshole father? I can relate," I said.

"Did your father beat your mother and cheat on everyone he's been with, too?"

A quick exhale left my mouth and my heart hurt for him. "Oh... No. He's not that kind of asshole." I rubbed his hand with my thumb. "I'm sorry."

"You didn't do anything. No reason to be sorry." Almost undetectably, he said, "It's my fault."

"George! How can you say that? Of course, it's not your fault."

"Just drop it. We're almost there."

My mind raced with a million things to say or not say and questions to ask or things to do, but it all seemed so inadequate. We pulled into a wooden boathouse leaning over the water. A large blue neon sign read "Lees on the River" with a flashing fish next to it. As soon as he parked the truck in the parking lot, I unbuckled and jumped across the truck to sit on him, straddling his lap. I gripped my thighs tightly around his waist and my arms around him, burrowing my face into his neck.

George sat still and stiff for a moment. Then, as if some ice cap melted, he gathered me into a bear hug tightly, burying his face into my hair. His chest rose and fell with each deep breath, and I could feel his heart beating strongly against my own ribcage. We held each other like that for a long time until he cleared his throat, breaking the silent, cold air around us.

"You hungry?"

Sitting back on his lap, I scanned his face, checking to make sure he was okay. "Yep."

Staring into my eyes without moving, he leaned

forward to lightly place his soft lips against mine. He opened the door, pulled me tighter to him, and stepped out of the truck before setting me down. We traipsed across the cracked asphalt to the wooden house made of graying cedar. The sun was setting over the water, creating a red haze that made it look like it was on fire.

"Red sky at night…" I murmured.

"Sailor's delight." George finished, looking at the scene with me. I smiled, pleased he got my reference.

The interior of the restaurant opened to a long, distressed bar fronted with grayed bricks and a barback filled with colorful liquors. One end of the restaurant opened to glass doors through which extensive wooden decks sat over the water. The enclosed patios were lined with white twinkle lights and space heaters.

"Inside or out?" the host asked as we walked in. George looked at me.

"Outside, I think," I answered.

George nodded. "My lady wants outside."

As we made our way across the red vinyl floor, the scents from the kitchen wafted to my nose and made my stomach growl. Fortunately, the decks outside were cozy and not cold, though the weather had been quickly hastening towards winter. After placing our drink orders, George looked quickly at the menu before setting it down.

"They have good catfish and beer cheese here."

"Okay, that sounds good."

Once we had our drinks, I planned to change the heavier subjects for something lighter, figuring George had given enough of himself on the drive there. Before I could ask which TV shows were in his top three of all time, George interrupted my thoughts.

"Kinsley, I didn't have a good childhood. I grew up trying to take care of my mother and brothers because my father… because of my father. He brought in lots of women, and they weren't always nice to me." He sipped his water and stared at me pointedly. I think I was supposed to interpret what he meant.

"D-did he beat you, too?"

"Nah, not really. The women, well, one woman he brought home… she wasn't *nice*. She caused me a lot of problems."

"Oh?"

George nodded. "Yeah." He took a big breath as if he were preparing to say something.

The waiter brought over our food. "Here you go! Do you see anything you need? Ketchup? Extra tartar sauce?"

"No, I'm good," I said quickly, so we could get back to what George had been saying.

George shook his head at the waiter, who left us. He took a big bite of his fish and chewed slowly. I waited. George swallowed. Just as I was about to give up and say something, he said, "So, you said your dad was an asshole. What was up with him?"

My shoulders dropped. Was he trying to change the subject? Maybe he had had enough emotionally tense conversations. I appeased him by explaining about my father's insistence that I always be the best, feeling like he'd wanted a son instead of me.

"And after the accident, he was so frustrated with

me not being able to do as much as I once did... He told me once that I wasn't even *trying* to get better. That's when I knew I'd never be good enough. No matter what. It was then that I decided to do for *me* and not for him."

I told George about Bethany being the final straw that broke my father and me apart. Each child he had with her, especially his son, made me realize how we were never truly a family.

"I never had one, either. I mean, I have my brothers, but they were more of something that was my responsibility."

"Why *your* responsibility, though?"

"Who else would care for them? My father wouldn't. My mother couldn't. It was just us."

"And now me."

George peered at me with sadness in his eyes. He held his arm out to the side of the table. I put my hand in his. He pulled me up from my seat and into his lap. Grabbing my plate from across the table, he loaded up a fork and began to feed me. It wasn't bad since we were the only crazy people that chose to eat outside. Otherwise, I'd be too embarrassed to sit on him if others were watching.

"It's good, right?"

Snickering, I replied with my mouth full, "Yes, it's good. You don't have to feed me."

He put his face into my hair and quietly said, "I want to." His gesture made me relax further into him. I let him feed me, and he seemed to enjoy taking care of me.

Once we finished dinner and paid, George said the surprise portion of the evening was about to begin. The night had set in and when I looked up at the sky, I gasped at the wonders of the stars. In the dark of the countryside, there were no disruptive artificial lights. Every twinkle from millions of miles away was visible.

George drove us to a gravel drive that turned into a dirt road. He slowed the truck, making a sudden left-hand turn into an overgrown field, running over small bumps of earth. I clung to the grab bar with one hand and my seatbelt with the other while George laughed. His wide grin made me think of how he must have looked as a little boy playing outside in the mud.

He pulled up next to the shadow of an old barn, almost collapsed from its age. Jumping out, he quickly made his way to the bed of the truck and pulled off the cover. Underneath was an air mattress already blown up. An extra-large sleeping bag was lying on top.

"Whoa! Do you bring a lot of girls out here?"

"Huh?" he asked.

"You just happen to have a bed in the back of your truck?"

He jumped onto the tailgate and held his arms out to lift me up beside him. "I like to sleep out here sometimes." Placing me back on the air mattress, he crawled up next to me. "Alone."

"You're not alone now," I said as I laid back on the built-in pillows.

George lowered himself next to me and rolled to his side. Cupping my face with a large hand, he gently pressed his lips to mine. "No, not now." Lying on his back, he watched the show. "Sins, there's a meteor shower tonight. It requires silence to fully appreciate. You think you can handle that?"

I slapped his chest with my hand, and he grabbed it. "Yes, motormouth. I can."

We lay together on our backs as the show began. Our hands were joined, and I was warmed by the heat of his enormous body. The light show was something I'd never experienced. Sharp lasers shot quickly through the sky, one after the other, in a dazzling display. My eyes couldn't understand that the beauty they were seeing was real. Each flash of white made my heart race with excitement.

"Kinsley," George said.

"Hmm?"

"Kinsley, I need to tell you something."

"Shh! I thought you said we have to be quiet."

George was silent. I turned my head to see what he wanted.

"Kinsley," he said.

"Yeah?"

George stared at me.

"Yes, George?"

He stayed silent, but pressed his lips to my forehead.

CHAPTER
FOURTEEN
GEORGE

FUCK. I couldn't say it. Words escaped me. As usual.

Kinsley, my stepmother is blackmailing my father and me. Blackmailing us for an accident that my father covered up. You know, the one that almost killed you. She wants to force you and me to have a threesome with her because she's a controlling cunt. I know you'll say no, but I had to ask.

Kinsley, I love you.

Everything was right there on the tip of my tongue. It all sounded horrible and wrong and would cause her to run away. Part of the reason for bringing her out to the middle of the field was so she couldn't. Not without me catching her and her needing a ride back to town, which would give me more time to explain.

Instead, I just stared at her as if her brain could telepathically collect my thoughts. I had to tell her the truth. But I wanted to be inside her one last time before I had to let her go. There was no way she would stay with me if she knew everything. If I even spoke the disgusting words, asking for a threesome with my ex-stepmother, she'd probably run all the way back to Northview. Not to mention probably hitting me for fucking Gianna like I'd cheated on her. Once she found out who my father was and what he did... that would be it for us.

Cuddled up next to me, I reached around her waist and unbuttoned and unzipped her jeans. She helped by shimmying them down her legs. I pulled my cock out and rubbed between her legs while we spooned and watched the stars. I kissed her neck as she grabbed my hand and started sucking on my finger.

"Oh, fuck." The sensation of her lips suckling the end of my finger made my dick stiffen. She humped my cock between her thighs, rubbing her wetness all over the shaft as she slid back and forth on it.

Turning her head to me, we kissed gently, tongues toying with each other. I panted breaths into her face, the steam from our mouths mingling in the cold night air.

Reaching between us, I lifted her leg slightly so I could push inside her. We groaned at the same time as our bodies linked together. My arms wrapped around her, encasing her with mine, and I plunged deeper inside.

"Damn, princess. Your cunt is so hot on my cock. It's like my own dick heater."

I slid a hand down her stomach to her wet cunt and rubbed her nub as I fucked her.

"George..." she moaned and writhed back against me.

"Shh, just let me fuck you." I hastened my hip

movements as she quivered in my arms, screaming out my name with her orgasm.

"I'm gonna empty my balls in your pussy, then pull your panties up to keep it inside you." I turned her face towards me so I could kiss her one last time while I came. Moaning into her mouth, I unloaded everything I had, everything I felt and wanted to be, into her.

I held her there. I didn't want to let go, but I had to.

"George, I lo—"

I interrupted her by sweeping my tongue inside her mouth. She couldn't say it. It would break her if she said it after she found out about me, after I left. *Fuck!* Why didn't I leave her alone? It was way too late now.

"You cold?" I broke our kiss and quickly asked her before she could get her bearings or repeat what she was about to say.

"N-no. Are you?"

"Not with you right here." I tugged up her thong, and she situated her jeans. "You okay to doze here for a bit?"

"Yeah. It's peaceful."

"It is. It's our spot, Sins. Peaceful and quiet here. You and me." We could always have this spot together, this night together. I could come back here and pretend. Pretend she was with me.

She nuzzled closer and her breathing evened out while I watched the stars. My phone buzzed in my back pocket. I inhaled deeply.

Pulling it out, I glanced at the notification.

> **GIANNA**
> Meet me now.

A moment passed, then another came through.

> And bring your girlfriend *kissy face emoji*

Fuck.

"What was that?" Kinsley woke up and looked behind her.

"Uh, I gotta get going."

"I thought we were going to sleep here."

"Um, something came up. I have to head out. Come on. I'll warm up the truck for you."

"George… What is going on?"

After I gathered up the sleeping bag, I held out a hand to help her down from the truck bed. As casually as I could, I shrugged. "What do you mean?"

"You keep getting these texts and then have to go suddenly. Is there someone else? Are you secretly married or have a child or something?"

"Wha-? No. Sorry, I just need to leave."

Kinsley wasn't buying it, and I didn't blame her.

We loaded into the truck, and I blared the heat for her. Making my voice as casual as possible, I tried to engage her in conversation the entire way back to her apartment, but she was silent for once.

It was the worst sound in the world.

Staring out the window, she would grunt a reply here and there. At one point, she reached over to my radio and turned up the volume. Once I pulled up to her apartment complex, she didn't hesitate. She jumped from *Serenity* without even looking back as I called out to her. She slammed the passenger door and bolted toward her building without a glance behind her.

My phone buzzed with a call... Gianna.

"Yeah?"

"Are you coming? You better be here within the hour."

"I was out of town. I'm on my way now." I hung up on her. Cracking my neck, I put the truck in reverse before speeding towards Springfield. When I reached the motel lot, I let my forehead rest on the steering wheel for a few moments, trying to gather the strength to make it inside. Taking a deep breath, I slid out and made my way to the room.

"Well, where is she?" Gianna threw open the door wearing high heels and a short, silky pink robe. Probably nothing else on underneath.

I sighed and stared at the threadbare carpet. There were so many stains it looked to be part of the pattern.

"I didn't ask her."

"So then you want to give me a baby?" She slammed the door behind me and locked it.

Roughly running a hand through my hair, I pulled it out of the elastic. "No."

"Those were your options. I'm running out of time for another pregnancy. You're off the hook tonight. I thought I was ovulating, but the test was negative. You missed your window this month."

My shoulders relaxed.

"But, there's always next month!" She patted my chest.

"So either I get Kinsley here for a threesome, or you want me to impregnate you?"

"That's the deal, Georgie." Her dark red stained lips raised into a smirk.

"Who's to say that you won't just demand I impregnate you after a threesome?"

"Yeah. Who's to say? I guess you'll just have to trust me." As her green eyes raised, she batted her eyelashes at me and smiled sweetly. "Or trust that I want *both*."

I pressed my palm into my forehead. Shit. This had to end somehow. I couldn't keep jumping through her hoops. It would never stop. Her demands would get more outrageous. What was next? A foursome with Kins, her, and Alenna together? Roping Aaron into this? Porn?

"I can't get it up tonight. If you suck me off, you're gonna taste my girl."

"Good." Deftly, she eased to her knees in front of me. "It'll prepare me for when I can taste her fully."

Unzipping my jeans, she fished out my flaccid cock. There was no way. I was in love with Kinsley. I couldn't do this. The nausea rolled over in my stomach when Gianna put her lips on the tip of my cock. Catfish threatened to come up. Running to the bathroom, I made it just in time to lose my entire dinner into the toilet.

Gianna's cackles echoed off the tiles. I couldn't stop retching.

"Poor, poor, baby Georgie." Gianna stood in the

doorway while I hugged the porcelain. I guess I was never going to eat at Lees on the River again. The thought of catfish made me throw up again.

"I can't do this, Gianna," I panted out.

In a rare motion of empathy, Gianna filled a glass from the bathroom sink with dirty tap water and handed it to me. It was so brown, I didn't drink it.

"Bring her. I want her here. I want to taste what you taste and share her with you. I want to break her like I broke you."

Had she? Was I broken? My head throbbed, throat was raw, and my stomach was filled with acid. Yeah. I felt broken.

Gianna stood back to allow me to leave. Maybe she would have pity on me this time.

"Your puke smell has turned me off. Hopefully you get her here before I ovulate, for your sake. Otherwise, I'm happy to have a big George the third." Her eyes blazed. "Maybe a Georgina."

She walked with me to the door and opened it, leaning up to kiss my sticky cheek. When I turned my head, a small woman with dark hair stood just outside in front of me with a look of murder in her eyes.

"Oh! Baby, you did bring her!" Gianna rubbed a hand down my chest as Kinsley glared at the two of us. My blood stopped moving in my arteries. She must have followed me. The impact of her eyes on mine was like two asteroids colliding. The explosion was more painful than anything I'd ever felt before.

Kinsley turned on a heel and stomped into the parking lot.

"Kins, wait! Sins, please!" She quickened her pace towards her car, which was parked near my truck. My long legs managed to catch up and get to the driver's side door before she could. I pressed my large body in front of it, blocking her from getting inside. "Please listen."

The darkness of the night was only broken by the neon light of a motel vacancy sign, and yet, I could still see how red her face was. Despite all the times I'd pissed her off or hurt her, this was worse.

"Move."

"It's not what you think."

"Get out of my way, George."

I swallowed. "Please."

I saw it happen in slow motion, but wasn't going to stop it. Kinsley reared back her arm and slapped my face with as hard a hit as she could manage. Her little arms tried to shove me out of the way with both hands gripping my chest. It would have been cute if I wasn't devastated. I had to let her go.

My knees hit the ground in front of her, no longer able to hold me up. The desperation within me to keep her was too great. Grasping her around the waist, I buried my face in her stomach and cried. "Please, please, Kinsley, don't leave."

Tears hadn't so much as formed in my eyes since the day my mother left. Now they were freely falling. A scream ripped out of my chest and into the dead air ending with a sob.

I was that little boy again.

Kinsley stood still as a statue, looking everywhere but at me.

"Please, I'm sorry. It's not what you think. I don't want this. Please don't leave me."

She managed to peel my hands apart and step away, then got inside her passenger door. I fell to all fours and huffed in breaths, weeping. The pain was unbearable.

Her car sped past me and she was gone. That was it. I'd never get her back. Gianna would force me to impregnate her. My father would ruin my mother and brother's lives.

It was hopeless.

))) ● (((

The next few weeks were not my finest. Kinsley never showed up for tutoring. When I asked, Dr. Torrad said Kinsley had "gone in another direction," but I knew the other tutor wasn't teaching her, I had asked him, so I wasn't sure what direction she had gone. Dr. Torrad wouldn't let me give her notes to pass to Kinsley, nor would she let me know her grades.

Kinsley didn't eat at the table with us for lunch anymore. I didn't feel like watching her avoid me, so I started getting my lunch to-go and eating in my truck alone. Enjoying the silence. In the safety of *Serenity*, I could pretend like my heart hadn't been shattered.

Every morning, instead of my regular gym workout, I tailed Kinsley while she ran. She never saw me, but I was there. Watching. Making sure no one came after her. Even if I couldn't be with her, I wanted to keep her safe. I'd caused her enough trouble. It would be my fault if something happened to her.

In the evenings, I followed her if she left her apartment. She kept up her routine of heading to the various university events. Throwing a hoodie over my head, I stayed in the shadows in case she needed me. Instead of dancing and drinking at the club on Friday nights, she looked sad and distracted. That made me feel conflicted. I was happy she seemed to miss me, but I didn't want her miserable, either.

Late at night, I had to perform for Gianna. Most nights, I would vomit so much I couldn't do it and she'd throw things at me or slap me, then kick me out. Usually, I made myself get sick just so she would. Other times I had to eat her pussy and once I had to fuck her, but had a condom on because she hadn't ovulated yet. That day was approaching.

My only personal time was when Kinsley finally went to bed. From the safety of my truck in her apartment parking lot, I would monitor that her bedroom window lights would darken around 11 p.m. Then, I'd go to Gianna, and after that, I let myself into the observatory.

Like an machine, I stuck to the schedule.

Sometimes I'd fall asleep on the floor of the auditorium, gazing up at the planets aligning. Other times, if the weather wasn't too cold, I'd sleep outside in mine and Kinsley's spot under a blanket of stars, always imagining she was there with me, using the sleeping bag as if it were her body.

When Thanksgiving rolled around, Aaron was allowed to come home for a visit. Normally, I'd go with Mason and Levi to Xavier's to smoke up and chill, but he was with his girl this year. Pretty sure Levi had other plans, too. I was glad to have my little brother home, but also worried he'd use the opportunity to try something stupid. Like drugs or visiting our mother.

After I dropped off a prepared turkey dinner at my mom's, getting an earful about how she didn't want me there and wished I'd never been born, I headed to the bus station to pick up my youngest brother. I forced Dan to join me, despite his weary excuses of having to hang out with his teammates that day.

"Too bad. Today's about family."

Dan snorted. "Some family."

As I drove, I wondered where Kinsley spent her holidays. When I followed her that morning, she had changed clothes after her run and drove to a nursing home. I figured she was visiting grandparents there. It only made my heart ache for her worse than it already did knowing how kind and caring she was for others. In my fantasy, I walked in and joined her there, holding her hand and meeting her family like someone important in her life.

But I wasn't important in anyone's life.

When Dan and I pulled up to the bus station, I scanned the crowds for Aaron. He said he would meet us out front, but I didn't see him.

Just as I worried Aaron had gotten lost, or worse, was off on his own doing something he shouldn't, Dan said, "Holy shit!" He gasped and opened his door, stepping down from the truck slowly.

I looked where Dan's head was pointed and saw a thick, muscular man with a buzzed head of blonde hair. Holy shit was right. Aaron looked like a completely different person.

Dan walked up to our little brother, and they half hugged. Jumping out of *Serenity*, I hurried over and grabbed him into a big embrace. Pulling back, I held his face with both my hands, staring into his light blue eyes.

"What did they do to you?"

He smiled broadly, confidently. "Took your advice. Been hitting the weights."

Dan slapped his back. "And the food, looks like. You look good, bro."

As I bent to grab his duffel bag, Aaron snatched it quicker than I could. "I got this." He slung it over his shoulder like it weighed nothing. "I have a bunch of laundry to do. I hate the machines there. Half of them don't work."

We piled into the truck and headed home. Dan drilled our brother about the details of his school, and I listened while glancing back in the rearview mirror at him perched between our seats. He was so different. And not just in his looks.

"Yeah, 6 a.m. every morning," Aaron replied to Dan's question about mandatory wake up time.

"Even Sundays?"

"Yes. I don't have weekends anymore."

"Dude, that sucks."

Aaron shrugged. "It's not that bad. I'm used to it now."

"How's your roommate?" I asked him.

"He's cool. Showed me the ropes when I first got there. Introduced me to some guys."

"What about *girls*?" Dan asked.

Aaron blushed and looked down at the console. "Ah, there's a school nearby." He swallowed. "I heard."

"You guys haven't hit that?"

"There's a few events throughout the year they have planned for us."

Dan huffed. "Planned events. *Great*."

I nodded at Aaron. "Sounds like you're doing real good for yourself there. Obeying the rules and all."

Aaron sat back in his seat and stared out his window.

"Well, I'm calling a few sluts over tonight, for sure," Dan said.

"Dan." I warned him, slapping the back of my hand against his arm.

"What?"

I shook my head. If Aaron didn't want that, we shouldn't push him. And I didn't want him to screw up on his holiday.

When we arrived at our house, Father was in the kitchen with his latest girlfriend. I didn't bother to learn her name. She had catered a big dinner in her attempts to play mom. Once we all ate, almost in complete silence, minus the silverware scraping on our plates, I followed Aaron upstairs to his old room, more for his protection from Father than anything.

"Hey," I said once we were alone. "I really am proud of you."

Aaron started taking out dirty clothes from his duffel to stuff in his hamper, picking up his room without looking at me.

"You okay?" He was being too quiet.

"George," Aaron moved behind me to close and lock his door. "Gianna visited me."

After a sharp inhale, I held my breath. Before I lost my cool, I steadied my voice. "When? Why didn't you tell me right away? What happened?"

Aaron sat on his bed. "She, um. She started flirting with me." He looked up at me through his long lashes.

I crossed my arms and waited.

"It was weird. I didn't know what to do."

"You were supposed to call *me*. I could take care of it."

"Well, she blew me and my roommate," he said flatly.

"What? When?" I could feel turkey and gravy rising into my throat. Swallowing hard, I willed my pulse to slow down.

"Two weeks ago."

Pacing, I ran my fingers through my hair repeatedly, trying to come up with something to say and to stuff my dinner back into my stomach.

"I'm not into her, man. If you are." Aaron stood up, narrowing his eyes at me, misinterpreting my anger.

I stopped in my stride and grabbed his shoulders. "Not. At. All. I'm worried for you. Aaron, you're underage." His face dropped and he looked guilty, like he'd done something wrong. "D-did you do anything more?"

"Like what?" His body stiffened at the question.

"Like have sex with her?"

Aaron relaxed. "Oh, no. Just the blowjob with my roommate."

"Are you okay?"

He shrugged. "It was just confusing, is all."

If I could take away that pain from him, I would. I knew exactly how he felt. An idea came into my mind. One I didn't like, but could work to help us both. "I'm gonna need something from you."

CHAPTER
FIFTEEN
KINSLEY

I WAS DOING OKAY. Running every morning helped. As did the evening jogs. And between classes if I could fit it in.

Skipping the cafeteria for lunch helped me to avoid *that guy*. Instead, I spent the time training for my next marathon or studying for astronomy before grabbing food at my apartment. Dr. Torrad was much more receptive to give me extra help when I hounded her office hours daily. She showed me some YouTube videos that were valuable, and I felt like I was better prepared for the final.

I kept up appearances at Manny's, Tony's, the Lounge, and even the Warehouse on Friday nights. Only Marissa guessed that there may have been something off, but she was often busy with Xavier. Elle was with a new boyfriend none of us could stand. Sharice was with Maurice and too busy sucking his face to party with us.

I was spending more time with Edith on the weekends, though her dementia prevented her from recognizing me. Sometimes she didn't know I was even there. I'd bring her favorite flowers to set in her room and talk at her while she laid in her bed, eyeing me suspiciously.

After leaving the nursing home one Saturday morning, I visited the Northview police station to copy any evidence from my hit-and-run. The accident report said that my car had skidded on the ice with no other tire tracks visible. When I asked to speak with the officer who investigated the scene that night, they informed me he had died two years prior. He was only thirty-seven.

My next stop was the tow company that took my car all those years ago, but they didn't keep records that far back. Another dead end, but I wasn't going to give up. That was the only good thing about what *that guy* had done to me. Rage was a great motivator.

I stopped along Main Street, but the stores either did not have video footage or had it and had turned it over to the police for evidence. When I asked earlier, however, the police station said they did not have any footage from that night.

Frustrated, I walked back past the local bookstore towards my car. Levi Joseph was walking out of an alley between it and an antique store, not watching where he was going. He bumped into me and started to apologize.

"Oh, hey, Kinsley!"

"Hey! What are you doing down here? In an alley?" I asked.

"Oh, I, uh. Just looking at the apartment there." He pointed above the antique store.

"I thought you lived at the Theta manor."

"I do. I just… What are you doing down here?"

"A fruitless adventure." I grimaced.

Levi seemed confused. "What kind of adventure?"

Levi was nice. He was always so Golden Retriever-ish. I wanted to talk with him.

"I was hit by a drunk driver a few years ago, and the police say they don't have any evidence of it. It happened right over there." I pointed to the four-way intersection. "But, I was hoping one of these stores still had some video from that night."

"Huh. That sucks. Well, hey, I just met the antique shop owner. Want me to ask if they have—"

"No, I asked. They said they didn't. Very hastily, if I may add."

"Let me know if I can be of any help."

"Thanks, Levi." He walked towards a rusted Honda Civic with bald tires. "Hey, Levi."

He paused before getting in his driver's door. "Yeah?"

"You and Elle… You okay?"

He smiled sadly. "I'm working on it." He drove away.

Elle was a very private person when it came to her dating life, but things had come out a few weeks ago when Levi messed up big time. It wasn't my place to push them back together, but it was easy to see how much he loved her. Especially with how hard he was trying to win her back.

Meanwhile, I hadn't spied a single blond hair from *that guy* that tried to ruin me. He played a cruel prank on me, made even more cruel by the fact he claimed he wanted a "truce." That was before he made me develop feelings for him, then fucked someone else.

I figured he had been fucking her the entire time. It was the only thing I could assume with him leaving me to meet an older woman, a *sexy* older woman, wearing nothing but a robe and touching him like she owned him. Some nights I couldn't *stop* thinking about her red fingernails crawling up his chest and her pouty lips touching his cheek.

None of that mattered. I was better than him. I just needed to focus on my redemption plan, saving Kinsley from her foolish mistakes. First, was getting rid of the cheap piece of jewelry sitting in my backpack that held no sentiments for me. Returning it would make me ditch some dead weight I had been holding onto.

It was two weeks before finals. I waited for Cale and Sydney after our Russian literature class. Digging out the old bracelet, I held it out to her as the two eyed me suspiciously.

"Here. I think Cale wanted to give this to you."

Cale took it from me and glanced at his girlfriend. "Thanks, Kinsley."

"Sure, no problem." I was going to walk away because Cale meant absolutely nothing to me, but I was on a mission. I needed a win. "Cale."

He exchanged a glance with Sydney, who walked to the classroom door to wait for him. "Yeah?"

"I'm sorry I waited so long to return it. Your anniversary probably passed. I wish you two all the happiness, but I have to get something off my chest."

He looked like I was going to give him a terminal diagnosis. He swallowed and squeaked out, "What's that?"

"You were so immature and vain to break up with me the way you did. Just because I have scars doesn't mean that I'm not beautiful in other ways. You lost the best girl you'll ever have only because you were too stupid to—"

"What are you talking about?" His eyes narrowed and his cheeks flamed red.

"I'm talking about you breaking up with me after my accident because of my *scars*."

"Kinsley…" He shook his head with his mouth open. "I didn't break up with you for your fucking physical scars. I just meant, like, you know, *mental* scars from what happened to you."

"What?" Now I was confused.

"After the accident, you shut down. You weren't the same fighter I knew. I mean, you obviously got that back now, but right after… you were *afraid*. And the Kinsley I knew was never afraid of anything. She was better than me at everything. Hell, I told you I didn't go to Harvard because I wanted to save money. I never got accepted. You were always better, better at everything… I-I was young, stupid. Didn't know how to handle it. I was jealous of you. I'm sorry."

"Oh."

"You—" He stopped himself and checked where Sydney was tapping her foot down at the entrance of the class. "You're beautiful… Um, hot, actually." His eyes traced my body, and I got weirded out. "I never even really noticed your scars when we, uh, you know." He cleared his throat.

"Okay." I regretted bringing it up, but now that he clarified, I felt some relief; a past hurt healed. I was also a little creeped out; I didn't want him to look at my body like he was. Not anymore. "Thanks."

"Thanks for the bracelet." He turned to walk down the aisle towards his girlfriend.

After class, I suited up for another marathon training session. The marathon was step two of my plan. I was going to beat my times and get another win. It was Thursday, so there wasn't much going on unless I decided to go to the Ginger Lizard Lounge later.

It was closing in on the end of the semester. The wind felt like knives cutting into my face. It was dark well before 5 p.m., which made my evening runs shorter. Aiming to get a few miles in before dinner, I chose my old high school, which had a well-lit track.

As I ran the circles, I thought of all I had to do over the coming weeks. Xavier Cardell's parents were hosting their annual holiday party, and this year, I was invited since I was friends with his girlfriend. Step three was looking stunning at the event. *That guy* would be there and I was not looking forward to seeing him, but wanted to leave an impression. Not that he had missed me. I had been just a hook-up. A toy. A fling. A game to him.

So why did he break down in tears in front of me if he was with *her*?

As a habit, I pushed that question out of my mind. It was the thought that made me have hope that we could be together, that there was an explanation that made sense. That somehow, I had misinterpreted what happened. I was only fooling myself.

Once I flushed the thought out of my mind, I ambled to the parking lot with my hands on my hips. When I walked next to the stadium bleachers, a figure jumped out from the stands and grabbed me from behind. It was the hard body of a man that grasped me around the mouth so I couldn't scream, though I tried. I kicked my legs back to hurt him and he grunted, loosening his grasp of me.

I took off in a sprint, but he was fast and caught me before I could get away. He snatched an arm, and I tried to pull away, but he gathered me up again, wrapping his hand around my neck and squeezing. Dropping to my knees, I let my body flail while attempting to pull his fingers off my carotids. It didn't work. The light of the track was fading, darkness was replacing it.

Not again.

☽ ☽ ☽ ● ☾ ☾ ☾

The first thing I was aware of was something tight wrapped around my torso and waist, preventing me from moving. Thrashing as much as I could, I knew I needed to escape. Strong arms grasped my shoulders.

"Shh, Sins. It's okay. I got you."

My eyes fluttered open, then shut. Then open again. A fuzzy George appeared with long blond locks falling in his face. He was staring intensely at me as if seeing me for the first time.

"You're okay, princess."

We were moving; the bumps of a road underneath us made my head hurt. Two paramedics were working an IV and checking my blood pressure next to me.

"Don't move," one of the uniformed women commanded.

I was strapped to a board and could barely turn my head.

"Wha-what happened?" I asked George. My voice was hoarse.

George brushed some hair off my forehead and my vision cleared more. His forehead furrowed and his jaw set.

"You were attacked. I was too late to stop it. You changed your evening running spot, and when I went looking for you, I couldn't find you. Took me too long to figure out where you'd gone." George's large thumb stroked my cheek, then my hand lying on my belly. "I'm so sorry, princess. It's my fault. I should have been there."

"Why should you have been there?"

George glanced at the two workers and closed his mouth. He turned his head to look out the back windows until we arrived at the hospital. After running me through the CT scan for my head and an X-ray for broken bones, I was allowed to remove the collar around my neck and board on my back once the radiologist read the results. Stuck on a gurney in a curtained off section of the emergency room, George never left my side for a moment, except when he couldn't come with me for imaging.

His large paw held my hand, while his head anxiously scanned the busy department. Continually making circles on my skin with his fingers and thumb, he looked lost, like my hand was the only thing grounding him.

"George."

"Huh?" His distant look faded, and his crystal blue eyes focused on me.

"George, what did you mean you should have been there?"

"Do you need anything? Water? Can you have that? Is that okay? Should I get a nurse?"

"No, they should come over soon. Sit." Snapping my fingers, I pointed to a small plastic chair next to the cart I laid on. He sat, but his body was so big, it was like a kid's stool he squatted on. Dragging it next to the gurney with one hand, his other held mine the entire time. At this height, his face was right next to mine, and I caught his manly steel scent, which was a welcome reprieve from the bleach and burning smell surrounding the hospital atmosphere.

"Kinsley, I've been watching you, well, guarding you."

"Why?"

His eyes darted left. "Someone slashed your tires. I thought... I figured you were in danger without me around."

"What are you not telling me? And why are you here? Shouldn't you be with that woman?"

His large shoulders heaved as he took a deep breath. "I know what it looked like, but it wasn't what it seemed." I wasn't sure I even wanted to listen to him. "That woman was my stepmother. From when I was in high school. She was..." The Adam's apple in his throat bobbed slowly as he swallowed, a look of sheer pain came over his face. He wasn't going to finish his sentence.

Stepmother... My mind raced, trying to put everything together.

"She hurt you."

His blond head of hair slowly nodded as his eyes shone with wetness.

"Did she beat you?"

He hesitated, then slowly shook his head.

"She..." I was confused. "She *molested* you?" I whispered the word.

"Well, I guess maybe it wasn't, 'cause I was 15 and a guy and..." He brushed some of his hair back out of his face.

"George, what are you saying? You were underage. *Of course*, it was molestation. Or... did she do more?" His face fell and my eyes filled with tears as I realized... "Did she? Ugh! She did, didn't she?"

Rage filled my bone marrow more than when I looked into Barrett Grant's face. I wanted to *murder* that bitch. Climbing over the bed, I crawled into his lap after untwisting my IV line. We held each other there, but I was still so confused and sat back shaking my head.

"How? How could you *be* with her?"

George's head fell backwards to stare at the ceiling. He sighed. "She's blackmailing my father. She's threatened me, which I don't care about as much as her threatening to hurt my youngest brother. Aaron's sixteen."

My face scrunched. "I don't understand."

"If my father loses his job, he won't be able to afford to give my mother money, which she barely has any of anyway. He only pays her because of us, his sons. I'm sure once Aaron is out of the house, he's going to cut her off completely. She won't be able to function. She'll die. Not to mention my brothers. Gianna already hurt Aaron and is threatening to make him impregnate her—threatened to make me do so, unless…"

A little breath caught in my throat. "Unless what?"

George's light blue eyes darkened to the color of a stormy ocean as his brow furrowed. "Unless I bring you with me next time."

"What?"

"Kinsley, I haven't wanted to be with her *ever*. It wasn't my choice. I love my brothers. It's my responsibility to care for my mother. I don't want to impregnate Gianna. I told her that. She said if I didn't bring you, then she'd force my brother."

"Why me?"

George ran both his hands through my tangled hair, holding my skull with his big palms so we were eye to eye. "Because I love you." Warmth spread throughout my body, but I was smart enough not to buy it, no matter how much I wanted to.

"Don't say shit you don't mean."

"You can believe it or not, but that doesn't make it any less true. You're my North Star, princess. My guide. My anchor. I was wrong about you being a white hole. I'm the one whose heart explodes every time I'm near you. You sucked me in until I couldn't escape your pull. And I don't want to. I love you, Kinsley."

Hearing the words, I couldn't accept them and shook my head slightly. I so badly wanted to believe it was true. He pressed his lips gently to mine, then kissed my cheeks to catch my fallen tears.

"Kinsley!" My mother's voice broke my emotion. Her hand was on my back, and I stood to give her a hug. "Oh my god, what happened?"

I explained a little about what I could remember as George stood behind me with a hand on my shoulder like he wouldn't break our connection.

"Are you the George who called me?"

"Yes, Misses, uh..." He stuck his hand out to her, but she pulled him in for a hug.

"It's Miss Monroe, but just call me Jan." She snapped her finger and pointed at the gurney. "Get back on that thing!"

The nurse I met earlier pulled the curtain back and said, "I agree. You need to stay there. The doctor should be in soon. Do you need anything? Pain doing okay still?" He fussed with my IV line as I got situated on the hard pad again.

"I'm good." The nurse left, snagging the curtain behind him.

The headache had subsided with an anti-inflammatory, otherwise, I felt fine. My mother stroked my hair off my face, and George stood at the foot of my bed, one hand gently massaging my foot.

"George was there to rescue me," I told her.

"George, I can't thank you enough. Kinsley, I'm disappointed you haven't introduced us yet."

"Oh, um. He's…" What should I say? Boyfriend? The guy who's fucked me several times now? My tutor? I still wasn't sure. I was still in shock about everything he told me. I didn't know if I wanted to give him a second chance or not. He had been doing everything for his family, which was admirable. But why wouldn't he just *tell* me?

Before I could figure out how to respond, my father breezed in with panic painted on his face.

"Kinsley," he said with an exhale, as if relieved to see me. I was surprised he wasn't upset that I was just lying there; that I wasn't curing cancer. He strode over quickly and kissed my forehead. "What happened?"

George cleared his throat and explained how he ran up on me as a guy was attacking me. The man, dressed all in black, ran off when George approached. George then called the ambulance and my mom from my open phone.

"Well, thank you, uh…" My father stood up, addressing George.

"Dad, this is George. He's my boyfriend." George

looked as shocked as my father. Both of their jaws dropped as they eyed each other more scrupulously.

"Oh, well, nice to meet you. Thank you so much for being there for Kinsley." They shook hands. "What are you studying, George? Play football? How long have you two been together?"

The doctor walked in, interrupting any answer I could come up with for my father. I was cleared to go without even a broken bone or concussion. I had to make sure not to play contact sports for a week and watch for any worsening headaches. There would be bruising from the fall, but otherwise, I was healthy.

A police officer was waiting outside the curtain to take a report, but I knew it was useless. The police in this town were corrupt. Who policed the police?

It was almost midnight when George held my hand as we walked out of the hospital with my parents. He put his huge winter coat over me since I was still in just a sweatshirt and leggings. It hung to my knees and swallowed my frame, but the scent of G filled me and that was the warmest thing I could have worn.

"Well, George, please stop by for Christmas in a few weeks. I'd love it if you celebrated with us. It's usually just Kinsley and me," my mother said. She shot daggers at my dad with her eyes.

My father said, "Bethany and I would love to have you over, too, George. We have a big celebration with our family. I think I'll be playing Santa this year. Kinsley used to love that." He was smiling his big, fake smile.

George nodded and smiled at my parents. "Thanks for the invites."

Once we reached his truck, my parents each gave me a hug, asking if I wanted to stay with either of them, but I assured them I was fine. I wanted to talk to George alone. There were still too many questions I had.

George placed me carefully in his passenger seat like I was a porcelain doll and grabbed the sleeping bag from the back to put over me. I didn't need it, but I appreciated the gesture. Once he clamored in, he put his hands on the steering wheel, but didn't drive.

He turned his head slowly and narrowed his eyes at me. "Am I?"

"Are you what?"

"Am I your boyfriend?"

I inhaled sharply. "I don't know. *Are* you?"

"I want to be. *Fuck*, I want to be more than that." My heart thudded in my chest. He leaned all the way across the cab and placed his lips against mine. "Girlfriend… I'll take it for now." His George breath flooded my nostrils as he said the words close to my face.

George sat back and drove to the main exit of the hospital's parking lot. "George, what did your father do?"

He quickly braced himself, like he'd been shot. "He did something really bad. And if I tell you more, it could put you in danger."

Maybe he was embezzling money from his company. George said he was a manager… Maybe he worked for Cardell Enterprises like most of the town. George came from money, so that made sense. The Cardells were *not* a family to mess with. If George's father had messed with old Cardell money, that could put George in danger, too. As angry as I had been with George, I did not want him dead. Especially before I could give him a second chance.

"I'll do it."

"Do what?"

"The threesome. I'll do it."

CHAPTER
SIXTEEN
GEORGE

"WHY THE FUCK would you agree to that?"

"Because I want to help you. I don't want you to impregnate her or be hurt by her anymore. I don't want your family hurt. Or your life to be in danger."

It was noble. She cared for me, but… "No, Sins. No. I'll figure out something. You don't need to get involved. I wasn't asking you to join when I told you her request."

"I want to."

Turning my head, I stared into her sparkling hazel eyes. Her face was set like flint. "Sins, no. I'm telling you no."

"And I'm telling you yes." I had no retort. "I'm going to do it. I could eat pussy, I think. Is that what she wants?"

"I can't discuss this with you." The nausea was hitting me again. What was worse was that someone like Mason would call me a fool for trying to talk my girlfriend out of a threesome. But this wouldn't be like well-produced studio porn. It would be nasty, homemade creepy porn with terrible lighting. It would be my dream girl with my worst nightmare.

"Well, we should. I got tested last week for STDs. I am clean. How long have you been having sex with her?"

"I never fucked her without a condom. She's been threatening me for months, but I'd never stick my raw dick inside her. I would never do that to you, Kinsley."

"Well, there's that. Good." Kinsley turned in her seat, angling her body towards me.

Grabbing her hand on the console, I pleaded, "Sins, I never wanted to have sex with her. I'm sorry. I should have told you sooner, but… I thought I could let you go and then it wouldn't matter. If I—"

"I get it, George. She's forcing you into this. But now we have to fix the issue."

"You're the bravest fucking person I know." She was. Kinsley was brave and forthright, and sharp as a whip. So was her tongue. But she also had no sense of self-preservation. "Even if you agree, Gianna could just force me to do it again some other time."

"I'm not stupid, George. I've already thought of that."

It dawned on me that Kinsley was strategizing a secret plan. "No. Sins. Whatever you *think* you can pull on her, don't. It will end worse for you."

A little vindictive smile crept across her face. I'd seen that look after she would prank me. "Or it could end worse for *her*. She can't get away with being a sexual predator and trying to ruin my boyfriend's life."

Even from my peripheral vision, I caught her swallow thickly.

"How would you feel seeing her and I together?" I asked.

She hesitated before she spoke. "Seeing you and her? Having sex?" I waited as she considered her answer. "Sick. Angry. Jealous… And also aroused."

"Yeah. I'd feel the same way." Thinking about it just made my stomach feel like I'd swallowed batteries. I didn't want to share my girlfriend. Especially not with Gianna. Being with my ex-stepmother always made me feel confused, sick, like I was broken and dirty. It was my personal hell and I didn't want to drag the love of my life into that pit with me. "Sins, I don't want you to do this."

"Too bad. I'm doing it. We are getting you out of this mess so we can be together, and so we can give that bitch what she deserves. Let's talk rules." We had reached her apartment and were sitting in the lot. "But first, I'm starving and need hot cocoa. Come up?"

"It's late, not sure how you can sneak a body like mine inside the girl's dorm."

"I know Mary at the front desk. You'll be fine."

"Stay right there," I said with authority as she put her hand on the door. Jumping out, I walked around to her side, and grabbed her so her legs surrounded my waist as she clutched my neck with her arms. It was our position.

Mary didn't say a thing to us when I carried Kinsley past the front desk. When she lifted her eyes in a question, Kinsley quickly explained I was helping her after an accident.

Dropping my girlfriend onto her bed, I pointed to her dresser. "PJs?" She told me which drawer to find them in. I got a glance at her colorful underthings, which made me oddly excited, like I was a twelve-year-old boy again. I handed her the T-shirt she asked for.

"I can walk, you know." Standing, she pulled off her leggings. Watching her undress made my dick twitch, but I willed it to calm down. She may not be ready to get reacquainted after what happened. I was still in shock that she was even talking to me. When she walked into her bathroom, I perched lightly on her bed, but she beckoned me through the open door with a finger. "I have an extra toothbrush. Come on."

"Y-you want me to stay?"

"Yes, of course."

We brushed our teeth like an old married couple, and my skin burned hotter than ever. It was such a simple thing that I never knew I was missing until it happened. Now I wanted it every night. She eyed me in the mirror and spat out her toothpaste, rinsing her mouth. I followed behind her. "Kinsley," I said as we returned to her room.

"Take off your shirt and pants. Come to bed with me. We need to talk about a plan."

"Kinsley. What are you doing? You were ready to cut me yesterday. Now, suddenly, you're okay with me being your boyfriend. A boyfriend that's fucking his stepmother?"

She sighed. "No. I'm not okay with it."

WHITE HOLE

My heart stopped.

She quickly said, "I don't want her in your life. George, she's an abuser. *She's* the problem here. You were trying to save your family, and I think that's noble, albeit I think you're taking on way too much responsibility." Propping herself against some pillows, she sat up in her bed. "*Your* problem was pushing me away. I want to show you how great of a team we can make when we join our brilliant minds." She held her hand out to me. "We can figure this out... *together*." When I still didn't move, she patted the bed. "Now, strip Big G, and get the fuck in the bed with me."

Quickly, I obeyed. I held my girl as we chatted about everything until the early morning hours. We discussed what sexual activities we would feel comfortable with, or what scenarios Gianna may put us in. We devised a strategy to take her down, but I was much less confident in our plan than Kinsley.

Kinsley wanted to hide a camera in her backpack and set it up in the room to video Gianna. She thought we could get Gianna to confess she had been blackmailing my father and had hurt me as a teenager.

Gently, I questioned her plan. Even if we caught a confession on camera, who could I hand it over to? My father? He'd never let the footage of his own son and ex-wife come out like that. He'd rather it stay in the dark than risk his reputation. I would do it anyway if we got the right confessions from her. I had to try something.

Our conversation moved from Gianna to our fathers. I kept things vague about Chief Turner's work, but shared a few stories from my vault. Kinsley held me as I told her things even Xavier didn't know. I talked about my mom, about the day she left us.

Kinsley told me about her recovery after her wreck in the hospital and her father's pressures on her. She confessed she felt responsible for her parent's divorce.

"That's ridiculous," I said, as we lay on our sides, facing each other.

"Almost as ridiculous as an eight-year-old boy blaming himself for his mother leaving?"

For a long time, I stayed silent. Boys were supposed to listen to their mothers. "She told me it was."

"Well, your mom sounds like a complete cunt." Kinsley paused. "Sorry."

"No, she is. She blames me for everything." Stroking her chocolate hair, I tucked a piece behind her ear.

"It wasn't your fault, George. Your father is a wife beater, serial cheater, and all-around asshole. Your mother couldn't put the blame where it belonged. It wasn't safe for her to do that, but she should never have put it on you. She's not your responsibility and their divorce wasn't your fault. You were just a kid. And then your father let that... *predator* rape you." She turned over and pushed back into my waiting arms, gripping mine as I hugged her. "I don't think I want to meet your parents, George. Not while I want to kill them both."

"If I don't take care of her, who will?"

"She's an adult human. Maybe she needs to figure it out. You know what? On second thought, I do want to meet her. Take me to her now."

A small smile crept over my face. Kins was in full

fired-up mode. I could imagine the two of them going head-to-head in an all-out verbal spat; it would be like two hot suns colliding. All the words I had been missing seemed to flow so freely from her mouth. "Relax, princess. We can visit another time." I kissed the top of her head and she settled as I held her.

As the night progressed and we talked, I'd never felt closer to anyone. I knew I could never be without her. Kinsley was becoming a necessity in my life. I'd never talked with anyone as much as I had with her. Each word I spoke out loud felt like it was patching up old wounds I didn't even know I had.

"You followed me." She spoke quietly as the sun was peeking under her bedroom blinds.

"Yeah."

"Why?"

"I had to make sure you were safe. After the tires, I knew you were in danger. I love you, princess. Gotta watch out for my girl." When I wrapped my arms tighter around her, she fell asleep, and I drifted off peacefully, too.

☽ ☽ ☽ ● ☾ ☾ ☾

It was several days before I got the text from Gianna. Kinsley and I had been hanging out in my room at the manor studying after spending the morning in bed making love. That's what it was. That cosmic energy exchange between our auras? It was love making. As much as the girl liked to irritate me by calling me 'Big

G' at times, she was *my* gravitational constant. I'd never felt safe or grounded with anyone until her.

"It's game time," I said to her, standing to kiss her on the cheek.

"Can you even get it up after this week?"

Taking a step back, I stood with my hands on my hips. "Jesus, Sins. I'm twenty-one years old, not seventy-five. I can get it up again, yes." Quieter, I said, "Only with you there, though."

"I'm just saying, I feel sore from the last few days of sexcapades. Didn't know if your rod was raw."

"Only because you're so fucking tight, yeah. Come on. She'll start bugging me if we're not there soon." To say my nerves were at an all-time high was still an understatement. Despite going over the gameplan several times, I was weary to go.

Kinsley grabbed her backpack, making sure the camera was well hidden and in place. Then we were on our way.

Once we arrived, I put her little body protectively behind me and knocked on the door.

"No girlfriend?" Gianna's eyes narrowed in annoyance when she opened the door. Kinsley peered around me. "Oh, there you are, precious! Come in!" Gianna grabbed Kinsley's hand and pulled her into the room. After shutting and locking the door, I strode over to grab Kinsley's backpack from her, setting it on the dresser at the right angle.

"Well, well. No wonder Georgie has been hiding you. You're beautiful. Kinsley, right?"

"Yes." I could tell Kinsley was trying to get a read on

Medusa. Her hazel eyes widened as she scanned Gianna's face.

"I'm Gianna. We are going to have so much fun together. It's been too long since I ate young pussy. And now I'm starving." Gianna put on her most seductive smile, bright red lips parting to display her full set of white teeth.

Kinsley glanced at me for a second and took a deep breath. "What do you want me to do?"

"You ever been with a woman, precious?"

"N-no. I'm not opposed to it, I'm just not that interested. I mean, I prefer penises. Well, I prefer George's penis. And George's body. Not that you're not pretty, I am just not…" God, would she stop talking? As if she read my mind, Kinsley clamped her mouth closed and bit her lip. Sidling up behind her, I brushed her hair back and placed my hands on her shoulders, gently massaging.

"Aw, she loves you, Georgie." Turning her eyes back to my girlfriend, Gianna said, "Enough to share you?"

Kinsley nodded. Gianna slid her fingers through some long brown strands from Kinsley's hair, and stroked it before placing her full lips against my girlfriend's. Some weird mixture of outrage, possessiveness, and heat rose within my core. Confusingly, my cock started to harden. Nausea rolled in my stomach at the sensation. I didn't want it, but I couldn't stop it. It was just like when I was a teenager. I couldn't pause to analyze the complex soup of feelings I was experiencing. If I did, I wouldn't be able to function, and this performance needed to happen to try to get any confession from the bitch.

Kinsley's body relaxed into my stepmother's lips as I stood behind her, rubbing her arms. Gianna ran her fingers around the back of her head and pulled her into a deeper embrace. Kinsley put her arms around Gianna's waist and the two began to make out. Sensing Kinsley's body ease into their movements, I slid over to the second bed to watch them. My jaw was clenched, my body ready to jump up and stop them at any moment. If Sins showed a moment's hesitation, I would end this whole scene.

Gianna moved Kinsley to the edge of the bed with her hands gently gripping her waist. She sat Kinsley down, then sucked her lips down the side column of her neck as Kinsley tilted her head, her hazel eyes watching me. I wasn't letting her stare go; I was going to keep that bond between us the entire time. Gianna helped my girlfriend remove her sweatshirt, then her tank top and bra, until her perky breasts were exposed. Kinsley's pink nipples were on point as Gianna licked one, while pinching the other between her fingers.

Disgusted with myself, I reached down to palm my dick in my jeans, trying to ease the strain there. This was how Gianna always made me feel: nauseated, aroused, and guilty. Watching Kinsley's eyes flutter shut and exhale a little pant when Gianna moaned on her nipple made my stomach flip. It was hot. I was hot. I took my hoodie off and tossed it on the bed.

Gianna unbuttoned Kinsley's jeans and helped her slide them and her panties down.

"Oh, my." Gianna turned her head to see me. "She's perfect, Georgie. Good job. Spread your legs, little girl. I want to see how pretty you are."

Kinsley's eyes flashed to mine as if asking permission. I gave her a nod, but it was all up to her. She was controlling this situation; I'd already told her as much before we arrived.

Kinsley opened one thigh, then the other, and Gianna kissed her way down her stomach between my girlfriend's thighs. Gianna's long red nails stroked up her chest, and her palm gently caressed her breast, then pushed until Kinsley laid back on the bed. Gianna licked her pussy once and Kinsley's head shot back up to glance down at her with a gasp.

"That feel good, precious?" Kinsley nodded quickly. "Good." After a few minutes of snacking on Kinsley's pussy, Gianna stood up and helped my girlfriend slide back on the bed while pulling down her own panties. "Georgie, be a good boy and help me out here, huh?"

When she bent over my girlfriend to consume her, I knelt behind Gianna and began to eat her cunt. As I slicked my tongue through Gianna's folds, fucking her with my tongue the way I knew she liked, I heard Kinsley stifle a moan as her thighs collapsed around Gianna's head.

"That's a good girl. Just relax. Let me make you come." Gianna's voice was muffled between my girlfriend's legs. Just as Gianna writhed on my hand from the addition of my fingers to both her pussy and ass, Kinsley panted and humped her head. The two women exploded almost simultaneously in cries of ecstasy. It was like music to my ears, hearing them orgasm at the same time, and my cock responded by growing to its full capacity. Now that Gianna had come, I wouldn't have to worry so much about her and could get on with the rest of the procedure, getting out of here as soon as we could.

Reaching down, I undid my jeans, releasing my aching dick.

"Oh, my god, Georgie. She's so precious. Look how her cheeks flushed."

Kinsley sat up on her elbows with a look of guilt on her face, like she didn't expect Gianna to make her come or even want her to. I met her eyes and tried to let her know that it was okay and that I understood that feeling. Very well.

Gianna stood to pull down my pants the rest of the way, and I stepped out of them. She knelt in front of me and stroked my cock. "Come here, precious girl. I want you to taste my pussy on your boyfriend's lips."

Leaning over, I pulled Kinsley to my side while Gianna sucked me off. Grasping the back of Gianna's head with one hand, I grasped my girlfriend's with the other before kissing her ferociously. She whimpered in my mouth, our tongues caressing each other's. While Gianna's mouth soaked down my length, I gazed into Kinsley's sparkling hazel eyes. I didn't want to say it in front of Gianna, but I tried to telepathically communicate with Kinsley, let her know I loved her. Pressing my forehead to hers, Sins bit her lip and nodded as if she heard me.

Gianna tugged Kinsley down to her knees and

handed her my cock. Kinsley's eyes met mine, and I stroked her face with my thumb. Fuck, I loved this woman. My cock was wet from Gianna's spit, but Kinsley swirled the tip with her tongue anyway. She stretched her lips as far as they would go to fit my head inside her hot mouth.

"Fuck!" I choked out as her tongue danced around me and she stroked the spot just beneath the tip. It made me lose my footing until I stumbled backwards. My knees almost collapsed when Gianna sucked my balls while Kinsley took my shaft, alternating with kissing down the length and toying with the end. I groaned, trying to stay upright. The sensation of the two of them working me over almost made me come right then. Gathering Kinsley's hair back and holding it at the base of her neck, I said, "Princess, if you keep sucking me like that, I'm gonna blow."

Taking a step back, I pulled my cock from them. "Gianna, get on the bed. On your back. Sins, crawl over top of her." I was done with Gianna calling the shots. She'd already gotten her orgasm and made my girlfriend come. She needed to sit down and know her place. "Nope, head the other way, Sins." She turned so they were sixty-nine with each other. There was no way I wanted Gianna to be kissing my girlfriend while I was inside her. "Yep, just like that." From this position, I could control the witch easier. I was stroking myself, but didn't need to keep myself hard because I hadn't had an erection like this since I was a teenager.

Gianna's head was near my girlfriend's pussy, and she flicked her clit with her tongue, which made Kinsley's back arch and a mewl escape her mouth. I straddled Gianna's face, which was almost hanging off the bed, and lined up with Kinsley's soaking wet pink folds. Running my dick through her wetness a few times, I pulled her hips back so I could enter slowly.

"Ahh... *fuck*! That feels amazing. Gianna, suck my balls." The feeling of Gianna's soft mouth suckling my sack and being inside Kinsley's tight pussy was something I never wanted to forget. I had to hold inside my girlfriend a full minute thinking of everything, but what was happening before I blew too soon.

Sins lowered her head in between Gianna's thighs, and Gianna hummed in pleasure around my taint. "That's it, princess. Lick her pussy." My stomach was so tight, it was hard to breathe. Gianna's tongue stroked up towards my asshole. I clenched my cheeks, so I wouldn't come.

Once I felt like I could settle down, I picked up my strokes and fucked my girlfriend. Gianna alternated between sucking my balls, tonguing my back hole, and flicking Kinsley's clit. Sins was snacking on Gianna's cunt, but I couldn't tell if she was enjoying it, or just me fucking her as her moans picked up.

I was going to put my cum inside my girlfriend and not give Gianna the opportunity to demand that I fuck her. "Fuck, girls, I'm gonna come."

Kinsley's head lifted, and she looked over her shoulder. I leaned over so I could kiss her while I filled her up. Gianna suctioned my balls, which exploded within the warmth and safety of my love's tight grip. Kinsley's pussy pulsated and she pushed back further onto me just as my cock throbbed and shot off. She screamed into my mouth as I held her face. I didn't care who was listening anymore. "I love you, Sins."

"I-I love you, too," she said breathlessly. I pulled my cock out and my cum ran down her pussy lips onto Gianna's waiting tongue. When I took a step back, Gianna French kissed my girlfriend's cunt, sucking all my cream out of her. I'd almost forgotten the witch was still there in my moment with Kinsley.

"My turn," Gianna said as Kinsley moved off her and picked up her jeans from the floor.

Pulling on my own clothes, I said plainly, "Nope. We're done here. You got what you wanted."

"No, I didn't. I get a turn on that thick pipe now."

"Yeah, not going to happen, Gianna. I'm spent." I shook my flaccid cock at her. "This is it for your game."

"I want your girl sucking my nipples while I fuck you cowgirl. You're impregnating me *tonight*."

Kinsley's face turned red. "You can't demand he do anything anymore, bitch."

"Excuse me?" Gianna reared on my girlfriend.

"I know about you. I know you molested him, took advantage of a young, hurting boy. You're an abuser. Not to mention trying to blackmail him and his father. Threatening to hurt his brothers. Admit it!"

Gianna laughed. "Oh, is that what Georgie told you? No, girl. He *wanted* it. He *has* wanted it." Turning to me and running a finger along my cheek, she said, "Pretty, but stupid, and too innocent, Georgie."

"I'm smarter than you, *precious*, and not innocent. Pretty, I'll agree with. You've had to manipulate him to get him. He was a *minor*! He's *never* wanted you. That must hurt really bad."

Gianna slapped my girlfriend in the face. Without a second thought, I shoved Gianna in the chest, so her body flew and hit the wall with a thud, then slid down it before crumpling to the floor. Kinsley went to go after her, but I stepped in between the two. "No."

Turning to Gianna, who kneeled into a protective crouch on the floor, I said, "Go ahead and expose my father's crimes. I'm over it. I *welcome* it. I'm done with you. Don't contact me again. If you fuck with Kinsley or my brothers, I will hurt you. Do you understand me?" She didn't move. I took the two steps to stand over her until she looked up at me with tears in her eyes. "Do you understand me?"

"Yes."

We quickly dressed, then I grabbed Kinsley's bag and her arm and pulled her out to *Serenity*.

CHAPTER
SEVENTEEN
KINSLEY

WHEN WE GOT into his truck, George hit the steering wheel repeatedly with the palms of his hands until the entire cab vibrated.

"Whoa, whoa!" I touched his arms so he would stop. He let his head hang, blond hair falling over his face.

"Fuck!"

"What? We did it! We got through it, and I got the video." I patted my backpack, which we had set up with a small hole in the front pouch so my phone could record the events.

"Kinsley, she didn't admit to *anything* on video. I never should have agreed to protect my father in the first place. What was it all for? For Aaron? For Dan? For my mom? Dan's a grown man and my mother *should* take care of herself once she gets the help she needs. You're right. I can't protect everybody all the time. I'm such a fucking idiot. I should have just been there with you. Just us."

George looked like his eyes were wet. Brushing

some of his long hair out of his face, my fingertips stroked his forehead. "Hey, hey, hey. You tried to do what you thought was best. Yeah, you should have told me, but we weren't really, um, together." He quieted down. I climbed over the console and got into his lap and held him, running my fingers through his hair.

His face was in my neck, but he mumbled, "Fuck, princess, I love you."

"I love you, too, George. We're together now, and together we can fight anything."

His lips were soft and tender when he pressed them against mine, but stubble was hard and tickled my jaw. Gigantic arms enveloped me, and he held the back of my head with both huge hands. My thighs involuntarily twitched as my stomach did a little flip. I could have stayed that way forever.

"Are you okay?" he asked me, leaning back to look back and forth in each of my eyes.

"Yes. Are you?"

"I tried to keep that connection—"

"Oh, I was there with you. I got it." I smiled. "I was just disappointed she gave me an orgasm. I didn't want to—"

"It's okay. It's just a physical thing," he said.

I nodded.

George cleared his throat. "I, uh, I noticed you went ahead with the whole cunnilingus thing. I thought you said—"

"I was in the moment. Figured I'd see what it was like."

George smirked. "Yeah?"

"Not my thing."

He laughed. "Okay." He gave the end of my nose a little kiss. "Let's get some food and head back to the manor."

I settled back in my seat.

George drove us to the diner near the motel and, of course, wouldn't hear of me getting out of his truck by myself. "It's your short legs."

"I'm not *that* short."

"You're like, what, four feet nine?"

I slapped his arm as we walked in, chuckling. "I'm five-five."

He grabbed my hand and pulled me into a booth next to him. I thought the weak plastic seat may tip over with his weight and mine combined, but it held up. I was starving. Who knew a threesome could burn so many calories? We both ordered pancakes, shakes, and burgers.

After I was finished, George delved into my leftover fries and the extra pancake when I sat back, rubbing my belly complaining of how full I was. It was nice having a boyfriend that could eat anything I couldn't. Food would never be wasted.

"Ugh. Now I'm full." George pressed against the seat and put his arm across the back. I leaned into his side, smelling his George steely scent while we waited for the check.

"Tell me more about stalking me."

"What?" George smiled and looked down at me, brushing his lips against the top of my head.

"You said you were following me. I want to know more about that. And why."

"Like I said, you were in danger. The tires, the attack in the woods... Even if I couldn't be with you, I was never going to let anything happen to you."

"Huh."

"Huh, what?"

"Because you love me?"

George snorted a laugh. "Yes, princess. Because I fucking love you."

"I love you, George." I kissed him as the waiter brought our ticket. George leaned his forehead against mine.

"Every time you've said that... It's the best thing anyone's ever said to me."

"No one's ever told you they love you?" My brow crinkled.

George shook his head. Stunned, I sat back while he pulled out his wallet and put his credit card on top of it. Looking at the table, I tried to take deep breaths so I could keep my tears back. I didn't want him to think I pitied him, but I did. My heart hurt thinking about it.

"Hey, hey. What's wrong?" George's large finger stroked my jaw, tugging my chin to look at him.

"I love you."

"Good. I love you, too."

"Your parents should have."

"Yeah, well, some people shouldn't be parents."

I didn't care that we were in a restaurant. Barely squeezing in, I scooted into George's lap and wrapped my body around him, hugging him tightly. The waiter came back and thanked us. George slid us out of the booth and carried me to the truck like his little monkey.

꩜

The next week, we never parted, spending time studying for our finals either at the manor or the library. Some nights we landed in my room and others in his. My bathroom was much nicer, but his bed was more comfortable.

"Fuck, you take my cock so well, Sins." I was bent over my dresser, gripping the back edge to steady myself as we watched ourselves in the mirror above it. "Wait just a minute."

George pulled out and grabbed the bottle of lube from the bedside table. He drizzled it all over my back hole and slid inside my pussy again with a groan. He pumped a finger inside my ass repeatedly. The sensation of his huge cock with his finger in my ass made me come so hard, I saw entire constellations behind my eyelids.

"That's a good girl." George added a second finger while I was still recovering from the intensity of my orgasm.

"Oh!"

"You're gonna take my big cock in your ass tonight, princess." He spanked me with a loud smack and I jumped forward. "And come again like the dirty whore you are. Your little pink hole is winking at me. You *need* my dick in your ass, don't you?"

I moaned, and he spanked me again. "Ouch!"

"Answer me. Don't you?"

"Yes, George. Put it in my ass!" My breath stopped, fear coming over me, but I focused on relaxing as much as I could. If there was any tension, I knew it would hurt. Anal was all about trusting my partner and I trusted him with my life.

I had wanted to try anal, just to see if I'd like it or not. George used his fingers a lot over the week, but now was the time to go for the whole thing.

The pressure from his cock's head was not bad. In fact, it felt good as he entered. I took a deep breath in as he slowly slid in further. "Oh my god, George. It's too big." I didn't know I could stretch that much. "Wait, wait, wait."

George held in position.

"Ugh, Sins. I wanna come in your ass so bad. I'm going to lose it. I gotta move."

"Wait."

George straightened his back as if trying to stop himself from thrusting. Another deep breath and I could relax more. "Oka—"

He pushed in all the way, and I screamed. His hips thrust rapidly as he spanked me once more. Reaching around, he rubbed my clit, then leaned over my back. "I can't hold it. You feel too fucking good. Come with me." With his large dick fully sunk in my ass, he was at an angle that hit my G-spot repeatedly. Before I knew it, I climaxed easily, but this only tightened my grip on his thickness.

"Fuck! Kinsley!" George's hot cum filled my back

hole. He stayed there for a moment, then slipped out of me slowly. Everything spilled out and ran down my legs. George kissed my back and neck, suctioning the skin inside his mouth while moaning in pleasure.

"I want to shower," I said.

"Let's go together."

We held each other under the stream of hot water, soaping each other's bodies and kissing.

"How was I?" I asked him as he washed my hair, his large hands caressing my scalp. The sensation was almost as good as my orgasm. I kept my eyes closed and leaned forward into him as he massaged my head.

"What?"

"Was I okay? With the anal." I peeked one eye open.

George laughed. "You want a grade? Sins, seriously. You're amazing. That was my first time fucking an ass. You definitely earned an A plus from me."

"That was your first time, too?"

"Yeah."

I grasped him around the neck. "I love you, George."

"I love you, my princess." He swatted my butt. "You took my cock in your ass like a pro."

"What other firsts have you had with me?"

He washed my hair as I soaped his chest. "I've never had a girlfriend before. I've never shared the stars with anyone." He tilted my chin up. "I've never been in love." He sucked my lips into his before we rinsed off.

The following day, George tried to contact the internal affairs department about the video we took of Gianna, but no one gave it much consideration. George said he was going to try something else, and we discussed what we would do if no one listened to us. Fortunately, Gianna had not contacted him or his brothers in the past week.

We devised a strategy for how we would handle things together. Finals were almost upon us. Between all the studying and setting our plan in place, we were both exhausted. Despite our hectic schedules, I still wanted to do one more errand before the holiday party.

"This is where she lives?"

"Yeah." George parked the truck in front of some dilapidated apartment building. I'd asked him to introduce me to his mother. I felt calm and hopefully wouldn't kill her. "You don't have to do this. I'm okay with you never meeting."

"No, I *want* to." His eyes met mine. "I'll be civil, I promise."

"Sins, you don't have to be."

"For your sake, I will."

We walked up the rusted, metal grated stairs to a wooden door. The place looked like it had been a motel back in some bygone era. George pulled out a key to let us in. A ripe, dank smell of rotten food and mildew greeted us as soon as the door opened.

"Mom," George walked into the main room of the studio, and I followed, passing a small kitchenette that seemed to be the source of the odors. A frail woman in her forties sat in a recliner with an unlit cigarette hanging from her mouth. She was sleeping in front of an older TV. Her eyes fluttered open, and she grimaced.

"I don't want you here—" As I peeked around my boyfriend's back, she stopped. "Who the fuck are you?"

"Mom!" George yelled, running hands through his long hair.

"I'm Kinsley, your son's girlfriend."

She settled back in her chair and lit the cigarette. "Yeah? You don't look like much. You—"

"*I* don't look like much? Lady, you're in dirty clothes and an even nastier apartment, watching a blank screen with a cigarette hanging out of your mouth, telling your beautifully caring oldest son you don't want him here. *You* don't look like much."

"George, you going to let her talk to me that way?"

George smirked, but kept his mouth closed.

"George doesn't *let* me do or not do anything. I do what I want. He won't be coming over here to *fix* you anymore. He deserves better. Better than you ever gave him, that's for damn sure."

"Listen here, little girl. I gave him birth. He only took my life away from me, the ungrateful bastard. Just like his father, he is—"

"George is nothing like him! He is kind and protective, intelligent, capable... He has taken care of you even when you treat him like shit." I moved closer to her chair without realizing and George took a step between us. I peered around his big body at her crinkled face.

"You don't even know him! Think you know everything, don't you? Think you're smart. George, why even show up here with her? The two of you deserve each other."

"Mom, don't say a bad word about Kinsley. That was my only warning."

"Oh, so she needs *you* to stick up for her, huh—"

I interrupted. "No, I don't. I am smart. And we do deserve each other. You *never* deserved him. He's done with you."

The woman burst into tears and wailed. If I wasn't so shocked, I may have felt bad. Maybe even apologized. I glanced at George. His nostrils flared and his face burned red. Her tears didn't seem to be a manipulation.

George put his arm around my shoulders and pulled me into him. "She's right. I'm finished here. I tried so hard to make you love me until I didn't even care if you did or not. For a lot of years, I was angry about it, but now, I just don't give a fuck. When I gave up caring, this woman found me. She loves me, and I get the privilege of loving her. Goodbye, Mother."

George turned and put his hand on the small of my back, leading me out the door. I hadn't wanted to blow up at her. The entire visit got out of hand. My control slipped the minute she opened her mouth.

"I'm sorry, George." As he placed me in the truck, he kissed my cheek.

"Why?"

"That didn't go how I planned at all."

George shrugged and walked around the truck to get inside. "Meh. It went how it should have gone. I feel great. I'm free."

A white flash caught my eyes and both of us looked up to the balcony of the second floor of the apartments.

His mother stood in her long, fuzzy robe, gripping the metal railing, staring down at us. She lifted a hand in a slow wave goodbye. George started the truck and drove away.

☽ ☽ ☽ ● ☾ ☾ ☾

By the weekend, we hadn't had much time to plan our outfits for the Cardell's annual holiday party. Only the rich and famous in town were invited to the event of the year, but being friends with Marissa and Xavier had its benefits. George tapped repeatedly on my bedroom door while I finished putting in my faux diamond drop earrings. My dress was a pale mint color made of silk. It had full sleeves with a deep-V neckline that reached toward a peplum waist, ending in a watery fabric skirt that grazed the floor. The color accentuated my dark brown hair nicely.

"Holy fuck, princess. You look even better than at Halloween. We got time." George pointed to my bed. "Get back in there."

I slapped his hand down. "No, we don't. Let's go. We're going to be late." Although seeing him in his tuxedo made me wet between my thighs. His cologne made me reconsider how important it would be to arrive on time or not. "Come on. Maybe we can find a moment away from the crowd."

The party was like none I had been to before. No expenses were spared. The Cardells had even turned their backyard pool into an ice-skating rink.

As soon as we walked into the large white tent set up on the grounds at the back of their mansion, I scanned the room and found her. Gianna. It was like she was waiting for us to enter. She left the side of a tall man to come over and greet us.

"Well, hello, lovers."

George placed his hand over mine, which was resting in the crook of his elbow. "Gianna. I see you came with your employer." George nodded in the direction of the man she presented with.

"Oh, yes. I want to introduce your girlfriend to him. You don't mind, do you?"

"Actually, I do," George said, but Gianna grasped my arm and tugged.

"Gianna, please. Please, don't do this." George was trying to keep his voice down, but there was a desperation there that made my stomach tie in a knot.

Gianna's long, red velvet gown got trapped under my heel as she hurried us towards her date. I almost tripped and when I did, I caught a glance of my boyfriend. George seemed stuck to the floor where we entered, clearly in a panic, head turning side to side to glance around for help.

Pulling me up with her, her date slowly turned his gaze upon us. His eyes were like steel in their intensity. Immediately, my back tingled with a sudden sense of danger. I was trapped and wanted to return to the safety of my George.

"George, darling. I want you to meet someone very important in your son's life… Kinsley Whittemore, this is George Turner, *senior*, the chief of Northview police."

She let my arm go and smugly smiled as if waiting for a play to begin.

"The *chief* of police? Turner? Wait… George is your *son*?" I couldn't even tell if I spoke the words aloud or if they were just in my head. My face scrunched up, heart pounding rapidly in my throat.

"Gianna, what are you doing?" Chief Turner's brow furrowed at his ex-wife. "Uh, nice to meet you, sweetheart. Please excuse me." He turned his back, shutting me out of the circle of men he was conversing with. One was Mayor Grant. Unable to contain myself, I tapped the chief of police on the shoulder.

"Excuse me." He didn't move. Gianna laughed. "Excuse me!" I shoved and pushed my way into the circle of men standing there. "Do you know me? Do you recognize me?" My anger flared, and I lost any ability to think rationally. My boyfriend was there and pulled me away.

"Please, princess—"

"George, get her out of here," his father said sternly.

"No! You know, don't you?" I pointed at George's father. "And you!" I pointed at the mayor. "Your son tried to *kill* me! Did you know?" I lost it. I started laughing, along with Gianna, hysterically. "Oh, my god. You *all* know. You're *all* in on this." Twisting out of George's grip, I pointed at another man in the circle. "Who are you? Do you know? Are you in on this conspiracy, too?"

"Sins. Come on. Now." George forcefully moved me away from the circle. "I'm sorry, my girlfriend's a little drunk."

"I'm not drunk!" But it was too late, we were halfway toward the exit. I'd had enough of his pushing and dug in my heels to stop our momentum. Spinning around, I put my finger in his face. "George *Turner*, chief of Northview police's *son*. You fucking bastard!" I didn't care who heard me. "*You* knew! You've known all along. Did you help them to cover it up? What other crimes have you helped to cover up, *Turner*?" I spoke loudly so everyone around us could hear.

"I-I was trying to protect you," George said softly, as if he could get me to lower my voice. He glanced around at all the people watching. We were on the dance floor near the middle of the room. It was a big production, and I didn't care. My rage was fueling my performance.

"Wait, wait. The *blackmail*—it was for *my* hit-and-run? For what Barrett Grant did to me?!"

"Kinsley, please stop talking. Please for once in your life. Stop."

"No! Everyone needs to know. And you're a prick for covering it up, too." I had to reach up, but I smacked him hard across the face, then turned around and swiftly walked to the mansion.

Before I could reach the entrance to the house, however, Mr. Cardell got up and made an announcement. Standing near the door, I listened as Xavier proposed to my friend, Marissa. Despite the absolute beauty of the moment, it made me want to cry and run away. Wiping a few tears from my eyes, I walked back to congratulate the happy couple.

Putting on a happy face, I hugged Marissa, wishing

her a happy new life. George stood near the back of our group of friends, away from me. If he came any closer, I may have slapped him again. Shifting from foot to foot, I plastered a fake smile on until it felt like I could leave without making an even bigger scene than I already had. When the timing was right, I slipped out of the party unnoticed.

CHAPTER
EIGHTEEN
GEORGE

IT ALL CAME CRASHING DOWN, imploding like a dying sun. I watched Kinsley run away and didn't stop her. Why should I? It was always going to end up this way.

My best friend was there with his girl proposing, and I couldn't even congratulate them. Xavier's eyes met mine and I nodded. He winked.

Others surrounded the happy couple, and I let myself get pushed to the back of the crowd. We were called to our seats for dinner. Millie Cardell must have forgotten my hatred for my father because my assigned seat was next to him. The mayor was on the other side. Barrett Grant sat to my right with an empty seat between us where my date would have sat. Barrett's smug face stared at me as I grabbed my water goblet and chugged. I needed something stronger.

Barrett kept his eyes on me as I looked around for a waiter to bring me some whiskey. "What?" I finally asked, annoyed.

"Told you she was trouble. Saw the whole thing."

He wasn't wrong. She was trouble. I shrugged my shoulders at him. Barrett moved away from his date and into the seat left for Kinsley. Leaning in closer, he spoke softly. My father and his were also engaged in a quiet conversation.

"We can take care of that trouble."

I lifted my eyebrows. Curious, I waited, wondering what he had in mind.

"Yeah. I mean, your play to fuck her into submission was a good one, but obviously not good enough." He glanced up at his father. "We've had someone following her." I waited for him to continue. "Are you in this with us?"

A large hand clasped my shoulder, and my father spoke quietly in my ear, "Listen to Barrett, son. We need to end this problem."

My face hardened, and I popped my jaw. Nodding slowly, I agreed. "She deserves it."

Barrett's smile widened. "Fuck yeah, she does."

"Bitch thought she could embarrass me in front of everyone. Leave me like everyone else does." I spoke through my teeth, mainly to myself. The waiter finally brought a whiskey. "Bring me another." Downing the double, I slammed the glass onto the table. "What's the plan?"

"How far do you want to go?"

Before I could speak, my father and the mayor left the table. They knew. They probably had told Barrett to plan this. "Far."

Barrett nodded. "Have dinner with us next Friday,

my father and me. I think your father will be there, too."

"Where?"

"We'll send a car for you. You live at Theta Rho Zeta manor, right?"

I nodded.

"Stan will pick you up at 8 p.m."

))) ● (((

Somehow, I made it through the week and finals without failing. Kinsley's Chanel scent was everywhere in my room, despite me doing laundry. My lowest point was jerking off with her pillow over my face, huffing the smell of her hair like it was a can of spray paint. No, that was probably the second lowest. The worst was when I slept with it every night, pretending she was there with me. I even found myself saying her name one night, waking myself up and reaching for her, only to remember she wasn't with me.

When the mayor's car came to pick me up, I was prepared. Ready for everything to be over. I needed it over. Nothing would stop me. I had nothing left. This was revenge.

I wasn't even angry anymore. All of that had gone away. In its place was resolution, confidence, focus.

Once I arrived at the mayor's house, I was searched by a black-suited security guard before I even entered the house. He patted me down roughly and made me hand over my phone. When he felt up my dick, he paused and looked me in the eye. I stared him down. *Yeah, man. It's all me.*

He backed away. I walked in the front door and another guard led me into a dining room. The mayor and my father sat at the head of the table and nodded at my entrance.

Barrett stood and shook my hand. "Welcome. Come in." He held out his arm like the table was a buffet, but there was no food served yet. I wasn't hungry; food would only distract me from what I needed to do later.

I took a seat next to my father. "Son, we know you got yourself entangled in this mess. But it's time to end it." George spoke to me, using his commanding voice.

"I agree." Everyone seemed surprised, except for Barrett.

Mayor Grant cleared his throat. "You agree what?"

"I agree that the *problem* needs taken care of. Ended. I didn't show up here just to help; I want to be the one to do it."

The mayor seemed pleased. "Well, that's great. You realize what ending it means, right?"

I hesitated. "I think so."

My father eyed the mayor, then turned to me. "Son, we need her dead."

"Kinsley?"

"Yes."

"Got it. You want Kinsley Whittemore dead because of some stupid wreck? I want her dead because she broke my fucking heart." My voice cracked when I spoke, despite struggling to not show emotion. "I'm putting that cunt in the ground."

"Well, you won't have to." Barrett spoke up.

"We have it handled, Junior." Mayor Grant said at the same time.

"I appreciate your efforts, George, but they have some people on it already," said my father.

"What do you mean?"

Barrett said, "We have one of our guys picking her up now. She jogs about this time in the park. We got a new guy to handle it instead of those petty criminals. A professional."

"You got a professional to kill Kinsley?" Heat rose up my face. I cracked my neck. This was my job to take care of, not some professional.

"Yes. A retired member of the force. We've played around enough with her and need to finish the job."

"Take me to her."

Barrett slicked his tongue over his teeth. "Told you he'd want to do it himself." He laughed and his father smiled. Barrett called someone on his phone as the tense silence at the table continued. "It's me… hold off for a bit. We got someone that wants to finish the job… Oh? Yeah, she's a bitch like that. Just tie her down until we get there."

Barrett ended the call and laughed. "Guess she kicked the shit out of his nuts when he grabbed her. Let's go."

Our fathers stayed behind as Barrett and I were driven to an old industrial park near my mother's apartment complex. An abandoned metal warehouse as big as an airplane hangar stood on the banks of the water there. A light was peeking through the dark night from a crack in a large sliding door when we got out of the black Mercedes.

My steps were steady as we strolled into the building. Inside, there was a man dressed all in black, clutching his jaw. He stashed a gun into the back of his jeans as we approached. He looked bored. Behind him, Kinsley was sitting on a metal chair. She was blindfolded and had duct tape around her mouth. Her hands were behind her back; her feet were taped to the legs of the chair.

"We have lover boy here, Kinsley." Barrett laughed.

She turned her head to hear us better.

"I can't believe you guys didn't just do away with her a while ago. Ended my misery before I got involved with her," I muttered.

"Well, now you can."

"Maybe if you hadn't gotten so wasted and driven that night, I'd be okay."

"Maybe if *she* hadn't been in the way, I wouldn't have hit her. You ever think about that?"

I shook my head at the prick. "And now you want her dead."

"Yes. Kill her and be done with it." He smiled. "I'm going to enjoy watching the chief of police's son commit murder."

Kinsley moaned behind the tape. She kicked and tried to move.

"Can I get that piece?" I asked the guy with the gun.

He nodded and handed it over.

I ripped off Kinsley's blindfold and her head whipped around until she could focus on me. Kneeling in front of her, I let the tip of the gun drag over her face while tears rolled down her cheeks.

"Not so mouthy now, are you? Finally quiet. Going to be quiet forever." I stood and pressed my lips to her forehead. "I love you."

I spun around and held the gun up at Barrett. "You piece of shit really thought I could kill the love of my life? You're dumber than you look." Barrett's jaw dropped.

"What are you doing? Kill her." When he saw I wasn't moving, he raised his hands and nodded to the guy in black. "Get him."

The man pulled a gun off the table and held it up at Barrett. "Keep your hands up." He got behind Barrett and grabbed his arms, holding them behind him. The pipsqueak tried to get away, so the guy had to use his force, punching him in the back of the head to get him to comply. Laying on his body, the guy used zip ties to handcuff Barrett. "You're under arrest for conspiracy to commit murder and I'm sure they'll also get you on that hit-and-run, too, as well as covering it up."

"What the fuck?"

I quickly ripped the tape off Kinsley's mouth while the officer continued reading Barrett his rights. Four more FBI agents entered. I kissed my woman, brushing her hair back off her face.

"I love you, George." She eyed the officer trying to undo the tape on her hands. "Did you get them?"

"Yes, ma'am. We got them. We got them all. Prisoners won't take kindly to police chiefs and mayors on the inside." The agent smirked.

As soon as her body was freed, she jumped into my arms, and I cradled her against me. "I love you, Sins. We did it. You're safe now."

"I'm safe with you."

"Uh, we need that, um, audio, sir." The agent stood and held out her hand while politely not staring at my crotch.

"Oh. Yeah, hang on." I dropped Kinsley for a moment, turned around and dug into my boxer briefs. I pulled out the wire and recording device the agents had given me before dinner. "Sorry, it's a little, um, sweaty."

Kinsley jumped back into my arms.

"Do you two need a ride?" one of the FBI agents asked. I held my girl against me as we walked out to the unmarked government car. Rubbing my hands rapidly over her arms, I tried to keep her warm.

"Ma'am. You'll have to sit in the seat with a seatbelt," the officer instructed Kinsley once we were in the backseat. I didn't want to let her go, but reluctantly let her slide over to the seat next to mine. We held hands until we reached the manor.

"And Gianna?" Kinsley said as I led her inside the house. Once we were in the foyer, Xavier walked down the staircase with his signature smirk.

"She's um…" I glanced at my best friend.

"I think she moved. To another country. Far, far away. Not anywhere close to here," Xavier said nonchalantly as he waltzed past us into the kitchen.

"*Oookay*. I don't want to know."

I nodded. "Let's get you upstairs."

Once we reached my room, I threw her little body

on the bed like I loved to do. She was so pliable. I jumped on top of her, but before I could kiss her, she said, "I can't believe our plan worked! They ate it up!"

I nibbled her neck. "Yeah."

"Gianna never suspected anything. I thought I did a great job with the acting. And Aaron's video didn't even need to be used, I guess."

I nodded and sucked her earlobe. She moaned.

"Did I slap you too hard at the party?"

I couldn't even think about the party right now. "Sins, I've been without you for a fucking week. Longest seven days of my life."

"Sorry." She kissed me deeply, then pulled away. "The scariest part was telling the FBI. I didn't think they'd listen to us."

"Well, Levi came in clutch."

"Yeah, he sure did."

Levi had found some security camera footage from the apartment he rented. The old renters had a doorbell camera, and he asked if they could look back to when Kinsley's accident was. Sure enough, they had a snippet of Barrett's car driving past at a high speed, heading straight for Kinsley's car. The FBI seemed to be aware of Mayor Grant's activities for quite some time. They wanted a bigger crime, but ours was good enough to bring him in and try to pin other charges on top. He certainly wouldn't be mayor anymore.

My father was arrested along with the mayor. Aaron was at home, on break from school. I'd asked him to record Gianna if she tried anything with him again. He got her on a phone recording, asking him to have sex with her. It didn't matter; Xavier's people took care of her. And where she was… was no place I would want to be.

Dan was in his dorm, probably. I'd talk with my brothers later. I figured Aaron would be thrilled to ditch the academy once he found out Chief was locked up. We could get him in online school or public school. I already discussed with Xavier that I'd be moving back into our house next semester so I could watch out for him. The house was paid for, so I was banking on my father allowing me into his accounts to pay the bills while he was in prison. Hopefully, for the rest of his life.

"I think we should celebrate." Kinsley sighed and leaned back, stroking my hair out of my face.

"That's what I'm trying to fucking do, but you won't shut the fuck up." If I were honest, I hoped she would never shut up. I couldn't stand it when she was quiet. Somehow, her words went from annoying the fuck out of me to being something I needed. Kinsley had given me the words I never could say. I only wished she would shut up now so I could rail her into the next train station.

"I just—"

Before she could get the sentence out, I kissed her and ripped her pants down. I couldn't wait any longer. I needed to be inside her. I missed her way too fucking much.

Not even checking that she was wet, I plunged in, and she arched off the bed. "Damn, princess. You pussy is so fucking hot and tight. I gotta stretch you out again."

"Please."

"Please stretch you? My fucking pleasure." As I pumped inside her violently, all the longing I had built up over the past week entered my cock, expelling with every thrust.

Sins lifted her hips, so we connected as deeply as possible. "So fucking big." She was out of breath, gasping at the shock of my size. Her pussy squeezed me so hard I was suctioned back inside every time I pulled out.

"Your pussy doesn't want to let go, does it? Come all over it, princess. Own it. Ride this dick like it's your toy." *Fuck*, watching her get off on my body almost made me explode inside her before she had a chance to. I slowed down, and she worked me, humping my pole like a crazed stripper. Gripping the back of her head, I kissed her, tangling my tongue with hers. I couldn't hold back any longer when I felt her inner muscles contract around me and she screamed in my mouth.

"Can't fucking last." I swiveled my hips one more time and held my cock close to her womb and filled her up with a week's worth of cum. Well, if you didn't count handjob jizz. Which I didn't.

"I love you, George," she panted. I collapsed on top of her, and she made a choking sound. I'd let her breathe in a moment, but I needed to catch mine first.

"I love you, Sins. You're mine." I leaned up on my elbows again to stare at her face. "Say it."

"I'm yours."

"And I'm yours."

EPILOGUE
KINSLEY

I WASN'T NERVOUS. Okay... I was. I had a good strategy, though. If I didn't make it into my first choice, I could easily make it into my second or third. Or anywhere, really. It was a sure shot. I shouldn't be nervous.

My husband's palm was sweaty in mine. His leg bounced up and down as his giant thumb twisted my wedding ring around and around my finger. Placing my hand on George's thigh, he stopped it's rhythmic bobbing and darted his blue eyes to me.

"Relax. I got this," I whispered to him.

He tapped his lips to my temple. "I know you do, princess."

"Kinsley Turner-Whittemore."

George squeezed my hand as I stood up and walked down the aisle to the front of the class. It was Match Day, when we would find out where I would be sent for my specialty training. In my case, neurology residency.

My first choice was Georgetown University, because George worked as a NASA engineer at the Goddard Space Flight Center.

Once I stepped to the front of the room, the dean handed me a white envelope and I ripped into it. "Georgetown!" I screamed and ran at George, who stood up. People clapped as I jumped into his arms and wrapped my legs around his waist. We kissed desperately.

"Told you, Sins. We can do anything together."

"Yes, we can." I kissed him again, then he let me down, so I slid down his body.

Aaron grabbed me and pulled me in for a tight hug. "Congratulations, sis!"

"Thanks, little man." Aaron was stationed nearby. He finished his private academy for high school, choosing to go back. George Turner, senior, had agreed for George to take over the family funds, and George was able to pay for Aaron's schooling. Once he graduated, he entered West Point, wanting to continue his military education with the Army. And despite my teasing nickname for him, he was now George's size.

Dan looked like a skinny kid next to his two giant brothers. He still played baseball, but in the minor leagues for a Brooklyn, New York team. After slapping George on the back, he kissed my cheek. "Let's eat." Due to an injury, Dan had a few weeks off, so he didn't care what he was consuming.

"I made a whole big buffet spread at their house," my mom said. My mom moved to live closer to us. Her townhouse was only a few miles away from our house.

Shortly after she moved, she met Hugh, an older man that treated her like royalty. Things were getting serious between them. Unfortunately, he had to work late and couldn't make it to my event.

"Fuck, I love your tater tot casserole, Ms. Monroe." Dan threw an arm around my mom.

"Language, Danny," my mom scolded him. Since their own mother was still back in Northview, my mom had become their secondary mother.

George's mom was doing better. She had gotten treatment for depression and called once a week to talk. George said I was the closest person to her now. Some days I did consider we might be friends. Other times we would bicker too much.

George's father was not doing well. Constantly in fear for his life in prison, we were informed he had to spend most of his life sentence in solitary. None of us visited. He was someone none of us ever thought of, except on Father's Day. On that holiday, George and I usually planned some fun activities together, like watching all the *Star Wars* movies or the show *Firefly*, his favorite.

"Have you heard from your father, yet, Kins?" my mother said as we loaded into George's truck. Dan and Aaron drove separately and followed us back to our house.

"He is coming next weekend." Even though we still didn't get along well, he loved George and was putting in an effort to try to restore our relationship. He had visited us a few times *without* Bethany or his other kids. When I visited for holidays (mainly to catch up with

Levi, Elle, Marissa, and Xavier), it wasn't as terrible with George by my side. If I had to admit it, I was even enjoying my half-siblings.

"Well, just a few more weeks until we call you *Doctor* Turner-Whittemore. How does that feel, Kins?"

"It will feel weird. And terrifying. And like I finally reached all my goals. Which is sad in a way."

My husband laid his hand on the console, and I took it.

"Well, at least you guys can finally take a honeymoon—a proper one," my mom said.

Glancing over at George, he smiled. I knew exactly what he was thinking about because I couldn't wait for our company to leave, either, so I could jump on him the minute they were gone.

We had plans to visit Greece for two weeks before I started residency. I'd also stopped my birth control pills two months ago. We needed to fuck as soon as I was ovulating. Which was tomorrow. Which meant if we had sex in about ten minutes, we could aim for a boy. I'd considered if I wanted a boy first or a girl first. Either way, we needed to get it on soon. I needed to get pregnant immediately. That way, I could give birth during a December break. Then I could get back to work in February and have our second in my third year (a measured twenty-four months apart). I would only need to make up three extra months and wouldn't be too behind in my residency training.

"Stop stressing," George said, sensing my mind racing.

"We need to get home."

He lifted our hands and kissed mine. "I got you."

When we pulled into the garage, George helped my mother get down from his massive truck and led us inside. She walked into the laundry room, but when I went to follow, George grabbed my waist and pulled me back and slammed me up against the wall.

"Fuck, hurry," I said.

He groaned on my neck and lifted my skirt. "*Ughhh*, princess. No panties?"

"Figured they'd just get in the way."

"Good girl." He unzipped quickly and shoved inside me. I tried to stifle my moan. As I gripped his neck, he thrust against me, pushing me hard against the wall. "I'm gonna fill you with my seed, princess. You ready for it?"

"Mmm-hmm." I locked my legs and rubbed my clit on his pubic bone as he stayed deep inside me. As I felt his cock pulsate, I came, too.

"I love you, Sins."

"I love you, too, George."

He kissed me. "Was that quick enough?"

I nodded and he let me slide down. Straightening my skirt, he pulled up his pants. Lifting my chin with a finger, he said, "Go lay in the bed for fifteen with your hips up. I'll make an excuse."

"That's just a myth."

"I just love the thought of my wife laying there with my cum inside her that long." My husband smirked.

"Well, then I'll do it. Tell them I had a Victorian era headache."

As I walked into our laundry room, he spanked my ass.

"Good job with the sex."

"Sometimes I miss the days when you didn't talk."

George laughed. "Right back at ya, princess."

The End

AFTERWORD

Want to know what happened to Gianna?
Did she finally get what she deserved?

Sign up for Kitty's newsletter to receive the extended epilogue and the exciting, **very dark** conclusion to The Color Series!

http://authorkittyking.com

ACKNOWLEDGMENTS

To my best friend and partner in writing, Jen. Thank you for always suggesting to add more penis. I cannot do this without you.

To my friends who beta read for me, thank you for putting up with another of my books and always being so hype about them. It's been thirteen years since we all met and I cannot imagine life without you.

To my new beta reading team, thank you for taking the time to analyze my words and help me craft a great final version of this work. I appreciate you not just for reading, but for being my biggest cheerleaders, especially when things get tough.

To Sarah, my editor, who is diligent, speedy, accurate, and sends me great messages when she's dying of laughter at my silly lines: thank you.

To my husband for helping me with *Star Wars* details and watching all the *Star Wars* movies with me that first weekend you moved in ten years ago. Pretty sure we didn't get much viewing done, but it was fun nonetheless.

Most importantly, I want to thank you, reader. As I type this, I have tears in my eyes. I had no idea how amazing the reception of The Color Series would be. But you made *Red Night* a bestseller in new release,

BDSM, **and** romantic erotica. Not only that, but it won a KDP All Stars award. All your messages, likes, comments, reviews, edits, videos, and purchases motivate me to keep going. I wouldn't be doing this without you. I appreciate you tremendously.

I will truly miss these characters and am sad to end the series. But I have left things open in case I want to revisit Northview University again in the future. I've heard your pleas about Mason and even James. They will be added to my "may be developed" list! I love that you've fallen in love with them as much as I have.

The Color Series will always be where I got my start. I was nervous, scared, and as insecure as Marissa when I wrote *Red Night*. I needed Xavier to be strong and omnipotent to guide me forcefully through the rigors of the writing world. Once the first book was finished, I relaxed and enjoyed the ride with Levi and Elle in *Blue Film*. After that, I started to want to *say something* with my writing. Hence, *White Hole* was born.

And now, dear reader, I hope you hang with me for the next **big** journey into the **dark** and disturbing city of Gnarled Pine Hollow…

ABOUT THE AUTHOR

Kitty King is a bestselling romance writer by day and a psychiatrist by night. She is the author of the International bestselling title *Red Night: Xavier's Delight* and *Blue Film*. Kitty enjoys reading erotic romance tales just as much as writing them. She is usually described as "a badass" by her husband, "dramatic" by her parents, "the best teacher" by medical residents, "livid" by previous video game mates, and "hysterical" in her own mind.

http://authorkittyking.com

ALSO BY KITTY KING

THE COLOR SERIES

Red Night: Xavier's Delight (Book 1)

Blue Film (Book 2)

White Hole (Book 3)

STANDALONE

The Wrong Man

THE COMPASS SERIES (COMING 2024)

Full list on Amazon author's page:

http://amazon.com/author/kittykingauthor

Printed in Great Britain
by Amazon